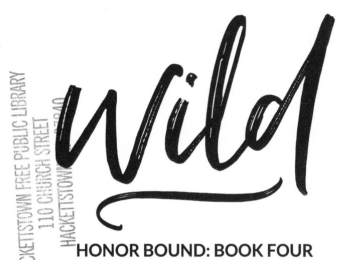

Wild

HONOR BOUND: BOOK FOUR

ANGEL PAYNE

HONOR BOUND: BOOK FOUR

ANGEL PAYNE

WATERHOUSE PRESS

*For Thomas – Because you see my wildness,
and love it.*

*And for all the readers who loved Garrett,
Zeke, and Ethan enough to clamor for more.*

*Special thanks to everyone who wanted to see
Wyatt and Josie's story.*

This one's for you!

RAZE THE BARN

Garrett Hawkins and Sage Weston-Hawkins

CHAPTER ONE

"Damn it."

Sage Hawkins angrily wiped her eyes. Snow fell over the outside world, a sight she'd waited so long to see. From her vantage point on the second floor, she stared at the trees and fences glistening with the fallen flakes and the cornfields turned into lush blankets of white. The Iowa countryside looked like a Currier and Ives print, silver, peaceful, and magical.

She let out a heavy sigh as more tears stung. If it was all so damn magical, why was she so miserable?

She and Garrett had deliberately waited until the break between Thanksgiving and Christmas to visit his parents and his beloved Uncle Wyatt and Aunt Josie. Garrett had been adamant that Racer, their baby boy, experience part of his first winter on earth in Iowa, with all the traditions of the season, and especially the snow.

Sage beheld that youthful joy on her husband's face as he and Wyatt trudged into the yard, returning from their quarter-mile trek to retrieve the mail. After dropping off the pile at Wyatt's house, they headed for the barn situated between the two Hawkins houses. With Racer bundled in a baby carrier on his chest, Garrett looked like a reverse-hunchback. That didn't stop the man's eyes from gleaming like fresh-cut blue quartz or the tawny stubble on his jaw from giving way to his charismatic grin. Yeah, the one that made her heart tumble over itself, even in her present condition.

Her present condition. Egghh. She longed to scratch her skin off and start all over again in another body. She didn't do "conditions." She'd been in disaster zones. Skydived with soldiers. Survived a year on the run from slave traders. Had her wedding crashed by a lunatic on a revenge campaign.

But none of that had mattered to fate.

It was determined to give her a "condition."

The logic in the decision shouldn't have been a huge shock. Just when she thought the cosmic dues had been paid and her pregnancy would end in a day of stress-free joy and love, a vacation to Los Angeles had turned into a nightmare that brought Racer to them a month early. The "break" that Garrett's Special Forces Group was expecting on that trip? Never happened. They'd ended up assisting the CIA on a terrorist plot to bury the West Coast under a nuclear cloud, with her husband as the first casualty of that feat. Even now, she shuddered at the memory of Garrett's face, so strong yet still, lost to the huge hit of sleeping gas he'd endured to save her. She'd kissed him with so many desperate pleas to wake up as Racer Joseph put the pedal to the damn medal in her belly...

She gasped as the helplessness pulled at her all over again. Clawed her soul like a monster on grief's playground, cackling at her to abandon hope and jump on its merry-go-round of desperate fear.

"Go. Away." She seethed the words, a luxury she hadn't been given the day Racer was born. Once they'd escaped from Ephraim Lor and Cameron Stock, Racer had lived up to his name, clamoring for his grand entrance despite her pleas otherwise. With her best friend at her side, Sage had given birth to her son without knowing if his daddy would ever wake to hold him.

It's over now. Done. Lor is dead, and Stock is at the top of the FBI's most wanted list. They'll find him and lock his ass away forever.

Which meant she only had to worry about the next lunatic who wanted to go at her husband with a bomb, knife, gun, rocket, or chemical canister. And the one after that. And the one after that.

Over?

It was never going to be over.

She bolted off the seat, straight to her well-used pacing path on the carpet of her in-laws' guest room. "Get a grip. You fell in love with an SF guy. You love him for what he is. You love him for all of it. You knew the drill before you accepted his ring."

That was all before she'd lain next to him for hours, her head on her husband's chest, wondering if his next heartbeat would be his last.

The tears came again. She pulled in a shaky breath, mentally kicking at the asshole on the merry-go-round. She couldn't let him win. She wouldn't.

Why did it get harder to believe that every day?

Garrett called to her from outside, his baritone filled with happiness.

"Sage." His laugh mixed with Wyatt's from the yard below. "Sugar, you in there? Go to the window. You have to see this!"

Grabbing a tissue and mopping up the new tears, she commanded her self-composure back to the emotional battlefront. "Fake it till you make it," she whispered, forcing a smile.

She curled a knee back onto the window seat and looked out, searching for her husband. It was the world's easiest feat.

The man consumed over six feet of the frosty air, melting it into an obedient glow for his golden-haired, broad-shouldered, undeniably virile presence. The effect was hit by an extra injection of sexy thanks to the bulk of his parka, the thick stubble that now populated his jawline, and the longer line of his legs due to his boots. He was hot farm boy mashed with hot soldier, officially turning him into mouthwatering man, a concoction that literally made her thirsty with longing for him.

Every muscle in her body yearned to jump him.

Right before she swore to kill him.

The idiot stood there grinning down at Racer, who was on the ground in the mud and snow. Correction—rolling around in the muck, squealing with laughter. God only knew where his Thomas the Tank Engine snowcap had gone, though Garrett had managed to keep the little mittens on his hands. That didn't help the man's cause very much.

"Hey!" he yelled. "Look. He wants to make snow angels already!"

She made sure he got a good look at her glower before she whirled away from him, snatched her jacket, and headed downstairs.

CHAPTER TWO

Garrett laughed like he'd just helped bust an opium farm and decided to stay for lunch. Not that he'd ever touch the shit, but he imagined this was how good it felt. His cheeks hurt from smiling. His heart was about to fissure from being crammed to capacity. This was the best high in the world.

He hadn't been back to the farm since last year, before the Special Forces mission that had changed everything for him. Deep in an East Asian jungle, a continent away from where she'd supposedly died, Sage had walked out of his dreams, into his arms, and back into his life. The story of their miracle had captivated the world, resulting in a media storm that kept Sage busy even when he was deployed to a new op soon after. Her positive pregnancy test was the perfect beginning for their new life together, though it didn't help in slowing down the pace. Being back in his boyhood home, settling into calmer routines and simpler pleasures, had been just what their new family needed.

Maybe it would return the happy sparkle to his wife's eyes, too.

Hope lifted his heart when she disappeared from the window. She'd barely left that perch for two days. Maybe Racer's delight had gotten through and she finally wanted to join the fun.

She bounded out of the house so fast, the screen door slammed back against the wall.

It didn't look like she wanted to make snow angels. A snowball rolled around a few rocks, maybe. Probably aimed at his head. Or worse.

Shit.

He gave a shot at a grin anyway. "Hi there, beautiful. Did you come out to join—?"

"Are you out of your damn mind?" Sage snatched Race up and dragged the edge of her scarf across his face. Their baby scowled and batted at her hands.

Garrett drew in a careful breath. He'd fallen in love with this woman for her spirit and fire, but for the last couple of months, she'd given new meaning to the words. The Native American tribes in Washington, where he was based out of Joint Base Lewis-McChord, had beliefs about spirits intervening with women in childbirth. Perhaps he needed to do research about what happened almost six months after the fact. Maybe some trickster mountain spirit decided it was fun to slide down the summit and fuck with the new fathers in town by turning their wives into completely different creatures.

Or maybe, shit-for-brains, you have to sit her down and have a serious talk about postpartum depression.

Now was definitely not that time.

"Sugar, what's the—"

"*Don't* 'sugar' me." Her face bunched up like she held back tears. Again. "Oh my God, look at him."

He frowned in confusion. "That's exactly what I was doing. And he was having fun. It's just a little snow and mud."

"It's in his *mouth*, Garrett."

"And we're in the middle of the yard, not the barn with the chemicals and cows. It's not going to hurt him."

For a second, her face cleared. A glimmer of hope filled

him. Maybe the mountain demon had finally jumped off and she'd be free to look at herself with objectivity. She'd have a good laugh at her paranoia and then suggest he ask his parents to watch Race for a bit so they could head upstairs together...

And maybe the clouds would open up, and God would invite him upstairs for a beer and a chat. Preferably about where the fuck He was hiding the confident woman once known as Sage Weston-Hawkins.

"He's not some recruit for your team, Sergeant. Keep my baby out of the damn muck."

More snow wasn't due until late tonight, but a sleet storm moved in on his heart. Fury and bewilderment tangled with each other even as he battled a thick erection watching Sage's ass during her retreat into the house, still wiping Race as she went. *Damn it.* He'd never been so enraged and in lust with someone in the same breath. It'd been weeks since they'd done anything more than kiss, a fact that hadn't been earning him the customer satisfaction award from his cock. Now it seemed he was due for more of the same frustration.

All of that fueled the glower he swung at Wyatt and Josie as they approached. His uncle held their eighteen-month-old girl, Violet, who lived up to her name with blue eyes featuring sparkling flecks of purple. Garrett's cousin flashed a gap-toothed grin over the head of her princess doll. Despite his irritation, he ran a gentle hand over her strawberry-blond curls.

"Guess we need to debrief." Wyatt's tone held a smirk, but his eyes didn't fuck around.

"No," Garrett countered, "we don't. Thanks anyway."

Josie let out a delicate snort. "How's the view down in that hole, whelp? See anything fun?"

Whelp. The only time either of them used his childhood handle was either with deep affection or irritation. In this case, it wasn't complicated to rule out the former. "I know what's going on, okay?" he snapped. "I know that Sage and I need to... talk."

Josie switched her indignation for a smile. "It's not a dirty word, G."

"Though talking's probably only the start." Wyatt added with calm that edged on grim.

Garrett narrowed his eyes. "What the hell does that mean?"

"Tell him, Josie."

His aunt, who looked happier than he ever remembered, turned a tender look up at him. "About four months after Vi was born, I started exhibiting a lot of the same behaviors you're seeing in Sage. I couldn't sleep. I'd be fiercely protective of Vi one second but push her off onto Wyatt the next, locking myself in the bedroom for hours to hide from the world."

"Sound familiar yet?" Wyatt injected.

Garrett glared again. His uncle chuckled. *Asshole.*

"To be simple, I felt overwhelmed," Josie went on. "And unworthy. And insane. I had no idea what I was doing with an infant at my age. I railed at God for giving me such a precious gift when He could so easily take it away." Her next words brought a painful twist to her lips. "And...I thought a lot about that night when Sage, Rayna, and I were captured by King and held aboard his yacht. I put on a brave face for those girls during those hours, though deep in my heart I was prepared to die the next morning." A sheen of tears glowed in her deep-green eyes. "But even that fear paled to all the things I suddenly felt for my daughter. The terror of losing her, along with the knowledge that some things in life are beyond our control..." A desperate sigh tore past her lips. "It was too much to wrap my head around. So I didn't. I dropped out and fell deeper into my depression."

Garrett clenched his jaw and swallowed hard. So much of what she'd relayed, behavior-wise, matched what he'd witnessed in Sage lately. How much of the rest was the same? How much was probably worse? Sage hadn't spent just one night in King's chains. The man's Thailand dungeon had been her home for weeks.

He dragged a hand through his hair to help push past the despair toward something more constructive. A plan. "Okay, you obviously didn't stay there, right?" he demanded. "In your depression?"

Wyatt arched his brows. "You think I'd allow that?"

He let his uncle observe the grin he barely held down. "No, Sir."

"Damn straight."

"Language!" Josie shot the rebuke with a laugh while Wyatt handed Violet, now squirming for Mommy, back to her.

"So what happened?" Garrett questioned.

"Hauled her ass to the doctor right away, that's what happened."

A blush warmed Josie's cheeks as she gazed up at her husband. "Hmm. Not *right* away."

Wyatt cracked a wolfish smile. "Someone had to remind you about who was calling the shots, missy."

Garrett watched as his aunt bowed her head and pressed it into Wyatt's shoulder. How many times had he seen her do that, never fully understanding its meaning before now? It was a beautifully submissive move, made more eloquent when

Wyatt tenderly lifted her face for his kiss.

Josie turned her smile back to Garrett. "I was resistant about looking for help," she explained. "Like a lot of the world, I thought postpartum depression was only something that struck a woman soon after birth. I had no idea it can hit up to a year after the baby comes. Like every good army wife, I wrote off my feelings as a rough patch and tried to move on." She leaned against her husband again. "Thank heavens I got a little push from my man."

Garrett smirked a little. "You mean your Sir."

Shit.

Impulsive and unthinking, meet mouth. He fell into silence, uncertain about how his aunt would react to that. Had Wyatt told her he'd come clean to Garrett about how the D/s dynamic existed inside their marriage? He hoped so. That heartfelt discussion had taken place over a year ago, but Garrett remembered it like a conversation from yesterday. His uncle's confession had been fifteen minutes of a world-changer for him. Wyatt had opened a window about what a Dominant's boundaries and discipline, given with command but tempered with love, could mean to a submissive who'd been tapped out on doing things like that for themselves.

At the time, he'd finally seen that Sage was such a sub. She'd begged him to explore the dynamic because she'd endured a year of simply trying to survive, and the chance to "turn off the switch" was her idea of paradise. He'd finally realized that and, in doing so, had given himself an amazing gift too. Being able to relieve a fraction of her trauma-infused precious solace to his soul and the guilt that would never fully let him forget the hell she'd endured.

Josie's delighted laugh hit the air, relieving his tension.

"Yes," she affirmed, "my Sir." She giggled more when Garrett felt an idiotic blush rise up his neck. "Don't stress, whelp." This time she threw out the nickname with warmth. "There's not a lot Wyatt and I keep from each other. Besides, *I* heard you spying on us when you were a kid, too."

His flush turned into an inferno. "Fuck on a stick."

"*Language.*" After the admonishment, she shrugged. "You were a curious boy in puberty. I think I would've been shocked to *not* find you lurking one night. And as much as I love your parents, you sure as hell weren't going to get the four-one-one on the birds and the bees from *them.*"

Garrett kicked at the ground. "Now that the two of you have embarrassed me worse than the karaoke contest debacle, you gonna help me figure out what to do about Sage?"

"Hey," Josie protested, "you were good!"

"I sucked ass. In front of Ellie Macallister."

Wyatt grunted. "Who got knocked up by Jason Yearborn before your senior year was up. We saved you from that tramp."

"Fair enough. How about helping me hang on to the jewel I *did* find?"

Wyatt scowled. "Wasn't that what we were doing?"

Before Garrett could pile another layer onto the perplexity sandwich, Josie cleared her throat with diplomatic timing. "Master, may I speak boldly?"

Wyatt nodded. "Sounds like a damn good plan, pet."

The woman took a moment to set Violet down, encouraging her to find magic snowflakes for Dora the Explorer and the Snow Princess. When she straightened, there was a glimmer in her eyes that conveyed a message of nothing but naughty. "Tie her down, command every sound she makes and every breath she takes until she can't string two thoughts together, and make her see the light." She lifted a grin back at Wyatt. "How was that?"

The man burrowed his face into the cowl of her jacket and openly nuzzled her neck. "Beautiful, darlin'. Simply beautiful." He twisted his head when Garrett returned nothing but a tense silence. "What now? You *still* having trouble understanding the directive, nephew?

"I understand it fine." He toed the ground again but put angry force behind the move this time, sending the snow into a fan that delighted his squealing cousin. "I just think there's going to be a few issues with the mission execution."

"What?" Josie retorted. "Why?"

Wyatt's own response wasn't so mystified. "Shit." He drew out the word as he pulled away from his wife. Garrett swore he hadn't seen such a glare out of his uncle since he was thirteen and accidentally flipped one of the tractors into a ditch of sludge. "Are you telling me the only action that play room of yours has seen lately is from the dust bunnies?"

Garrett averted his gaze. It'd been a lot longer than "lately." The last time he'd taken Sage to their BDSM play room, he'd been home on a fast three days of leave between the battalion's missions, and Sage was just starting to show the bump where his son was growing. "Well, they're bunnies," he finally murmured. "So if they need a place to get their kink on, the Hawkins play room is—"

"Goddamnit, Garrett," Wyatt growled. "Don't make light about this. Haven't you been talking to Zeke about any of this shit? He's an experienced Dom. I expected him to advise you better."

He huffed in exasperation. "Gee, so sorry, but Z and I are usually discussing other things, like how to take care of the scum-nuts threatening our national security while assuring our own balls come home intact. There hasn't been a lot of time to talk about how completely lost I've been on how to touch my wife since she delivered our son while I lay unconscious three doors down in the hospital."

"So you've just decided not to?"

Josie's query didn't accuse like Wyatt's, but the implication clung. Heat spread up his face again. At this rate, he'd be able to shuck the parka and get a goddamn suntan out here. "I'm—I'm afraid of hurting her, okay? Her body's been through a lot. Her heart's been through worse."

Josie shook her head. "But you haven't given her any safe ground to express that."

Pain radiated through his jaw as he clenched it...as his aunt's words knifed into his heart. Sage had come back to him from death last year, but in many senses, he'd murdered her all over again. His wife, so used to being in control and "on top of things," didn't know how to access her vulnerabilities by herself. That was why their dynamic as Dom and sub was so important to her. She literally needed to be told it was all right to let go.

And he'd gone AWOL on her.

A growl full of self-loathing tore out of him. "Guess I've dicked this one up pretty good."

To his surprise, Josie grinned. Not so shocking was her little hop forward, followed by pulling him into a tight hug. "Good thing we're here to help you un-dick it."

He threw her a sarcastic glance. "Oh?"

The glee behind his aunt's smirk gained more steam. "Sir, I think it's time to show the whelp what improvements you've made to the barn."

Wyatt chuckled. "You took the words right out of my mouth, pet."

"I'll handle the rest." Josie flashed one more grin at Garrett before picking up her daughter and heading back toward their place. "This is going to be so much fun."

CHAPTER THREE

Sage had feigned sleep when it was time for dinner. The excuse wasn't far from the truth. After losing it at Garrett in the yard, she'd tromped in and asked his mom to watch Race, knowing Maya Hawkins would cancel tea with the Pope to spend time with her grandson.

Less than ten minutes later, Sage had gone back upstairs, put on sweats and a T-shirt, and buried herself in bed. She'd been there ever since.

For the first hour after that, she'd tried to cry. Thrown her hardest concentration into it. Instead, every time the strips of her mental flogger came down on her soul, she'd taken the pain in a disoriented fog.

You don't deserve to be his wife.

She felt nothing.

You're not fit to be a mother.

Nothing again.

You can't handle all this. Maybe the only place you truly have value anymore is with those slavers in Thailand.

She immersed herself beneath the covers and escaped into sleep. Though she'd roused a little when Garrett came in to check on her, bringing the savory scent of pot roast and fresh-baked bread with him, she quickly slipped back under.

Through her groggy consciousness, she'd listened to Maya giving Race his bath. Baby squeals. Her mother-in-law's laughter. Garrett's husky chuckles joining in.

A world she longed to join.

A reality she didn't deserve.

In little stages, the house fell silent. She shifted, tucked the pillow back beneath her head, and curled back into a ball, steeling herself for the invisible flogger to return. She needed to stay strong. She couldn't bend. She wouldn't break.

The bedroom door opened. The strong boot cadence told her it was Garrett once more. His normal spice and pine scent was enhanced by the crisp kiss of fresh snow, denoting he'd been outside not long ago. She also smelled food. Against every will in her body, her stomach growled like a rabid Doberman.

"Sage."

For a split second, she thought about continuing her charade. Stomachs could sound like flesh-craving canines even when somebody slept, right?

But something about her husband's voice pulled her up like a physical force. A blend of tones she hadn't heard for an achingly long time. Darkness. Demand.

Dominance.

Holy shit. He looked the same way too. His hair was slicked back from his face in some Euro-lux look, though he'd left the stubble on his jaw, which was now steeled as he stabbed his ice-blue stare at her. He wore a gray Henley that showed every magnificent line of his torso, which topped formfitting black leathers finished with his heavy motorcycling boots.

Despite her exhaustion, which didn't feel like that anymore, her eyes widened and her pulse jumped. Damn, those pants...on the tree trunks that did double duty as his legs...*wow*. Where the hell had he even found them, out here in the middle of Iowa? And did she really care?

"Uh...hi." Her voice was raspy, sounding as stunned as she

really was.

Garrett didn't return the greeting. After turning on the lamp next to the bed, he ducked into the hallway and reappeared with a lap tray loaded with food. Slices of the pork roast she'd smelled earlier were joined by seasoned potatoes, spiced apples, and pecan rice. Occupying a separate plate on the tray was a hunk of hot, heavenly-smelling bread, and another dish held a slice of chocolate cream pie that was destined to settle humanity's "pie or cake" debate forever.

"Sit up." The words were light-years away from a request. Her husband's face, unchanged from the unyielding stare with which he'd entered, backed it up. As soon as she complied, he set the tray over her lap. "Eat. Every bite."

"But I'm not—"

"Hungry? The fuck you aren't. *Eat*."

"Yes, Sir."

It spilled out with barely a thought, as automatic as the sweep of her hands toward the knife and fork. She would've giggled if not for the deep breaths she took to wrestle down her astonishment, puzzlement, and...*hope*?

God, like she could even dare to think that his kinky dream makeover meant something. They weren't at home. They weren't even in the same state. The play room wasn't downstairs. Most significantly, they were parents now. Apparently, her new status as Mommy had canceled out her role as subbie. Not that she'd given Garrett any reason to want that from her anymore.

He settled into the chair next to the window and watched as she took every bite. Sage fought against stealing glances at him, but between the silvery light from outside and the golden lamp glow from inside, his usual masculinity was transformed into a double-gilded vision of pure power.

Ohhh, hell.

She rubbed her legs together under the covers. The motion provided just enough friction to turn the tingles in her pussy to full-bore arousal. Forget about the flurries outside; her gut twirled with enough climatic turbulence for the whole county. And food was rapidly becoming the last thing on her mind. "Honestly, I can't get through all of this," she finally confessed, letting the fork fall.

Garrett rose to his feet, looking like a tower of liquid flame brought to life. Despite what the sight did to her clit and its friends now, she huffed in resignation, assuming the return of her careful and understanding husband was surely near.

World's biggest mistake.

"Not acceptable." He punched every syllable with command. "What were my instructions about the food, Sage?"

She couldn't help cocking her head and arching her brows. "Instructions?" But even her snarky take on the word didn't stop her vagina from clenching again or her heart from speeding to a new tempo.

Garrett's reply came with matching attitude. "You go right ahead and keep up that sass, sugar. It'll just make it more fun to show you why you're gonna need every ounce of nutrition on that tray tonight."

The remark was a sweep of raw arrogance, rendered on purpose by the only man on earth who knew what it would do to her. She didn't try to hide her aroused whimper from him now. Garrett let a single soft chuckle out in acknowledgment but made no other sound until she started on the pie. Sage smirked in vengeance as she lifted the bite of pastry to her mouth but licked it all off the fork instead of biting it, making sure Garrett saw every purposeful inch of her action.

A sound spilled from him mixed between a groan and a grunt. A fast glance to the beautiful bulge in the crotch of his leathers proved she'd gotten the upper hand she wanted, if only for a moment.

When she dipped her fork in for her second bite of pie, Garrett snarled, "Stop."

Sage flashed a gloating smile. "Yes, Sir."

He walked back to the bed with steps that were more authoritative than before. Without warning, he yanked the pie off the tray, leaving the fork behind. After ducking back out into the hall, he returned bearing her snow boots and what looked like a floor-length parka made out of decadently warm, thick material.

He stood next to the bed for a long second before speaking again. When he did, the words were definitely not what she'd expected.

"Are you wearing panties?"

Sage straightened and gawked up at him. "Excuse me?"

He expelled a long but controlled breath. "Are. You. Wearing. Panties?"

"Yes." She didn't filter her irritated embarrassment. "Of course I am. What the hell—"

"Are they wet?"

Now she blatantly sputtered. "Garrett, what kind of—"

"All I want is the answer. Yes or no. Are your panties wet? Are you aroused right now, Sage?"

She fumed and picked at the coverlet. "All right. If you have to know, then yes. They're wet. You'd turn a diehard lesbian into a puddle right now. Happy?"

"Considerably." He punctuated his sentence by brushing

the hair from her forehead, and a sigh escaped her lips. As his hand continued into the rest of her hair, gently tugging the strands to turn her face up to him, she groaned. Past his subtle smile and all that delectable scruff, he directed, "You're going to get up now. You're going to go check on Race before returning to this room, where you'll get completely naked. Put on this parka and the boots and then join me in the barn in ten minutes. There'll be discipline for tardiness." He released her and stepped toward the door but turned back, eyeing what must have been the most stunned stare she'd ever worn in her life. "Better pull back the hair, sugar. Wouldn't want to tangle it in the equipment. And yeah...bring the panties."

Without another word, he left the room. The silence that descended in his wake didn't provide any buffer from her continuing jolts of sheer shock. Nor, she realized, did she want it to be. Though her heart thudded hard enough to make her shake and her lungs ached from holding her breath, every word of her man's commands rolled through her senses with exhilarating promise. There was going to be equipment. There was going to be discipline.

At last.

CHAPTER FOUR

Garrett relished the powerful crunches of his boots against the barn's hay-strewn floor as he descended from the loft. It was chillier down here despite the space heaters he'd started to crank up an hour ago, but that was okay. The loft was warm and, by the end of the night, was likely to be downright torrid. That was completely fine by him.

Why the fuck had he waited so long to do this?

Bewilderment spurred the question more than regret. Tonight wasn't for compunction. It was for reconnection. Reclaiming every inch of his woman. Stamping himself anew onto her body, spirit, and mind. Giving her senses the freedom they needed so her soul could fly.

He silently thanked the Big Guy upstairs for Wyatt and Josie's intrepid wisdom. But when Sage walked in, he realized the message to heaven was incomplete. Even in Josie's poofy parka and the big furry boots, the woman looked like an angel sent just for him. Aside from the knowledge that she was completely nude under the garments, he was captivated by the golden cloud of her upswept hair, the reverence of each step she took, even the sweet uncertainty across her spun-from-the-clouds face. She was breathtaking. She was also completely his for hours to come—if his erection didn't go into battering ram mode on his leathers first.

Wordlessly, she approached him. Her gaze never rose higher than his chest, indicating she'd already started to piece together what his summons was all about. Like he was going to let either one of them forget? The corners of her mouth tilted up a little, lending to the overall mien of peace that palpably flowed from her. Damn. The way she glided right back into her submissiveness... It astounded and humbled him. She didn't just want to submit to him. She *needed* this. And as she dipped her head lower, offering everything she was to him, the realization slammed that he needed it too. He would never deny either of them again.

"Fancy seeing you here, mister," she said softly.

His first temptation was to flip a cute jibe right back. Instead, he firmed his jaw and held out a hand, palm up. "Panties?"

Dutifully, she dug in the coat's pocket and pulled out her lace thong. Once she pressed it into his hand, he ran his thumb over the material until he found the damp patch in the crotch. *Fuck.* Just a few minutes of their verbal foreplay had made her pussy produce quite a puddle.

After he rubbed the spot a few times, he lifted his thumb and licked it with slow enjoyment. Sage's high mewl was as perfect to his ears as her taste was to his mouth. "Delicious," he murmured. It was the total truth. He loved knowing how her body responded to his power, how wet her cunt became for him. He showed her his pleasure by leaning down to kiss her, deliberately giving her just the tip of his tongue with the contact. He wasn't in a hurry to take back every inch of the body and desire that were his alone to control.

"Mmmm...more." The pleading cry had clearly been smoldering in her and finally exploded out. Garrett witnessed the conflict on her face and stifled a chuckle. Perhaps not *every* part of his wife was fully on board with re-embracing her submission. That was all right too. He'd have more than enough pleasure showing her the way.

He gently tilted her face back up, giving her another teasing kiss. But when she sighed and parted her lips, coaxing his tongue in, he pulled back.

"We're just getting started, sugar." He made it more an admonishment than a reassurance this time, which turned the grass of her eyes into a dark forest of desire. So goddamn mesmerizing. He was able to tear himself away after a few long seconds, taking one of her hands and pulling her toward the stairs that led toward the loft. Once they stood at the bottom, he couldn't temper his grin in response to her puzzled glance. The fact that his aunt and uncle's "dungeon" was hidden in one of the highest points on the farm was an irony nobody had missed. But at this point, with his woman looking this fucking irresistible, he wouldn't have cared if the play space was in the middle of the front drive.

He beckoned her to start climbing in front of him. If she tripped or lost her balance, he needed to be on the right end to catch her. She made it up without a problem and then stood in place, waiting for him—though when he joined her, he saw that her stillness had less to do with obedience and more to do with amazement. Couldn't blame her for that. He'd fired the same reaction at Wyatt this afternoon when his uncle brought him to help with setup. Wasn't every day that a guy got invited to play in the Kinky Barn, where velvet blankets atop strategic hay bales became an instant spanking bench, an old Hawkins wagon wheel was transformed into a bondage lattice, and an equally ancient plough was outfitted with a pillow and leather straps that would place a cute subbie into a very interesting position. In addition, a fucking swing was suspended from a rafter next to a wrought-iron bed that had been Wyatt's splurge, custom-ordered from a local lifestyle furniture maker according to the exact space specs of the loft. Garrett had wasted exactly two seconds being stunned Wyatt had found such a guy in Iowa before focusing fully on what he wanted to do to Sage on that expansive leather pad.

Ohhhh, yeah. He'd started formulating his plan that very moment—and tossed it all out the window within the last fifteen minutes. It was all he could do not to congratulate himself for the new plot with a snicker, though his grin must've given some of his wicked intent away, judging from the way Sage threw her gaze between him and the bed...and what he'd placed on it.

Time to remind her who called the shots tonight.

"Eyes back here, sweetheart." His blood heated as she complied, though she looked a little anxious about it now. The feeling of having her trust, even in the face of her uncertainty... It heated his blood, powered his fortitude, moved his soul. "Thank you," he murmured, kissing her forehead.

"Thank *you*," she returned, raising a radiant smile. "This is all...amazing."

He took a step back from her, filling the simple move with purpose, extending his arms to his sides and leveling his shoulders. "I appreciate the words, sugar...but now it's time to show me your gratitude."

Her breath caught at that. He savored the sound nearly as much as the gift she gave him next. With ballet-like grace, Sage unzipped the parka and let it fall from her body. She pulled out of the boots next. After stepping away from the mound of clothing, she lowered to her knees in front of him. Garrett let her hear *his* lungs stopping now. She'd spent the last

ANGEL PAYNE

five months in embarrassment about what the pregnancy had
done to her body, moaning that she wasn't the size of a starving
model anymore. He used this opportunity to tell her exactly
what he thought of that bullshit now.

"Holy Christ. You've never looked more beautiful."

She answered by rolling her eyes at his kneecaps, which
sent a spear of fury straight into his chest. Gripping her chin
in his hand, he forced her gaze back up at him. Defiance fired
in her eyes, almost daring him to challenge her on this subject,
which she'd been pretty damn vocal about since Racer's birth.
But he was ready for that dare. And ready to do a lot more than
challenge her on it.

He let a low growl unfurl before demanding, "Who are
you when we're together like this?" After a few long seconds of
her tight silence, he repeated. "Who. Are. You?"

Her jaw trembled beneath his fingers. Her surrender
wasn't so easy when it meant capitulating the control on her
warped body image. Garrett waited again, watching the war of
her will and her desire play across her face. At last, in a tiny
rasp, she responded, "S. I am S."

He relaxed his hold a little, stroking her cheek with his
thumb to indicate how deeply she'd pleased him. "And who am
I?"

"You are Master."

"The Master who's still staggered by what your body did
to bring our boy into the world. And the Master who's insulted
every time you speak a word of shame against it. So from now
on, whether you're in the grown-up play room with me or the
toddler play room with Race, the second you trash-talk your
figure is the second you've earned yourself twenty swats with
the slotted paddle."

Her face constricted. Her eyes glittered like angry emeralds. "Twenty? Are you serious?"

"Serious is one way of putting it." He flattened his lips. "You insult me when you attack your body, S. And I don't take insults lightly."

"You also don't take safe words lightly."

"No, I don't." He returned her victorious smirk with, "But I have a damn good recollection of how much my little girl loves to be edged on orgasms." After she shot him a furious groan, he murmured, "I take it we're square now?"

Her mouth stiffened too. But she replied in a mutter, "Yes, Sir. We're square."

"That's good, because it's time for you to honor your body in another way." He nodded meaningfully toward her slice of chocolate pie, which he'd placed where the pillow should be on the bondage bed. "You haven't finished your dinner yet."

After pulling her up with care, he tugged her over and watched her gaze get bigger upon approach to the other item on the bed: a triangle-shaped positioner cushion. Normally, Garrett would instruct her on what he wanted, but tonight was all about stamping *I Am Master* all over her psyche once more. Without hesitation, he lifted her and positioned her to lie facedown, with her waist caught by the pillow's apex. Before she could get out one huff of protest, he'd yanked open both of the leather wrist restraints clipped onto chains that attached to the bed's sides and secured her into them.

She'd been beautiful at his knees.

She was breathtaking now.

With her arms stretched out and her ass in the air, she had to spread her knees a little to maintain balance. Garrett secretly smiled when he anticipated her having to widen them again once he gave her his next command.

"Lift your head, S...and eat your dessert. Every bite. I'm watching."

CHAPTER FIVE

Was he freaking kidding?

Sage received the answer to her internal rant pretty fast, in the form of her Dominant's firm steps around to the head of the bed—right where she could lift her head for an eyeful of a beautiful erection defined by soft black leather. She could've sworn his cock pulsed as she gazed at it...not the most helpful observation in her fight to win back a little dignity here.

Was she really going to do this? Eat a slab of chocolate cream pie like some tethered slave girl?

But if she did...would that make him harder? Bigger?

There was only one way to find out. And damn, the pie *was* good.

She tilted her face and let the tantalizing cocoa smell draw her toward the plate. Since he'd given her no choice, she had to use her tongue as a fork, dipping into the sweet filling and scooping it into her mouth.

Garrett sucked in a hard breath. And the crotch of his pants stretched tighter.

Sage sighed in return. She took another bite, willingly this time. She suddenly realized that it wasn't such a tragedy to shove aside her pride when the reward was her Sir's clear gratification.

One bite went in. Then another and another. Garrett said nothing else as she ate, but his tight grunts conveyed a thousand words apiece. Each was filled with deepening volume, growing need.

When she looked down on what was sure to be her last two bites of the pie, Garrett tugged on her scalp to force her back. "Very good, little girl. You've done so well that you'll enjoy the last of your dessert in a special way."

As he made the promise, he unzipped his leathers.

Sage combined her moan with his as his erection burst free, powerful and huge, a milky drop already filling the slit at the top. Garrett braced his thighs against the latticed iron of the bed frame in order to take care of his promise with two hands. One fist claimed the base of his stalk, including his balls. With the other hand, he worked the pie's filling up and down his length. The sweet stuff clung to every inch of him, making her gasp as the matching parts of her body reacted to his hedonistic perfection. Rich chocolate and the taste of his cock... The man was going to kill her with temptation.

"Oh, Sir." After the words fell from her lips, she kept them parted in need. "I'm suddenly very hungry."

Even Garrett's arrogant hum didn't stop her from craving the special treat he'd created. "Then who am I to disappoint my girl?" He guided his broad head to the tips of her lips. "Get every morsel, S. Believe me, I'm still watching."

His directive, as thick and decadent as the cream that met her tongue at first lick, brought tears of happiness to her eyes. She'd missed this so much. Had longed so deeply to serve her Master again, to know he desired her like this, to feel needed in this way. She just hadn't known how to ask. When she'd first attempted to talk about adding Dominance and submission to their relationship, Garrett had been so conflicted that it nearly tore them apart. Though he'd at last seen the deeper connection it could bring them and embraced his Dominant side, it seemed the switch was thrown the other way after Race's birth. He'd been more than ready to touch her as soon as it was medically okay to do so...but their play room door had stayed shut for months.

With hope surging in her heart, she tongued and nipped at him. With heat conquering her blood, she savored his heady flesh mixed with the dessert's decadence. With joy swooping across her soul, she listened to him shove out a tormented growl.

"Oh, my little S...you're so good to me." He pushed himself into her mouth, just the crown, teasing her. "Show me more. Open wider. I need to fuck your mouth."

She had barely released a moan of acquiescence before he filled her completely, pushing relentlessly toward the back of her throat. She shut off her brain and descended into a state of pure animal reaction, taking breaths through her nose as she welcomed his invasion. When he drove into her again, she sucked him harder. On the third time, his balls slammed her chin.

Through a fog, she heard Garrett's harsh grunt. One of his hands twisted into her ponytail, using it to deepen his penetration. She loved every hot, primitive second of it. Rejoiced in being the sole instrument of his desire. Savored every sweet and salty inch of him, stretching her mouth and throat to their limits. Pushing her as nobody else could.

"Fuck!" His voice was nearly all breath as he pulled away. He left her in that position, forcing her to stare at his glistening, dark-red length while he composed himself. "Naughty S," he growled. "You did that so well, I almost shot my come into your mouth. And I am *so* not done with you yet."

He demonstrated that point by circling around to climb

onto the bed, positioning himself behind her. Because of the spread-eagle way he'd bound her hands, there was no way she could indulge even a peek at what he had in mind next.

But oh God, were her ears working.

When a low, repetitive hum filled the air, she couldn't hold back her whimper of gratitude. The sound was better than a classic disco remix to her, and Garrett knew it. She had no idea if he'd borrowed the pulsating wand or brought their unit from home, and she really didn't care. She just needed it in her pussy...about five minutes ago.

Her Master had other plans. *Damn it.*

While leaving the wand on, Garrett slid a couple of fingers along the cushions of her labia. "Well, guess who's soaking wet."

The untamed edges of his tone were gone. His baritone was a silky strand of control once more. It turned her on even more than his growl and dipped her spirit deeper into the dark perfection of her submissiveness.

It was from those shadows that she rasped to him, "S, Master. It's S who's wet and ready for you."

He pulled his hand away from her pussy and braced it against her hip, making her writhe in more urgent need. "I'm glad to hear that...but S isn't getting anything until she has a little chat with Sage. She needs to deliver a message to Sage for me."

At this point, she'd agree to fly to the moon for him. She was halfway there, anyway. "S agrees. Dear God, she'll do anything for you."

He took his time about answering that. *A lot* of time. Those extended minutes were filled with the magical teasing of his hands, roaming her entire body. He stroked her shoulders and dragged his nails along her neck. Cupped her breasts and played mercilessly with her nipples. Swept his big palms over her stomach, down her thighs, even along her calves and over her feet, playing with each of her toes. "You need to tell Sage how much I adore this body...but, more importantly, how much I treasure the mind, the heart, and the soul inside it. Sage has been denying those needs for far too long. She'll agree to talk to someone about her depression as soon as we return home to Seattle. Does Sage understand?"

She paid back his pause with one of her own. It wasn't intentional. Words were hard to form when one's heart was bared as much as one's body.

She searched that heart for a scream of resistance, a snarl of how-dare-you. She should hate him for doing this, tying her down and arousing her to the point of quaking need, but she didn't. Garrett had finally embraced his Dominant side out of love for her, and they'd rejoiced together about the realizations it brought him: that when Master and S came together, they were committed to being naked for each other, emotionally *and* physically. Bringing her up here tonight equaled his version of opening up to her about how worried he really was for her. It was a step of honesty from the heart of her hero, and she owed him the same in return.

Swallowing against the tears that welled and spilled, she finally managed a whisper. "Yes, Master. Sage understands."

Garrett leaned and set her wrists free from the cuffs. He kept his big body pressed over her, his erection throbbing against her back. "Thank you." He said it against her neck before biting her gently there.

He pulled away once more but grasped one of her hands as he did, guiding her to sit up so he could scoop her off the bed.

The command ingrained onto his face was plenty reason not to protest what he had in mind next. His erection, filling the V in his opened leathers, stressed the point even more.

Another reason to gawk at him? As soon as he set her down in front of the plough, he peeled off his Henley, exposing the tawny magnificence of his shoulders, chest, and stomach. Now his erection had some company—and her mouth had something new to water for.

Before she could entertain the fantasy of licking him from neck to navel, Garrett nodded toward the plough. "Down you go, sugar. Your head rests on the pad, and your ass fits into the opening between the handles." A smirk lifted his lips. "I'll take care of your legs."

Despite the confidence of his orders, she threw him a frown. "My head...goes down *there*?" Her stomach flipped when Garrett made like Thor with a glower and a cross of arms. "Okay, all right," she muttered. "Yes, Sir."

With his help, she lay back in position. The angle wasn't horrible, raising her body into a thirty-degree slant rather than the forty-five she'd expected, but with the way the headrest was positioned, she might as well have been blindfolded in terms of seeing anything Garrett had planned for her from the waist down. Or in this case, the waist up.

But what she couldn't see, she could certainly feel.

He tethered her arms first, using a length of soft rope for the task. If the feel of the bindings and his knots weren't enough of a taunt, the man made sure to stand between her thighs through every moment of the task, letting his erection once more press against her abdomen, directly above her sex. Driven crazy by desire, she tried to lift her hips, hoping a direct plea from her pussy lips would help hurry him along.

Wrong move. Garrett lowered his palm in a firm smack to her mound, making her yelp in a crazy mix of pain and arousal. "One more move like that, little S, and I'll forget I charged up the wand."

She clenched her teeth. "Yes, Sir."

Garrett, the letch, gave a chuckle as if they were out on a Sunday picnic. How could he be so damn tranquil with a hard-on that spectacular? She quivered just thinking about him fucking her with it, filling her pussy until she screamed from the perfect pain of it, but he continued latching her into the leather leg straps, around her upper thighs, knees, and ankles, like he had all night to drive her to the brink of insanity. *Numerous* times.

"Comfy?" he finally drawled while checking the buckles on each strap again. Even the feel of him doing that made Sage wet with anticipation. With the exception of turning her head left and right, she was unable to move. Locked down, completely at the mercy of her Master. And sweet shit was he into the role tonight.

Even knowing that, she couldn't control the snarky bite in her reply. "Just fucking peachy."

Would she *ever* learn her lesson?

Garrett rained two hard swats onto her pussy this time. "Still hanging on to the 'tude a bit, sugar? That's just fine with me. I have more where those came from. How 'bout you?"

Cocky bastard. He had to rub in the burn from the spanks by pressing at the outside of her labia, didn't he? Sage gasped and let out a groan as he dug in both thumbs, knowing exactly where to press so her clit was teased to the max.

"Oh!" She let it out just as he bent another finger in to spread her more intimate tissues, exposing that trembling ridge fully now. "Oh, please God!"

"He's likely around here somewhere, but why don't you try talking to me, instead?"

Cheeky, cocky, infuriating, sexy bastard.

"M-Master...I'll behave. I promise. I just n-need..."

"What?" he prompted when she stammered into silence. "Tell me, S. What is it that you need?"

"Ohhhh!" At first it was all she could muster, due to her Sir's utterly abysmal, completely perfect timing. Since he'd chosen to finish his question by moving the pulsating wand to the first inch of her vagina, the Hold button on her brain got punched again. "More," she finally squeaked. "I need more... inside me...this is driving me crazy..."

"Mmmm." He circled the toy in a bit farther before teasing her clit with a tender pinch. "Those words are prettier'n a song from the first bird of spring, baby girl." His voice dipped to a curious cadence. "But can you be more specific? Inside you, sugar? Where?"

Sage squeezed her eyes shut. She wasn't sure if her senses swam due to her upended position or his ruthless seduction, but her mind started an incredible flight. She was unable to focus on anything but every inch of skin he touched, every sexual nerve he awakened. "My—my pussy," she stammered. "P-Please..."

"You want me in your pussy, sweet S? You want me to fuck you with my cock?"

Wasn't that what she'd been saying? Yeah, for all she knew, she was spewing out the weather report right now. "Y-Yes! T-Take me hard, Master, please!"

His answer came after a maddening pause. "I'm more than happy to oblige, sugar." He shifted, settling his hips tighter inside of hers. "Just wouldn't want a fully charged pulsating wand to go unenjoyed by my beautiful S. Hmmm, what to do?"

His roguish tone gave him away. He knew exactly what he was going to do. But so did Sage. Her sex was wide-awake with the electric certainty of it.

So was her ass.

Sure enough, a significant *click* broke the air. He'd flipped open a plastic bottle. The naughty, slightly coconut scent of lube hit her nose in the moment before he slicked some against the rim of her anus. She released a tense hiss.

"Relax," Garrett encouraged. "Take a deep breath, S. Push out. You know how this works."

"I haven't known for at least a year," she countered. Her voice shook, though she knew Garrett would discern the arousal in it as well as the anxiety. This risqué aspect of submission had begun as one of her least favorites but quickly became a naughty delight after Garrett trained her ass to take it. Even when he'd been out on deployment, she'd had instructions for using plugs to keep her ready for his kinky fun back there.

Fun that had stopped as soon as she hit her second trimester with Race.

Which he'd clearly forgotten, since he dispensed more of the liquid now. He didn't bother with coating his fingers first, either. The lube hit her hole with the force of its straight-from-the-tube chill.

"Aaahhh!" She instinctively fought her bonds as the liquid slid down to new surfaces in her tunnel.

"Mmmm." His approval didn't lessen the shit-eating satisfaction in Garrett's voice. He accompanied it by swiping a finger around the ring of her hole, gently pushing as he went, gradually stretching her. It was a little painful. A lot sinful. And made her feel even more wildly wicked for him. "Goddamn," he murmured, intensifying the effect. "Your naughty little rose is so perfect."

Sage could only hiss again in response, because he began to work the tip of the wand into her entrance. There was another cold invasion as he poured lube along the length of the toy, silently confirming that he planned on getting the entire thing into her ass.

Holy shit.

"M-Master...it'll never fit."

Instead of a verbal response, he only inched the wand in deeper. Right before he turned it on.

Sage cried out in surprise and fury—and then awe.

The setting he'd picked was a forceful one, awakening every cell that lined her erotic tunnel. With every other surge from the wand, she was forced to open wider. Between the beats, her muscles retaliated, clutching the wand tight. Like a disco light on the fritz, she was filled with blinding light one moment and plunged into tight darkness the next.

It was an experience her ass would never forget—and she soon discovered that her pussy wouldn't, either. Every throb from the toy rocked straight through her inner walls, vibrating her womb in tandem with her anus. Her thighs clenched against the straps, rattling the buckles as her vagina cried in need. It felt like a subsonic bomb of lust had been detonated in her body, decimating her mind and her will in the blast, along with everything else.

"Fuck me, sugar. You're like something out of a dream."

His growl sifted into her mind. Part of her completely agreed with him. Her senses swam as deliriously as her balance. The walls and ceiling of the loft ceased to exist. She'd be sold on the whole I'm-dreaming-this angle, if not for the pulses that served as blistering, beautiful reminders of her awake, alive state.

She was going to add insane to that list if he didn't fill her body with his soon. She tried to tell him as much in a beseeching wail. Surely he saw how her muscles quivered for him. How her pussy dripped. How her body hovered just a match strike between flame and inferno.

I need to burn up. Master, please!

Above her, Garrett readjusted his stance. He dug his fingers into one of her hips, lifting her a little and releasing a long, low growl. "I need to be inside this beautiful cunt."

He wasn't getting any argument from her.

Nevertheless, the barn rafters filled with her shriek as soon as Garrett thrust all the way into her. Yes, she'd craved this. But no, she hadn't considered how her body would be pushed to its limits, stuffed full by two throbbing staffs united in one quest: to send her over the edge of sanity and into bliss.

They sure as hell succeeded. Thoughts and concerns, worries and cares, even her damn name, were all evaporated by the incredible heat pounding at both her illicit orifices. Garrett's strokes, along with the pulsating wand's incessant cadence, turned her into something that transcended logic, a living prism. Every color in the world blazed through her, set alight by the force of his passion and the magic of his love.

The joy of it made her mouth part into a giddy sob. Her pussy flickered with a completion she'd never dreamed possible.

"Master." It tumbled from her on a gasp. "I—I'm going to—"

"Oh yeah, little girl...my beautiful Sage. Do it for me."

Her head rolled back and forth. "I'm scared. It's so much. It's too much. I don't know—"

"Of course you know. And of course you can. Give it up for me, S. All of it!"

The firestorm grew. More colors ripped through her, this time with exposed edges, tearing off pieces of her resistance as they did. *No. Bring it back. It belongs to me!*

She had no idea she'd let it spill out loud until Garrett snarled a countermand. "No. It belongs to *me*. You'll give it over to me. All of it." He began to fuck her differently. His strokes were longer, harder, deeper. "Right now, you exist to please me. And you're going to please me by coming for me."

"Y-Yessss, Massss—"

She couldn't say anything else. Her lungs seized. Her heart stopped. There was only Garrett now. His grip was her steel-strong anchor. His snarling breaths kept her alive. His cock, thick and dominating, injected new fire into her body with every ruthless thrust until the blaze consumed her whole, incinerating her from the inside out.

She screamed. Or thought she did. For all she knew, she'd just sung "The Star-Spangled Banner" as her body imploded and her mind was pulverized into stunning silver dust. Garrett's bellow of completion became a part of that mindless mix before he shot his torrent deep inside her, searing her walls...completing her soul.

While he still rocked inside her, he switched off the wand and carefully slid it out of her ass. The ropes around her arms came next. With a few deft tugs, they were loose enough to fall free. After unlatching her legs, he pulled her up by the elbows and guided her arms to encircle his neck. From instinct, Sage wrapped her thighs around his waist. The feel of his body inside her, around her...the knowledge that he was here, strong and alive... It brought a moment of peace she never dreamed of enjoying again.

The comprehension swept over her like a surprise thunder squall. And her heart hadn't brought an umbrella.

"Don't make me let go." The words were barely a whisper, but his deep sigh told her he'd heard.

"Hang on as tight as you want, sugar. For the rest of our lives."

The gift of his strength, wrapped in such perfect softness, snapped off the last latches on her self-control. The sobs came, heavy and profound, raining from her heart in a devastating mix of fear and joy, heartache and elation, terror and triumph. She let it all crash over her as Garrett quickly unlocked her legs before carrying her back to the bed, continuing to hold her close.

It was one of the most miraculous moments of her life.

The realization made her spit out a giddy laugh. Yeah, she was a mess. She'd pretty much expected that. What she hadn't foreseen was getting into the thick of this breakdown and having a moment of such surreal clarity, it made her openly gasp—and laugh.

She'd spent the last five months wallowing in a swamp of self-pity when what she'd really had was a *life*. The universe had brought her back from the dead, into the arms of the man with whom she shared a soul, with a *kapow* of everything life was supposed to be: the lows as well as the highs, the uncertainties as well as the securities, the tear-filled goodbyes...as well as the treasured hellos.

Just like the one she gave her husband now.

"Thank you for rescuing me." She settled a kiss on his

sinfully rugged lips. "Again."

Garrett returned the kiss and kept his head dipped to keep her eyes locked on him. "You're welcome, but you know it's not all over yet. You'll go see Shrink Sally once we're home, Sage. It's not a request anymore. You need to process some heavy shit, stuff I'm not mentally set up to help you with anymore."

"I know." To prove she meant it, she framed his face with her hands and nodded emphatically. "I do."

"Yeah, and about *that* little phrase." He swept up her left hand and kissed the wedding ring on it. "You're also ordered to start putting together that damn *Princess Bride* wedding you want to have, before I change my mind about agreeing to look like fucking Christopher Columbus."

She didn't hold back her jubilant smile. "Readily obeyed, Sir! I prom—" Her own gasp sliced into the thought. "Holy shit, Master. Is that a fresh flogger between your thighs or has Renaissance fashion become a new fetish for you?"

Garrett curled his lips in a sensual smirk. "I don't fuck around with fetishes, woman." The grin dissolved as his jaw clenched, his forehead furrowed, and his cock pushed against her aching walls. "That's just my wife's tight, sexy pussy making me hard all over again."

She gasped in delight as he lowered his grip to her waist and began pumping her onto his staff with defined purpose. Her thighs tingled; her clit stiffened; her body melted for him anew. "Well, one good ride certainly deserves another..."

"Abso-fucking-lutely, my little S."

He sent more heat through her sex by raising one hand and tugging the tie of her ponytail free. Her hair cascaded over her shoulders and teased at the tops of her breasts, guiding Garrett's fingers to explore her rock-hard nipples as she kept up the sensual pace he'd set. The warmth didn't stop in her pussy. Her entire being glowed with the renewed fire of their love, made possible by the boldness and bravery of her amazing husband...her Master forever.

She gazed at the carved, perfect angles of his face and kissed him again with the force of her adoration. "My hero," she whispered.

"My heart," he whispered back.

TIE THE KNOTS

Zeke Hayes and Rayna Chestain

CHAPTER ONE

It was a dark and stormy night.

Zeke Hayes jutted a mental middle finger at the cliché. "Dark and stormy" he could deal with. This torrent was more like an all-access pass to Mother Nature's water park, without the Churros and cheesy Beach Boys mixes. The deluge had hit the highway right at midnight, forcing him to pull his truck off at the exit for his apartment instead of Rayna's house.

At least the Guy Upstairs had waited to drown the earth until after Sage and Garrett's wedding. Correction: makeup wedding. Sage had pulled out all the stops to compensate for her and Hawk's first attempt at formal vows, which had been ruined by a madman who'd nearly killed Zeke and had almost dragged Rayna back to white slavery in Thailand. Though Garrett had marched Sage off to a civil ceremony in order to put the legal seal on things before their next deployment, Sage had insisted on something with pomp, circumstance, flowers, food, music, and even her guy on a horse to sweep her off on a ride into the sunset. She'd gotten it all, including Garrett on a beautiful gray stallion, actually looking damn cool in the Renaissance wedding clothes she'd made them all wear. Yeah, it had been a pretty awesome day, until the second fucking flood of Noah.

As he and Rayna rushed from the car, the clouds growled and the rain fell harder. Z snarled back before tugging Rayna into the elevator. Shit. Her costume was made mostly of velvet, which meant she now wore every chilled drop that had fallen on her. Despite his best efforts to warm her, his firebird was frozen to the bone.

"Fuck," he muttered. The oath spewed from him a couple more times when they got to the door of his place. "Sorry, bird. I'm not used to the lock."

Every word of it was true. He could easily count the number of times he'd actually spent the night here in the last year, keeping the apartment mostly as—

What?

A place of his own to "get away alone with his thoughts"? Negative on that order, kids. His thoughts weren't exactly the kind a guy invited over for a few beers and a gut spill.

A restful retreat between missions? More sarcastic laughter echoed from his brain. If he wanted quiet, he headed for the cabin in the Cascades into which he'd sunk most of his design and decorating dollars. And if he wanted real peace, he slept at Rayna's.

A "Master Zeke bachelor party pad"? He didn't bother to let that one even play with the grenade pin. When he wanted to play Dom, the walls of the Bastille Club, where he was a staff Dominant, held more than enough equipment for his needs— all exercised on the willing body and soul of the woman by his side.

They truly had come so far together in a little over a year.

The best damn year of his life.

The fire-colored jewel that dangled from her black leather collar twinkled at him as affirmation of that. They'd made the most of every chance they had to feed the flames of their love, making sure the kindling of their friendship supported the bigger logs they'd placed on top. The result was a blaze that fed him, mind and soul, more completely than he dared admit.

And terrified him more deeply than he wanted to acknowledge.

As the lock finally gave for him, the woman scared him in other ways. Her teeth chattered like Morse code for *freezing my nipples off*. The tendrils of her fancy hairdo were soaked slashes against the beautiful angles of her cheeks. Her lips and exposed shoulders began to match the peacock blue of her gown.

"All those p-people b-beheaded by K-King Henry and Qu-Queen Elizabeth?" she stammered. "Th-They must have b-been the fashion d-designers for the c-c-court."

He gave her a tender smile while cranking on the heater, though it was impossible to stop his gaze from wandering to the cleavage formed by her tight-laced corset. Sage's dress had been more of a demure bridal thing, but the maid of honor had free rein to be more provocative in her purple and red gown, featuring a lacy neckline that pushed her breasts into very grab-worthy areas. Holy fuck, it was all he could do not to imagine just pulling them free from the fabric and then pinching them until they were as red as her dress before shoving her skirts around her waist and—

"Sorry, bird," he muttered instead. "I'm banging on the heat now." He also walked over and turned on the flames beneath the artificial logs in the apartment's excuse for a fireplace. "Isn't as nice as what we have at the cabin, but it'll have to do for now."

An awkward silence arced between them. Neither of them had to speak the reason why.

Isn't as nice as what we have at the cabin...

We. The word had never flowed naturally off his lips

unless he was referring to something that had to do with the guys on his Special Forces team. He sure as hell never thought he'd be including a woman in the phrase beyond an invitation to one of Bastille's private play rooms—let alone confusing one by looping her into a comment about his personal, solitary sanctuary.

Personal. Solitary. The words were a damn good credo for him. They'd served him well since the age of ten when the streets became his home and then gained more importance when discovering his kink gene nine years later. Hadn't taken him long to learn that like many other things in his life, he reveled in sensual Dominance the most when dealing it hard, fast, and rough. That was just peachy, but most of the time, he had to chill on his cravings for the sake of being a good Dom to his many submissives. And basing a lasting relationship on the affinity? That was like a wolf hooking up with a dolphin. Unwise and unnatural.

Yeah, the wolf card was best played with the "lone" part securely attached. Everyone knew their parts. Nobody got hurt. Pain was only best when it was consensual and clear.

So when the fuck had that all changed?

He grunted as he stomped down the hall to grab some dry towels for Rayna. *Who says anything's changed?*

He'd opened his pie hole on the wrong words. That was all. Rayna knew where he stood, where *they* stood, and she was fine with it. Happy, even. Just because she'd been along for the ride the last few times he'd been up to the cabin—

The last five times.

—which didn't mean shit beyond the fact that she was being his dutiful subbie, and—

Like she remembers good "subbie" behavior when she kicks

your ass in burping contests during the drive up the mountain or reads you jokes in different voices to help you relax.

—which still didn't mean anything, beyond the fact that they'd started this thing out as friends and now—

And now what?

What did *now* mean to her, if he kept dropping bullshit bombs like that? Was she getting ideas...the *wrong* ideas? Was he steering her down the same road he'd taken with Marie without realizing it? Was the day coming, perhaps soon, when he'd tell her he'd call as soon as he could during the deployment, only to find a thousand excuses not to? Would he promise to pick her up for a night at the dungeon, only to claim car trouble, last-minute training, or some other line she'd instantly see through...as her heart was breaking?

Just imagining it, picturing them apart, led him to a more terrifying question.

What if it wasn't *her* heart doing that breaking thing?

The second he rounded the corner back into the living room, clarifying that answer was shoved to the bottom of his duty roster.

The *very* bottom.

Rayna stood in front of the fireplace, wearing nothing but the historical underthings that went along with her lady-in-waiting garb. Lacy. White. Wet. And sheer. Good Christ, he could see every puckered, hard inch of her breasts, the delectable curve of her waist...and the V between her thighs, leading to the sweet treasure he adored so much. Her face was that of a fucking goddess, circled by intricate braids that were made more brilliant by the fire's glow. She took his breath away as she stepped from the puddle of her soaked gown and spread her soft arms, making a beautiful web in the air with the long length of red rope she held.

"I was looking for a blanket and found this instead." Her lips quirked in that shy, tentative smile that clutched his heart and jerked at his cock. "But I'm thinking it'll warm me up just as much as a blanket...Sir?"

CHAPTER TWO

The towels fell from Zeke's hands. He released a savoring growl along with them. While the sound gave her shivers in all the good ways this time, Rayna had to compel herself to meet his gaze as he stepped across the room like his gorgeous ass was on fire, hoping he didn't detect the lie she'd just told.

Okay, it was more of a little fib. She *had* found the blanket before the rope but only by seconds. The coil was tucked right beneath the cashmere throw, almost as if it wanted to be found tonight. It was a luxurious Japanese weave, intricately woven for one purpose alone, and it certainly wasn't to tie down luggage on the car. The stuff felt like silken sin against her wrists and fingers, making her wonder how it would feel against the rest of her body. Around her arms and thighs, pressed to her breasts, framing her pussy...

She'd be bound. Subdued. Zeke's prisoner in so many senses of the word.

Prisoner.

She forced her mind to repeat the word.

Yes. Prisoner. Because you've chosen *to be. Because you trust this man with every drop of blood in your body and every ounce of love in your heart.*

Zeke stopped in front of her. He didn't make a single move to touch the rope. His massive chest expanded with every one of his harsh breaths. He showed no mercy in his long and steady scrutiny of her. When he spoke, his voice was just as austere.

"Why are you offering this to me?"

She'd dropped her gaze to the formidable knot of his Adam's apple. She lifted it again, obeying the implicit command in his tone. There would be no playing coy about what he meant by "this." They both understood it referred to much more than the physical rope.

"Because I want to," she offered. "Because you love it, and I trust you, and I want to please you." She unhooked a hand from the rope to form a silencing cage around his lips. While keeping him locked beneath her fingers, she persisted, "And because it's time, Sir."

His eyes darkened to the shade of unpolished copper. She took that as her cue to let her hand drop.

"It's time?" he charged. "You've just decided that now? Tonight 'it's time' and that's that?"

There was a shitload of subtext beneath that query too. He was clearly referencing her few—make that about a million—issues around things like confinement and immobility, thanks to the year she spent running from white slavers and then being shackled like an animal once they'd caught her. But she'd been tackling it in careful chunks with the help of Sally Sadler, the base therapist. Though Z usually asked her to recount the sessions for him too, those requests had ceased during the last eight days.

The week leading to his best friend's wedding.

If the man thought she wouldn't make the connection there, he had a thicker skull than she'd thought. He hadn't pressed to search through her mental baggage because he'd been a little busy lugging *his* around. It'd been plastered across his face through every minute of the preparations for "the big day," every second of the rehearsal, every moment of the ceremony itself. While Z had been jubilant for his buddy, even playing the bridegroom's wingman had made him look ready to pass out a few times.

His bravery on his friend's behalf had touched the depths of Rayna's heart. It was a big reason why she'd picked this moment to hand over this piece of trust to him. She longed to banish that fear lingering in his eyes. Yearned to hear him snarl in her ear with the full confidence of his Domination again... with the certainty that his subbie treasured the collar he'd placed around her neck far more than any ring he could slip around her finger.

"It hasn't been *that* sudden." She smiled indulgently. "I've been talking to Sally about it for a while." Her lips lifted a little higher when thinking of the bespectacled psychologist who, along with Sage, had become one of her most trusted confidantes. "I've been working on it because I know how much you love to play with ropes. You gave that up for me, Sir. Now I want to give it back."

She opened her hands, letting the rope slip from her hands to his.

Zeke was unnervingly silent for a long moment. A sound built somewhere near the base of his throat. Deep, low, conflicted. "Ray-bird—"

"You mean subbie, don't you?"

This time, he full-out growled. "Rayna Eleanor, listen to me."

With a little snarl of her own, she sank to her knees. And didn't stop there. Desperate times called for desperate measures. With her forehead atop one of his Drool-worthy Francis Drake boots, she rasped, "Let me listen while you wrap those ropes around me. Let me hear you with every knot and feel you with every inch of trust I give. Please, Zeke. Please, Sir."

His hard breaths vibrated down through her. She whimpered a little as he settled one of his big hands over her head, his fingers kneading in an outward show of his conflict. When she risked a glance up at him, his tight scowl awaited. The bold cliffs of his face were beautiful in the fire's amber glow.

"Damn it, firebird." He slipped his hand down to cup her chin, the rope brushing her body with the movement. "Those eyes of yours could hypnotize me into robbing a goddamn bank."

It was a morsel of bait she couldn't refuse. And didn't want to. If he was going to make her push him, then that was just what she'd do. "Really?" she quipped. "A whole bank?" She ran a finger along the hem of his damp jerkin. "That would mean a *lot* of shoes for Sage and me—"

"Dear fuck."

His interjection gave her the chance to stifle her giggle, which was a good thing. He came out of the gate after that a man on a mission—an intense, don't-mess-with-me one. Without warning, Zeke dropped the rope in order to pull her up by both shoulders. As soon as she found balance on her feet, he shifted a hand to bracket her face, with his thumb on her chin and index finger against her jaw. If the commanding grip didn't melt her blood to butter, his gaze did. All the golden flecks in his hazels ignited at once, a thousand flames that seared everything she'd once called a pulse. The only thing still throbbing in her body was her pussy, screaming at her in need, moist folds surging in arousal.

As if he'd stared through her clothes to discover that fact,

Zeke kicked up one side of his mouth. It was the only warmth that sneaked onto his face. With his eyes still glittering like a damn panther, he murmured to her, "Go to the bathroom and get out of those things before you catch pneumonia on me, subbie. Then dry yourself off—and grab the lube off the counter on your way back in."

"Y-Yes, Sir."

She bit back the *damn it* that wanted to be added to it. Lube? That usually meant things were going to be inserted into places that required extra help. She winced as the thought dug in during her walk to the bathroom. *You had to get the rope out, didn't you? Had to wake up the man's kinky little itch.*

Which, she should've known damn well and good by now, was anything but "little."

Which, she should've also known, was capable of making her own skin feel a little tight and bothered.

The restlessness worsened as she pulled off the rest of her clothes and ran one of his big towels over her body. During that, she conducted a long study of herself in his bathroom mirror. She smiled at what she saw. Her figure had regained some curves over the last two years, the result of good nutrition instead of the sticks, berries, and bugs upon which she and Sage had existed during their year on the run in Africa. As a result, her breasts had gained a cup size and her ass now had a pleasant swell. The rain had loosened little tendrils from her wedding updo, framing eyes that shined with her growing desire for the man who waited to do wonderfully wicked things to her.

Zeke.

He'd made her this beautiful.

He'd made her this secure.

And she'd never stop trying to find new ways to thank him for it.

Tonight was going to be one of those times. She'd worked hard with Sally to get here, in this mental space where she could set aside the horror of the past and finally embrace the joy of her present. In many ways, it was a gift to herself as much as Zeke, no matter how strongly he'd object to that right now. But she was determined to convince him. She'd tell him with every second of her submission, every inch of skin she gave him to bind, every knot he secured...all of it now symbolizing her love instead of her pain.

With those conclusions helping her nearly float out of the bathroom, it was no wonder she dropped the lube bottle as soon as she returned to the living room. Her jaw followed the same trajectory. Her reaction was born from equal parts delight and dread. Z validated her on both reactions when he turned, letting the firelight caress the planes of his now-naked chest, and threw her a grin that matched his pirate boots.

"Merry Christmas," he drawled. "I had your present delivered here so I could hide it."

She saw his point. Though the seven-foot-tall aluminum tripod could be collapsed down into its own duffel, she would have instantly figured out his gift had it been delivered to her place once she saw the dealer's name on the box. They'd talked to the guy for an hour when they'd given the suspension truss a "trial run" at the lifestyle convention they'd attended during one of his three-day leaves between ops. She'd fallen in love with the apparatus. It could easily hold her weight, opening up sexy possibilities for their fun no matter where she and Zeke were. Granted, her Dom was the best at *Macgyver*ing any space into a play room, but having the truss would help him focus on...other things.

Judging by the smirk that persisted on his breathtaking features, those "other things" were already dancing across in his devious, kinky mind.

"Errrmm." She gave him a tentative smile in return. "Hate to be the bearer of crazy news, but you're three weeks early."

"Honey, in my line of work, we take the time we can get."

"Good point."

When she started to step forward again, Z halted her with a grunt. "You forgetting something, bird?" He nudged his chin toward the fallen lube. "Turn around when you pick it up. With your legs a little bit apart."

Shit. It never took much to rev the man's Dom engines to full speed. As the storm gained force outside the windows, so did the command in Z's voice and stance. His lips dropped the smirk but his eyes didn't. Those flecks of sensual pleasure gave her the incentive to obey his directive—while adding a saucy wiggle of her ass to finish it off.

She was only three shakes into the performance before he stopped her. In person. It took him just a couple of steps to lunge to her, slamming behind her and stilling her with his hands on her hips. His fingers dug into her skin, hurting her a little, turning her on a lot. As she gave him an appreciative groan, he fitted his chest to her spine and his chin to her nape. He grabbed the lube from her in a commanding sweep. His breath, hot and rough, flooded her ear.

"You're into trying all kinds of new things tonight, aren't you, bird?"

He finished the growl by scooping his arms around her, one under her knees and one around her waist. The room swirled by as he picked her up, spun her around, and carried her to the middle of the room, a few feet in front of the truss. The rope now lay in a tidy red coil next to the tripod, entrancing—and scaring—her more in this state than it had in a tangle. It was ready for Z to use on her now. To transform her into his complete submissive. His total captive.

And that was okay.

She was okay.

No matter how nervous he made her with his new and wicked chuckle.

She threw him a scowl. The pirate boots had definitely gone to his head. His grin was a naughty slash that parted his beard scruff, emphasizing the effect more. It was nearly impossible to concentrate on the large box he dragged off the hearth with one toe. She hadn't been paying the container much attention, thinking the truss had come in it, but she now realized the proportions didn't match.

The bullion flecks in his eyes, matching his smirk and his laugh, didn't relieve her disquiet. She tried to loosen the tension by quipping, "Another present?"

Zeke tilted his head, leaned in, and stared deeply at her. *Crap.* He knew what his version of the come-hither gaze did to her bloodstream and, right now, was clearly enjoying it. The firelight danced on his jaw as he murmured, "Santa was good to me, too."

Though he nudged the box's lid in a spirit of suspense, Rayna guessed the contents by the time he said "good." She remembered the other item they'd tried at the lifestyle convention. More accurately, *she'd* tried—while Zeke had watched with a growing surge in his crotch. Sure enough, as the imprinted tissue of the specialty boot maker was revealed, she barely stifled an anxious sigh.

She *had* to go and fall in love with a guy who'd lived on the streets for eight years but had a weird passion for ballet. More specifically, ballet dancers. More explicit than that, ogling *her* as a ballet dancer. The second she'd put on the fetish boots, which were like a ballerina's toe shoes with heels, her Sir had let out a low groan and openly adjusted himself there on the exhibit floor, his eyes betraying a craving to hike up her skirt and plunge into her while the crowd cheered. The reaction had gotten *her* so hot that she'd almost asked to be charged for the things so she could keep them on, teasing him all day.

That was before she'd tried to walk. And nearly broken both ankles, not to mention her neck. Zeke's reflexes had prevented both when he'd rushed and caught her so fast she'd almost looked for the rockets hidden in his ankles. Three minutes later, kinky ballerina was officially written off as a role from her past.

But *her* past always had a way of haunting her. And now its invasion was accompanied by the beautiful hulk of a man who crouched next to her, infiltrating her with his hot gaze, taking her breath away with the granite of his muscles.

Suddenly, a couple of ghosts from that convention didn't feel like such unwanted visitors.

"Wear them, Rayna." A tiny trace of supplication dotted his husky tone, letting her know the option to refuse was still hers. A *tiny* trace. "Wear them tonight...for me."

She swallowed and looked at the boots. They were stunning. He'd ordered them in a custom black-and-white patent style, making them look like a pair of Victorian lady's boots, a nod to her love for Steampunk. And even the pair at the trade show had made her feel elegant before she'd turned into an outright ele*phant.* "I guess I only have to stumble a few steps."

Zeke kicked up a corner of his mouth. "Who says you're 'stumbling' anywhere?"

"Huh?"

He answered that by pulling out one of the boots and sliding it onto her foot. She winced a little as the extreme arch forced her foot to go *en pointe*, but since the front laces were only for appearances, it took Z five seconds to yank the zipper along her calf, sealing her in. As soon as he did the same with the other boot, he leaned back on his haunches and took her in with a hooded, heated gaze.

"Holy fuck." He cleared his throat. "I've been fantasizing about what you'd look like in those and nothing else but..." His head started an appreciative back-and-forth roll. "My imagination sucks ass."

Her head fell lower, a natural reaction to the gruff edges of his voice. With her gaze fixated on his huge hands, now resting on the thighs that bracketed the strained bulge beneath his zipper, she adjusted to a position that best showed off the shoes for him. "Thank you, my Sir," she softly replied.

An approving rumble emanated from his chest. God, she loved making him do that. It always told her Z was on his way to his happy Dom space, trusting her enough to throw down his own walls and be the man to deliver the control she craved— and *he* needed.

"God*damn*, you please me." His voice was an extension of the thunder, rough and dangerous. It brought her head up a little, and her gaze was captivated by the gleaming lust in his.

"Then I'm happy," she whispered.

A deep breath expanded his chest. Warmth spread through her body before drifting to pool in the tender layers of her sex and the darkest corners of her vagina. That arousal thickened when he spoke once more, his graveled rasp transformed into a full Master's growl.

"You'll please me again by following me to the truss, little bird" —he rose and turned, clearly expecting to be obeyed— "on your hands and knees."

Her first reaction to that was...nothing. She didn't flicker so much as an eyelash, let alone a protest or glare. Deeper confusion set in. She should be enraged. Probably mortified too. Sure, he'd given her similar directives in their playtimes over the last year, but never something like this, literally trailing after him in a hands-and-knees crawl. It was an action of complete servitude, obeisance—of damn near captivity. So shouldn't the alarms of horror be pealing up and down her body?

But there was no such dread. Or fury. Or fear. No matter how hard she tried to muster the stuff, it wasn't there.

Instead, she took a little breath that vibrated with need. She uncurled her legs and recognized her moist desire in the cleft between them. She squeezed her eyes shut and felt only the mesmerizing pull of the man across the room...the Dom who'd ordered her to his side so he could lift her into unfathomable pleasure.

Hardly believing she did so, she moved into the position he'd ordered.

A smile of delight spread across her lips. Trusting him like this, pleasing him like this... It permeated her in wonderful warmth. The feeling intensified with every slide of her hands and knees across the carpet. The journey, along with the tight bonds of her new boots, wrapped the security of Z's Dominance even closer around her mind and heart, preparing her body for the same paradise. By the time she arrived at his feet again, she was ready for anything the man had in mind. "Putty" was a good word for it. "Pure goo" was another. But Z bested her on both accounts with the words emitted in his carnal growl.

"My perfect ballerina."

She knew he didn't expect an answer. That was a good thing. All she could do was sigh her thanks and press her head against his knees, repeating the sound as he brushed a hand along her hair—until he gripped her scalp and pulled hard. Her throat tightened to give him a grateful keen as he used the pressure to guide her beneath the truss. With the firelight playing across the carpet, it almost seemed like they were going to be playing Indians in the teepee—only tonight, she wasn't going to be the squaw. She was going to be dinner, hot and swinging on the sticks.

She couldn't wait.

"Up on your knees, honey." His voice thickened into magma that flowed straight to her core and coated her sex. She trembled in need for his next instruction, but after he widened her pose by nudging her thighs out with a boot toe instead of a spoken direction, instinct dictated he was shifting to "Stealth Zsycho" mode—another choice that would get no argument from her. When Zeke went silent, he became intense. The benefits, as she'd learned over the last year, were like sticking one's finger into a sexual light socket.

The thought, along with the anxiety that still nagged thanks to the pile of rope next to them, made her lungs pump and her limbs shiver. Though she struggled to calm herself as Zeke knelt behind her, she was certain he felt it all anyway.

"Breathe." The word was nothing but air in her ear as he drew the rope across her skin, beneath her breasts. She

ANGEL PAYNE

thought he'd caress her nipples as he did, but he scraped his hand between them instead, focusing on the space where her heart hammered her ribs. "Red light or yellow light if you need to stop or slow down. *Breathe*, honey."

Breathe. She could do that, couldn't she? All she had to do was focus on that. In, out. In, out.

The task was easy...for about a minute.

She was able to stay centered while Zeke wrapped the rope around her torso three more times. He maintained a silence that was nearly clinical, focused wholly on matching lengths of the rope and settling it around the places that would give her the greatest comfort.

That was all before he started peeling her comfort away. Inch by incredible inch. Moment by breathtaking moment. And, God help her, kiss by amazing kiss.

He began by folding her arms together behind her back, having her wrap her fingers around the opposite forearm so that binding her there would mean taking some of her balance...and a lot more of her freedom. She tensed from that recognition until he ran his lips along each arm first. With every touch of his mouth, her anxiety melted like honey in hot water. Once he finished tying her arms, he looped the ropes around her waist, caressing her skin in his intended path before he pressed each new length of rope against her.

With wet suckles to her nape and shoulder, he swept around to kneel in front of her. The world grew a few more shadows as he loomed close, eclipsing her view with his bulk. Rayna almost sobbed at how beautiful he was, hair tousled, jaw scruffy, face focused. His battle-toughened fingers brushed her skin as he created an intricate lattice over her breasts, waist, and stomach. Through every moment, he acted as though it

71

were a vanilla-style seduction too, stopping to give soft nips of his mouth and strokes of his knuckles, every move filled with intentional desire.

Despite her efforts to breathe evenly, air sawed in and out of her lungs like a rusty knife. Like she could be blamed. The man gazed at her with the force of a hurricane but touched her with the care of a summer breeze. Though his knots were secured tight, his kisses were as seductive as August stars. He might have resembled a mountain incarnate, but his concentration was an ocean, fathoms of strength beneath angles of dark beauty. She returned his attention with a gaze of awe...and arousal.

As he looped the ropes through the crevice between her thighs, his low growl confirmed he'd noticed the same thing. He captured her stare while pulling the lengths toward him, sliding the rope along the sensitive lips where she burned most for him. As Rayna expelled a pleading whine, she wondered how he could maintain his mien of silent composure. If anything, only his eyes changed, narrowing as if to chastise her for begging at all but obviously pleased with the magic his ropes had unleashed in her body.

Still without speaking, he jerked the leads a little tighter around her upper thighs. Once done, he wrapped them back toward her ass. Rayna swallowed, feeling small yet sheltered as he leaned close enough to push her forehead against the center of his chest. The powerful cadence of his heartbeat vibrated through her while his arms, massive and steady, bracketed her body. He stroked her back in slow but urgent sweeps, his long and mighty fingers working heat into her skin and muscles. As she sucked in a huge breath, so did he. Rayna moaned and gently bit his pectoral. Thunder rolled through his chest again.

He pulled her tighter, nearly locking her body against his. They swayed together, pulled by rising tides that were mastered by a moon of need...

And her Sir's wicked intent.

She should have recalled that he'd asked her to fetch the lube. He readily provided a reminder now, pulling the tube from one of the deep pockets in his historical breeches. Only the damn ghost of Shakespeare knew what else he'd stashed in there for his amusement, though she had a feeling she'd learn soon enough.

"Breathe," he whispered again.

Despite wanting to sling a retort, Rayna was powerless to refuse. Damn him, the man knew what effect his voice had on her when he lowered it like that. The magic of it was more intense because he had her physically at his mercy. Bound by his ropes. Submissive to his will.

Which now included the soft trail of his fingers into the cleft of her ass.

"Breathe."

Since she was chest-to-chest with him, the command literally echoed in her body. She successfully heeded his words while he circled the tender puckers at the rim of her asshole, as he slicked some lube along those dark tissues, even as he spread that forbidden entrance and started to push a finger inside. But she lost the battle when he fished in the pocket of doom again. His hand came back out quickly. Should that make her relieved or worried?

When he spoke, his voice rasping the air with nasty knowingness, she got her answer.

"You're such a good Girl Scout. Brand-new lip balm, right in the front pocket of your purse. Remind me to be a good Boy

Scout and buy you some more."

Worried. She needed to be very, very worried.

She expressed as much in another tight whimper, not that he let her get far with it. The sound became a full cry as he pushed the tube halfway in, giving it a little twist so the lube was spread too.

"Ahhh!"

"Breathe."

"Damn it," she snapped. "Stop telling me to— Ohhh! *Ahhhh!*"

As he spread her ass and seated the rest of the tube in, her body went taut to accommodate the invasion. Zeke's gratified growl, along with the way he started braiding the rope into a restraining harness across her ass, were little consolation for her new discomfort. "Sshhh," he admonished when she flung a frustrated huff. "Breathe and accept it, bird."

Her teeth locked. "I *am* breath—"

He severed her attitude by sweeping a hand up, yanking her head back, and crushing his mouth to hers in raw possession. In an instant, her brain was mush again. Her equilibrium vanished. The only elements keeping her upright were the cliff of his body, the haven of his kiss.

As he dragged his lips back, she struggled to pry open her eyes. Oh God, she didn't want to. Though her ass still hurt, the warmth in her blood made it better. And the heat in her pussy. And the firestorm in which her head now spun. She was achingly aware of the shaky sigh she emitted...and of Zeke's breath mingling with it as he moved his hand to cradle her chin, keeping her head aloft.

"Keep them closed." His voice blended with the storm, thick as thunder, silken as rain. "Surrender to the darkness, little bird. Lose yourself in it. Fly in it...for me."

Yes.

She was conscious of wetting her lips, struggling to summon the words to them, but nothing escaped save the breaths he'd been demanding of her every two seconds. She was nothing but air, light and fragile yet strong and essential, mastered by every move Z made, every touch he gave, every new knot he tied. As the ropes dug into her skin, the gates creaked open a little wider on her soul.

And she flew.

The floor disappeared beneath her. So did the pressure on her knees, even gravity itself. A dim corner of her brain questioned what was going on, but the gentle creak of the truss gave up the answer, along with Zeke's soft snarl. He'd bound her *and* suspended her.

And it was heaven.

She let her limbs go totally limp. Sure enough, the ropes kept her in place better than a safety net. She was weightless. Boundless. She felt like a precious treasure, an erotic jewel waiting to be claimed by her owner. New shivers claimed her vagina and sizzled through her pussy, especially as Zeke adjusted the suspension lines to spread her legs a little wider. Someplace precious and primal in her soul knew exactly for what he was preparing her, igniting every inch of her skin with new heat.

This was more amazing than she'd dreamed. She almost laughed from the realization. God, she'd been so worried about all the old shit this experience might stir up, it'd blocked her from considering the new vistas it might open. The incredible levels of erotic awakening to which it would help her soar...

The next moment, Zeke was there to show her just how

high.

If the panther-like sound from his throat didn't give away his arrival between her legs, the press of his thighs certainly did. From the way his massive muscles flexed against hers, opening her body more, she could tell he was standing now. He grabbed the ropes that bound her waist in order to slide her tighter back against him, which tightened the cinch against her ass. The balm tube slid in a little deeper, making every muscle clench around it...and sending a new ache deep into her pussy for good measure. She moaned, feeling her sex shiver as new drops of need formed.

"My beautiful little firebird." Zeke let both his hands trail down her suspended legs. His fingers roamed over the laces of both her boots before circling around to flow up again, teasing the backs of her knees and inner thighs.

Don't stop there. Please...please keep going...

She needed his fingers in her sex. Needed him to spread her labia with his big thumbs, stretching her for something even more massive after them. She needed his knowing strokes on the ridge of her clit, drawing her desire to heights that nobody else could.

She needed him. Only him.

At the first brush of his fingers between her legs, she moaned. As he plunged two fingers into her, she shrieked.

"Holy fuck." Z added a third finger, penetrating with more insistence. "Your pussy has never felt more perfect, subbie." With his other hand, he yanked at the loops of his breeches, which parted easily. The irony wasn't lost on Rayna. That those royal court designers decided to make men's crotches the easiest thing to unfasten, in an age where the queen's authority was based on her virginity, had to have been someone's idea of a joke.

His cock burned her tender cleft with new heat. Rayna trembled and mewled, incapable of moving much more than that. While the ropes kept her safe, they also rendered her more helpless than cuffs and chains ever could. By the sound of Z's sadistic grunt, he knew the exact same thing.

"You're shivering all over, bird. You cold? Need a blanket?"

His taunt, given as he dragged the length of his penis through her most sensitive tissues, brought a mix of hot fury and delicious frustration. She didn't know whether to yell or sob. In the end, a strained moan won out, courtesy of him guiding the barbell in his frenulum to the edge of her vagina and rubbing it there with excruciating leisure.

"S-Sir," she finally managed to rasp. "Oh, p-please!"

Sweet God, every inch of her craved him. She was on birth control and they'd gotten tested together, so technically there was nothing holding him back from driving all the way in—except that he was a rogue with an evil streak and the self-control of Saint Peter. That was fine, as long as he planned on letting her into heaven sometime soon too.

She keened again as he wiggled the ropes against her ass. The tight ache of his makeshift plug, along with the feel of his cockhead getting sucked by the first inches of her pussy, made every molecule in her sex go into overdrive. The ropes made it impossible to focus on anything else. She was his completely captive plaything.

"You know what the sight of this plug in your ass does to me, honey?" Zeke's voice was as unrelenting as his hands, which now used the ends of the ass harness to pull her back, giving her another fraction of his stalk. "Makes my cock leak that sweet precome all over your pussy. I know you love tasting me like that... Maybe the next time I let you fly, I'll let you suck on me a little before I spread you and fuck you. But right now, the sight of my juice all over your cunt just makes me want to do one thing.

"I'm going to fuck you good and hard, firebird."

CHAPTER THREE

With the ropes in his fists and her scream in his ears, Zeke heaved his little subbie all the way back, impaling her body with his.

He groaned, lost in the deepest pleasure he'd ever known. Her channel was soaking wet for him, a grip of heat and tremors that wrapped his dick in tight bands of ecstasy. With every thrust, it got better. He coiled more torque into one of his arms, using only that one to pull on the harness so he could be free to smack her sweet ass every time he yanked her back. As if his cock needed any more incentive. Her cries, growing more exigent each second, told him that the tube in her anus was working its magic too. That pressure on her G spot, in conjunction with his erection, made her damn close to climaxing from the inside out. Once she did, he'd be ready to layer it with the swipes to her clit that would send her over the edge.

There was just one hitch to that plan. The fact that every plunge into her pussy made his dick scream louder for release. He clenched his teeth with the paradise-meets-purgatory torment of it. He needed to think of something else. Maybe like...cleaning his gun. Goddamnit, that always gave him a hard-on too.

The wedding. Shit yeah, he'd think of the wedding, and— and—

Rayna in that gown. In that corset. With her hair all up,

and her lips giving him that I-can't-wait-for-you-to-fuck-me smile, and—

"Damn. Oh damn, Ray-bird. Nobody makes me feel like this...the way you do. Nobody makes my dick this hard, my balls this hot—"

"*Zeke!* Shit! Ohhhh, Sir!"

The words spilled out on sobs that coincided with the deep, powerful pulls from her vagina. All it took was a few knowing strokes to her stiff clit, and he dissolved the words into hoarse screams. As she reached her pleasure, he finally took his. The explosion was hot, blinding, dizzying. Orgasms were life's leading perk, but sharing them with Rayna had elevated these moments to a joy that far surpassed the release from his cock. Spilling his seed into her body made him feel... whole. Completed.

It made him feel like he'd finally found his home.

Fuck. *Fuck.*

The oath echoed in his senses at least a hundred times as he pulled out and leaned over her, murmuring his praise for her courage and beauty. He revised it to *what the fuck* as he yanked the fast releases on his knots, lowered and loosened her out of the ropes, and eased the balm tube out of her body. Though his panic eased during the familiar routine of aftercare, including Vitamin E oil on the spots where the ropes had chafed the hardest, the discomfort nagged the back of his mind like a top-forty ballad with a shitty but addictive chorus.

He blamed the mush attack on the wedding. Yeah, so he'd celebrated many weddings like this before. What better way to salute a buddy's demise than paying ode to bachelorhood with a mind-blowing fuck? But none of those buddies had been his *best* buddy...which had to be the logical explanation for the violins that crashed his mental rock concert.

"Hey."

The word, spoken with soft request, warmed the skin at the center of his chest. It matched the woman now sprawled atop him, her breasts pressed to his ribs, their legs tangled together in the blanket. Her voice was undemanding, filled only with her devotion. As he dipped his face to return her gaze, a satisfied subbie glow filled his vision.

"Hey."

Rayna traced his eyebrows with a finger. "What's going on up here, hot stuff?"

He let those brows drop. *Hell.* Just this once, he needed to dig deep and do what he'd never done to her before. Lie. If this circle jerk in his mind was giving him a gut punch, it made no sense to make her share the misery, especially because he was sure a good night's sleep would reset his control panel. Or so he hoped.

"Well?" Rayna abandoned his brows to sift her hand back through his hair. "Unless it's classified, you're spilling, Sergeant."

Z took her hand and returned it to his chest. He kept his on top of it. "I'm—" He huffed and rolled his eyes. He *really* needed a good lie right now. But all he knew with this woman was the truth. In every word or thought they'd ever shared, even the crappy stuff, they'd always had their honesty. "Rayna, I'm not top forty."

She reacted to that as he assumed she would. By giggling into his chest. "Thank you, Sir," she drawled. "Think I've got a good handle on that one by now."

He should've joined her in the laughter. Written the whole thing off with a bite of sarcasm, kissed her, and given her another mind-melting climax. But another memory from today haunted across his mind like a vindictive ghost, keeping him somber. "You cried today."

Her brows scrunched. "Well, yeah. Several times. My best friend finally had the wedding she wanted. I was happy."

"Not every time." He curled his free arm beneath his head, giving his gaze some elevation over hers. "Not *every* time, Rayna."

Brutal honesty. It was the hugest strength in their relationship and their most disgusting enemy. "Zeke, I—"

"During the ceremony," he cut in. "During that sappy Celine Dion song. You were looking down at your flowers, and your face was drowning in sadness."

Her gaze lowered. Her lips wobbled. "I just really like that song." A nervous laugh toppled out. "When I was little, I used to fantasize I was dancing to it with Justin Timberlake. He'd broken up with Britney and only had eyes for me. Of course, Finn and Shane tormented me endlessly about it. They even drew a mustache on my favorite poster of him, saying he'd 'thanked' them after all my lip gloss stains from kissing it."

He still didn't grab the bait of her humor. Instead, with his knuckles grazing her cheek, he murmured, "See? You want top forty. And honey, you deserve to have—"

"Ohhh, no." She bolted upright. He'd expected that too. And much to the regret of his churning gut, he also expected the renewed emotion in her voice. "You're not going there, Sergeant Hayes. We've *been there* already. You know how I feel! Why can't you get it through that steak you call a brain sometimes and realize that I am helplessly, hopelessly, in love with you?"

He released a heavy breath while scooping her hand back

in his. "And I with you, my little bird." After he gently suckled her knuckles, he ran his thumb along her ring finger. "But one day, you'll want the dance to Celine more than me. You'll need the ring and the *I do*s and the guy who comes home to you every night...and there's not a damn thing wrong with that... and fuck, how I wish I could be the guy wired to give it, but..."

He let his voice trail off, getting ready for what always came next in this dialogue. She'd twist her hand tighter into his and then hurl herself against his chest. After that, she'd tell him he had a Porterhouse between his ears again before begging him to take her to bed so they could screw each other into oblivion. After that, they'd be okay. He'd forget he'd ever been this morose on a day they should both be remembering only for its happiness.

But his brain got done running the scenario—twice—and she barely moved.

His lungs hurt. Her stillness...and the emerald pain in her eyes when she lifted her face toward him...tightened the terrible knots around his stomach, his lungs, his heart.

"Zeke, do you want to release me?"

That was no fucking help.

She gave the words, which evoked the D/s lifestyle's version of a breakup, in sparse whispers—but bamboo shoots under his fingernails sounded awesome in comparison. But the thing that sucked shit more? Her face was painted in the same shades of agony.

"Damn it," he snarled. "Of course not."

But he couldn't change who he was, either. He couldn't go back and park his ten-year-old ass in the middle of the living room so Mom wouldn't leave that night. What would've stopped her from pulling the same shit on a different night?

After that, even if he'd decided to take his chance on a foster family instead of living on the street, who knew if he'd have popped into adulthood any less fucked up? He had to live with the cards fate had dealt—but it was disgustingly unfair that she did too.

As if she'd watched that dialogue roll across his face, Rayna returned his hold with even harder pressure before rasping, "I'm not asking you to change, Z. I love this. I love *us*."

"I know."

He sent her a smile filled with gratitude and love and meant it. But as he pulled her down to him for another soft kiss, his heart's return shot was impossible to ignore.

How long until it's not enough? Until you want something different and I can't deliver?

In the army they had a word for situations like that.

Discharges.

CHAPTER FOUR

The wine was perfect. The candle glow was perfect. The crisp white table linen, topped by shimmering china and gleaming crystal, was perfect. The sweeping view of the city lights was *beyond* perfect.

Rayna let out a soft but heavy sigh.

Perfection was exactly the problem here. No, worse. It was fate's gigantic hand, hovering in the air between her and Zeke, getting ready to give her a five-fingered fister that was going to hurt like a concrete slab. She glanced at the other couples across the room. Everyone was marveling at the beauty of Seattle's newest chichi dinner and dancing club, glittering in their trendy finery. She wondered if any of them also wished they weren't here, swallowing against a chest that imploded in anguish and a heart that sobbed in apprehension.

Tonight, perfection was the beginning of the end.

After they looked over their menus and ordered from a waiter who was too damn dapper for his own good, Z poured her some more wine and then sipped from his own. "Hmm. That's good shit, for wine."

She nodded. His words were all Zeke; his tone was all park bench. Wooden and caked in crap.

"You look incredible tonight, firebird."

She nodded again and managed, "Thanks. You too." But he always looked amazing in his charcoal dress suit. The ensemble was cut so similarly to his dress uniform, he'd already been asked for his autograph once tonight. Seattle still loved their "Dark Knight," Special Forces style. She'd had a wonderful year since the adventures that had earned him the designation, being his lover, his submissive, and his friend—up until the muck-fest of a confrontation they'd had at his place three nights ago.

On two of those three nights, he'd headed to his cabin in the Cascades, no invitation to her extended. Yesterday, he'd actually stopped by the base health clinic to see her, along with a sweet invitation for this dinner. But after she'd readily agreed and hugged him, thinking her Dom had finally gotten his shit together again and was back for her, he pulled away and kissed her goodbye—on the cheek. His phone call a few hours later, stating he had to stay late at the base for gear inventory and would be sleeping at his apartment instead of her place, only solidified the dread in her heart.

When it came time to get ready for this date, she couldn't bring herself to get into anything besides funereal shades as well. She was pretty certain how this was going to go down and didn't see how cringing in the powder room, bawling her eyes into slits, was going to look great against winter white. The black dress she chose instead, with its scalloped neckline, sheer lace sleeves, and A-line skirt, was the ideal choice. Classy for dinner but practical for soaking up a torrent of mascara.

Just as they finished their shrimp-en-croute appetizer, the ten-piece band started to play. The group was known across the city for their ballroom-style takes on modern pop favorites. As a tango-influenced nod to Shakira's *Objection* ended and became a slow waltz version of *Bittersweet Symphony*, Z stood and held out his hand.

"Come on, honey. Dance with me."

She readily lifted her fingers into his. Never mind that the song was spookily appropriate; the sight of him encompassed everything she physically adored the most about him. His proud stature. His enigmatic smirk. His resolute jaw. And most of all, the magical blend of colors that turned his hazel eyes into her version of paradise.

She made it a point not to look at those eyes now.

The resolution was much harder to keep once they reached the dance floor. All too easily, memories flowed of the first time they'd ever waltzed, when Mua was still hunting her and they'd turned a muddy Cascades forest clearing into an impromptu dance floor. Z's possessive hold on her waist had all but ordered her eyes to meet his...and her soul to twine into his. Every time they'd waltzed since then, usually in the cabin with the real world far away, she was helpless to look anywhere but at him...letting him see the heart he'd captured not long after that magical winter afternoon.

Tonight, she gripped one of his broad shoulders while keeping her eyes riveted on the other. It didn't help her equanimity by a shred. She could still breathe in his scent, pine, spice, and musky man. She was still excruciatingly conscious of every huge muscle and hard angle in his body, especially as it took leadership of hers around the dance floor. She could still bask in his strength and warmth and try to accept the fact that this would be the last time she'd ever feel them.

Grief welled in her throat.

But hope fought back.

Maybe she was wrong about this. Maybe she'd connected all Z's dots backward and this picture wasn't what she'd assumed. Maybe all he'd needed was a little man-cave time, and this was his way of reconnecting after it. Granted, Z's definition of "reconnection" usually involved Nine Inch Nails on the speaker and her in cuffs and tethers instead of heels and earrings, but since she'd known him, the man had always been full of surprises.

She had to reprise all of it three more times before she believed it enough to raise her head.

It was clear Zeke had been waiting for her to do so. His eyes were dark as scorched copper. His lips were stiff as a mausoleum effigy. His jaw clenched until it reached the same texture. He took her breath away with his beauty...and his solemnity.

The song swelled through the air between them.

I'll take you down the only road I've ever been down...I can't change, no, no, no...

Every word burned as the truth in his eyes.

Rayna stopped dancing and shoved at him. Well, tried to. With that damn speed of his, he had both arms secured around her waist before she could get more than a step away.

"Honey." His voice was a determined murmur. "Okay, listen. I didn't want—"

"What?" Spitting it was a formality. She could easily supply that answer now, couldn't she? *Me. You didn't want me, right? And though I swore I wouldn't hate this time when it came, I do. I hate it. Because I love you, Zeke Hayes. Blindingly. Dangerously. You now have the power to rip my guts out and turn them into emotional coleslaw. And you're going to. Goddamnit, you're going to.*

He huffed through his locked teeth. "I just didn't want this to be shitty for us."

A bitter laugh spilled, piercing through the tears that finally came. "Put a pig in Prada and it's still a pig," she returned.

ANGEL PAYNE

"Buying me some shrimp and a good Pinot doesn't make this less shitty. Would you *please* let me go?"

He tugged her in tighter with one arm. With his free hand, he lifted her face toward his. "*Listen* to me. *I love you.* You're the submissive of my fantasies and the woman of my dreams. But damn it, I can't be the man of yours."

She wrenched her face away. "Now we can toss the pig into the river, because that's water under the damn bridge, Sergeant."

His face turned ferocious. "The fuck it is, *Sergeant.*" He let her go, though his vehemence was like emotional hot glue, still rendering her helpless to move. "You weren't the one standing there in that wedding, having to look at you struggle with your feelings for an hour. Having to watch all that longing on your face and knowing you yearn for that with me—"

"I don't *yearn* for it, all right?"

He stepped back, making her feel like an astronaut floating in the space where the sun had once burned. "I call bullshit." He shook his head, the wrath in his gaze joined by something terrible and twisted and full of fury. "Your ass may be the most delectable thing on the planet, but it's dunked in bullshit, Rayna Chestain."

She cocked her head in defiance. "Then maybe you need to take me someplace and spank it."

"And maybe you need to stop lying to me like this." His features broke into a snarl, a look she hadn't seen him use on anyone since the day Mua had tried to steal her back to Thailand. His torment had petrified her that day, because she'd known if the neurotoxin hadn't debilitated him, it would've induced him to kill Mua with his bare hands. His conflict terrified her even more now.

"Lying?" she sobbed. "Because I'm trying to save this? Trying to save *us*?"

"We can't be saved, Rayna." He roped his hands around her shoulders and jerked her close, towering over her. "*I* can't be saved!"

She didn't move for a long second. At last, she raised her fingers to his face, pressing them to his cheek as her chest compressed beneath the weight of wonderment.

The intense light in his eyes wasn't the fire of rage. It was the sheen of tears.

"I love you so much," she whispered.

"I love you more." His words peppered her face in harsh bursts. His stare never left her. "That's why I have to let you go." He pressed closer, dipping his mouth toward hers, before yanking back with a brutal choke. "I have to let you find your happiness."

As grief clawed at her soul, she curled her fingers in and raked at his face. Hot, wet stings tore down her cheeks. "Does this look like happy?"

When Z responded with nothing but grim resignation, she clearly recognized her position: at the base of his cliff of stubbornness, without any climbing gear or helicopters. He thought that this valley would bloom for her, make her happy, but the bastard failed to see a crucial factor in his warped plan. She made damn sure he knew about it now, though.

"You took away the sun."

A frisson of confusion twisted across his face. "What?"

Rayna gazed up at him once more. With shaking fingers, she reached up and unfastened the latch on her collar. As she pressed it into his wide, warm palm, her whisper was as broken as her heart. "You beautiful, amazing idiot. Nothing grows without the sun. Especially happiness."

★ ★ ★ ★ ★

She'd managed to turn and stumble away, though she'd be damned before returning to their table. Luckily, she found her way past the hostess stand and onto an empty outdoor patio.

The club was located at the top of a fancy downtown office building, which meant the views were spectacular on the three nights a year the city didn't get fog, mist, rain, or sleet. Right now, it seemed the elements had tuned themselves into her psyche and decided to bring on a mix of all four to match the freezing agony she'd once called her heart and mind.

She fell into one of the chairs, hard and wet without its cushion, and curled her knees up to her chest. The patio had a roof, but the air itself was a sponge. Within minutes, she was damp and chilled. That was good. Really good. She sat, shivered, and prayed for numbness. And begged heaven to make her body so cold that her heart couldn't feel anything either.

Heaven wasn't listening.

The bitter weight of her tears, spilling from her soul, confirmed that ruthlessly enough. She peered through the haze of them, seeing the world in a blur.

I have to let you find your happiness.

She had no idea how she was going to take her next damn step, and he wanted her to go Indiana Jones into the wilderness for *happiness*? She couldn't even take retribution by making him sit still for a *Raiders* marathon.

She palmed her cold cheek, feeling her lips quiver against it as she did, and rasped, "You still owe me that marathon,

Hayes."

And a trip to Comic-Con. And tango lessons. And a repair job on the broken shelf in her garage. And a thousand more things that their life together was supposed to be filled with. That their life could be *happy* with.

Grief tore through her chest and left her lips on a grieving choke. "Shit!"

"Not my favorite subject to discuss, but it's a start."

She was about to let the sob-fest commence when the voice, smooth and male and confident, slid across the patio. She looked up to observe a stranger who'd also scooted beyond the glass doors and now leaned against the wall in a stance as polished as his designer tie. The green-and-black-checked pattern of the thing was a trendy contrast to the stripes in his equally expensive-looking shirt, which was encased in a luxurious charcoal jacket. He looked like a guy who occupied one of the huge mergers and acquisitions offices below them.

And he eyed her like his next big-dollar deal.

Before Rayna could collect herself to respond, he walked over, pulled a chair next to hers, and sat down in it. That definitely jump-started a few words.

"Uhhh...as you can tell, I'm not great company tonight." She nodded toward the door. "I'm sure there's someone in the bar who's more your speed, my friend."

"You mean the bimbos in matching minis who just want to snag a guy from the tower?" He extended an arm across the chair behind her shoulders. "I was over that an hour ago, which was why I went to enjoy the band." His eyes, framed by a head of expensively cut hair, gentled. "As I walked in, you walked out. It appeared your night was turning out as lovely as mine." He put a scornful spin on the assertion.

Rayna averted her gaze to her hands, now meshed in her lap. "I don't want to talk about it."

Suit Stud didn't take the hint. He tucked a couple of fingers against her nape and circled them there. "For the record, he's an idiot." At her curious glance, he clarified, "The gorilla in the dark suit? You came here with him, right? He couldn't take his eyes off of you, either. Looked like you made off with his favorite teddy bear, which certainly begs the question why he let you walk away. Not sure *I'd* have been so stupid."

"I *really* don't want to talk about it." The glacial air wasn't so attractive now. She surged to her feet, intending to go in, ask to use the phone at the hostess stand, and call one of the girls from work to pick her up. It was well past Racer's bedtime, and part of Sage's treatment plan for her postpartum depression included regular sleep.

She had to slide against the wall to get back to the door. The wall that Suit Stud was easily able to use to his advantage.

As he straddled her head with both his hands, he pinned her lower body inside the cage of his legs. "Then let's not talk, beautiful."

He could *not* be serious. "I—I think you have things a little twisted, buddy."

He scowled at her. He was probably pretty cute when he wanted to be, and the bewilderment in his eyes spoke volumes about this being a tried-and-true tactic for him.

"King Kong dumped you, right? So screw him. Time to take back your life."

Damn. Okay, he *was* serious. "And you're here to help?" She quirked an eyebrow.

Suit Stud leaned closer, dipping his dark-blue gaze to her mouth. "Don't get mad. Get even."

"No."

The growl, so vicious that she wondered how it didn't visibly knife the air, made Suit Stud shift back a little. Two seconds later, he was forcibly hauled back by six feet. Even then, Zeke didn't let the poor guy out of his grip. He sat the man in a large decorative planter, face branded in wrath, lips curling in rage.

"The only 'getting' around here is lost, asshole. By *you*. If you dare even peek at her while you leave, I'll grab you again for a little neck-breaking practice, got it?"

CHAPTER FIVE

"Zeke!"

The horrified glimmer in Rayna's eyes cut deep into his gut. The stare was identical to the one she'd worn when he'd been ready to kill Mua's men for attacking her in the street outside Bastille last year. And God help his fucked-up soul, a lot of that same protective fire burned through him now.

After collecting himself on the dance floor, he'd scoured the club looking for her, needing to make sure she was all right. She'd left her purse at their table, and he didn't think she was distraught enough to leave without it, but he couldn't be sure, and that scared the crap out of him. Christ. Her collar had only been around his fingers instead of her neck for ten minutes, and he already felt as aimless as a lion tamer in Antarctica. Or perhaps the lion itself.

After prowling through the place, including a sneaky check of the ladies' room with his own eyes, he'd caught sight of her outside, being hit on by fifty shades of smooth operator. And his world had gone code red.

The color still fringed his vision as he parked pretty boy's ass more firmly in the planter. "Go inside, Rayna," he growled.

"Zeke, he didn't do—"

"*Go inside*, Rayna."

As the glass door *whooshed* open and then shut, pretty boy glowered at him. "Look, asshole. I was playing nice. I don't make women do anything they don't want—"

"Who the hell are you calling 'asshole'?" He yanked the guy up by his trendy tie. "Last time I checked, the umbrella of that definition was big enough to include dickheads who openly move in on someone else's woman." He leaned over the guy farther, grimacing at model boy's glare of defiance. "Does *that* sound like playing nice, pretty prince?"

The guy held up his hands. "Hey, I apologize if I misread the situation. I didn't know you two were just having a spat. Looked like a breakup to me. She's not wearing a ring. You can't blame a guy for making a play to be rebound man, right?"

A couple of new sensations curled through Z's chest. Shame. And regret. He swallowed hard before letting the guy loose. "No," he muttered, "I guess I can't." Hell. He'd definitely made plays to be rebound man a few times in his wilder days. Scorching sex, no strings; a coveted gig, indeed.

His stomach churned at the thought of doing something like that now. It roiled harder when he thought of anybody being *Rayna's* rebound man. Ever.

He mumbled an apology to pretty boy, which the guy easily accepted. But even after the man returned to the bar, his words clung to the air and chilled Z's bones deeper than the winter mist.

She's not wearing a ring...can't blame a guy...right?

His bones were freezing. But his spirit was galvanized.

With a pace he usually reserved for busting in on terrorists, he stormed back inside. As he'd prayed, Rayna was still there. She sat at their table with her coat on and her phone in hand, fixated on the screen as if debating who to call for a ride home. A knot of dread and urgency formed in his stomach. He rocket-boosted the speed on his advance. *Put the phone away, Ray-bird.*

As soon as she saw him, she stood. She wasn't on her feet for very long. He grabbed her, hauled her against him, and crushed her to him in a smash of lips filled with one purpose. Raw, pure possession.

"Ummm...huh?" she murmured when he let her go, many minutes later.

Z gazed at her, tugging at her scalp with the same unalterable command that laced his response. "I'm—" *I'm sorry. I'm so damn sorry. I was wrong. Worse than wrong. I was an idiot.* "I'm—"

Her eyes warmed with gorgeous green lights. "What?"

"I'm—taking you shopping tomorrow."

The lights disappeared. Her gaze narrowed. "Shopping? Why?"

"You're going to pick out a ring."

"I'm going to *what?*"

"You heard me."

Her whole face crunched. "No, I'm not sure I did."

The adorable pinches at the corners of her mouth were open temptations to kiss her again. Instead, he gripped her head tighter and made sure his gaze drilled deep into hers. "I'm saying...that...I never want this to happen again, okay? You're mine, Rayna—and damn it, I want the whole world to know it. So let's go do this thing. I'm ready."

Her expression only tightened more. Inch by excruciating inch, she slipped from his hold. As if fate knew he needed a helping hand, the band began a new song. He almost turned and gave the guys a fist pump of thanks. What could express things better in this moment than the classic Aerosmith ballad about not wanting to miss a thing about her? She had to understand things now, right?

Wrong.

The tangle in his gut cinched tighter as she stepped back again. "Thirty minutes ago, your story was different." She shook her head, the move as uneven as her voice. "How have things changed in the eighteen hundred seconds since then?"

He swallowed hard. Grimaced against the burn in his chest. He'd only known this feeling a few times in his life—every time the team had fallen short on a mission or lost a man in the doing. "Because they were the worst goddamn seconds of my life."

"Because I was outside talking to another guy?"

The burn became a growl. "He wanted to do more than talk, bird."

"No shit, soldier. But I was fine handling the situation on my own, okay?" She threw up a hand when he drew breath to protest. "You may know how to fillet a man fifteen ways and jump out of an airplane prettier than an angel, but I went through the same basic training you did, Sergeant. I could've turned his backside into a weed just as fast as you did. Remember that."

Her rant pushed him down the hill straight into frustrated and desperate, though not before bouncing over boulders of seriously turned-on. The conflict left him standing in a weird paralysis, hands curling into fists, eyes fixed on their dinners, which could have been lemur shit for all the appetite he had now. Like anything about this situation felt any more comfortable. Even the tense moments on the dance floor with her had been better. At least he'd been able to rehearse all that. But this, right here and now...sucked. This was his emotional backside, bare and exposed, hanging off the side of life's Black Hawk over the surface of fucking Mars. It was strange and scary, and he had no idea what to do except lift his head far enough to mumble back, "Duly noted."

The song ended. As the band announced they were taking a break, an uncomfortable silence descended. Rayna tugged at the cuff of her coat as she shifted from one foot to the other. "You know that I love you, Ezekiel Gabriel," she finally murmured.

Z let a dark rumble vibrate up his throat. "Yeah, firebird. I do."

"Then you also know I won't go shopping with you tomorrow."

She took a soft step closer, which made him look directly back at her again. Fuck, she was so beautiful in the candlelight. Ethereal...and sorrowful.

"You're talking about opening up a big chunk of your soul, mister—because as your wife, I'll demand no less. Less than an hour ago, that wasn't a change you thought you could make." She reached into his jacket pocket, where her collar was coiled at the bottom. She pulled it out and wound the leather strand around his fingers. "My heart is in your hands, Sir. Be true to yours in deciding what to do with it. I've earned that much from you, Zeke. No matter what you decide, I deserve your truth."

He couldn't reply. But damn it, there was so much to say. She grabbed him in the gonads now just as hard as the night they first met, when the nastiness of doing his job had faded beneath the awe of her serene strength, the enchantment with her frank humor. With the clarity of hindsight, he realized he'd started to fall in love with her right then.

Life had never been the same since. It would never be the same again.

Every stunning glimmer in Rayna's eyes told him that she

knew that too, which meant her demand deserved every shred of honesty he could give in return. She'd given him nothing less from the start, in her friendship, her submission, and her love—and she'd offered him that truth even after discovering how ugly his really was. She'd accepted him, even after seeing his street rat past and his extreme Dom present. She saw how it all meshed to make him the soldier she supported and the man she adored.

She loved him in spite of everything. *Because* of everything.

But he'd been making her extend that love from a distance, behind some damn high fences.

It was pretty fucking hard to get a ring on a woman's finger through a fence.

Could he take the ax out and do it? Let her into places in his life, in his heart, that nobody had been since his tenth birthday?

He owed her an honest answer to that—no matter how shitty the answer might be for them both.

CHAPTER SIX

For the six hundredth time in the last three days, Rayna was wide-awake at four a.m., thanks to the most masochistic question her conscience had ever created.

Why didn't you just say yes?

She shook her head and stared at the ceiling, wishing for an answer to magically burn itself there. An answer that made sense, anyway. Because when the man of a woman's dreams made her most precious fantasy come true, wasn't she supposed to shut the hell up for all answers except one? Wasn't she supposed to thank fate for the gift, unwrap it as fast as she could, and clutch it selfishly forever?

"No."

She deliberately voiced the assertion aloud, breaking the thick silence of her bedroom. She didn't yell or sob it. She only needed to hear it, soft and steady with conviction, reinforcing the power of *no* to the very depths of her heart. Sometimes, *no* had to be okay. Sometimes, *no* was for the best. She refused to settle for *yes* out of desperation, fear, and Z's misplaced jealousy. She was better than that. *They* were better than that.

She knew Zeke got that part, at least in his heart. But forcing his soul to slog through years of baggage for it too? Making the man look at parts of himself that hadn't been vulnerable since he was a kid? Telling him he had to shuck the backpack of pain that he'd carried for twenty years and then jump off the ultimate cliff of commitment with her?

As the days went by, she started losing hope about a happy answer to that.

The conclusion, as quiet as her affirmation, somehow ninja'd past her composure and gashed into her heart. The tears she refused to shed were now impossible to fight, racking her as she grabbed for another pillow. His pillow. Every inhalation was filled with the smell of him. Every exhalation ached with the loss of him. She cried until exhaustion overcame her, dragging her into a sleep as bleak as her heartbreak.

★ ★ ★ ★ ★

What a weird but wonderful dream.

The trill of an Irish whistle floated on the breeze, and a choir sang along with it. They sounded incredible, harmonizing perfectly on one of her favorite Celine Dion songs. Even the doves sounded pretty, cooing together as if trying to echo the chorus themselves. Crazy Mrs. Hopper from next door babbled something about them being hungry and she'd be right back after grabbing some bread crumbs for them...

Mrs. Hopper? Talking to a bunch of *doves*?

She bolted upright in bed.

Okay, she was awake now. The drool and tearstains on Z's former pillow were proof of that. But the choir was still singing. And the doves tried to warble with them again.

"What the hell?"

She shoved her hair off her face while shrugging into her robe. While she stumbled into the kitchen, she stubbed her toe. Since three out of the five toes on her right foot now screamed in pain, she determined she was really awake. Yet the music continued. Where was it coming fr—

"What. The. *Hell?*"

It was the last thing she stammered before her mouth popped open in shock. Perhaps permanently.

The choir, probably twenty or thirty strong, stood on her front lawn. Their red and gold robes matched the dozen standing candelabra that flanked her front walk, all draped in red satin with their tapers alight. The sidewalk between them was swathed in a plush red runner. Standing in the middle of that runner was someone who vaguely resembled Zeke Hayes.

"Vaguely" was an understatement. The man had slicked back his hair and shaved his scruff. His shoulders looked even more enormous with dual gold epaulets that draped over a fitted crimson jacket with military accents. His legs, encased in black pants, were covered to the knee in black Hessian boots. He looked gorgeous and nervous and sincere, a breathtaking prince right out of a fairy tale, which made her feel five kinds of perverted for wishing she could rip all of it off him and have her way with him right there on the sidewalk.

Wild fantasy aside, her hand shook as she waved at him through the big front window. As he smiled back, a little of the Zsycho smirk appeared. He approached the porch while she opened the front door.

"My queen, Rayna." As soon as he murmured it, the choir faded their voices into soft hums.

Her hand still trembled as he pulled it between both of his. "Errmmm...my king, Zeke?"

She wanted to giggle, but his mien became even more solemn. She'd rarely seen this kind of intensity in him outside the Bastille's dungeons. It made her knees turn to mush...and her pussy turn to fire. Thank *God* she was wearing a robe. And underwear.

She had no idea what to expect next, but this man taking a knee before her certainly wasn't it. His pride, forged as a boy in the crucible of the Seattle streets, was the one thing Zeke never relented to anyone. But here he was, bowing his head to kiss the tips of her fingers before he swept the incredible fire of his gaze back up to her.

"You asked if I was willing to change for you, Rayna. For *us*." One side of his mouth lifted a little. "But the truth is that I already have. You've changed me with your light and your love in my life and in my heart." He pulled back to retrieve something from his pocket. Her collar. Though he only pressed it into her palm, the cool caress of the leather brought new tears to her eyes. It felt like heaven. Better still, it felt like home. "I love you, Rayna. And I need you. Kneeling at my feet as my submissive...standing at my side as my wife."

She barely suppressed a sob as the choir fell silent. A breeze kicked up down the street, but all the candles stayed amazingly lit. Zeke barely moved. She wasn't sure he even breathed.

"If she doesn't say yes, gorgeous, you just bring that scrumptious ass over here."

Everyone broke out in laughter at Mrs. Hopper's flirtation. Through her giggles and her tears, Rayna looked down at the hulk who'd transformed into a prince for her. The soldier who'd fought so many of her enemies, including his own demons. And the Dom who'd set her free from her own dark nightmares.

"I think I need to go get dressed," she finally told him.

Zeke's brows waggled. "You look just fine to me, honey."

"Not if I'm going to let you take me shopping, Sir."

Zeke's grin split his face apart as he surged to his feet and conquered her mouth in a consuming kiss. Cheers rose up, including Mrs. Hopper's gleeful screech, as the wings of fifty doves beat the air in celebration. As Zeke kept kissing her, the choir started singing again.

Aerosmith had never sounded so good.

DIAMONDS IN THE RAIN

Ethan Archer and Ava Chestain

CHAPTER ONE

"Hello, Rock."

Ava Chestain made sure to issue the greeting beneath her breath even though her fiancé, Ethan Archer, was all the way across their suite at the Ritz-Carlton Half Moon Bay. He wouldn't be happy to hear her talking to her engagement ring again. And he'd be outright seething, in a not-so-yummy-Dom kind of way, if he learned what she was calling the thing. But she couldn't help it. The ring had at least twenty clear diamonds arranged in a burst pattern around a four-carat yellow diamond that had been custom-cut for the setting. Ethan had slipped it on her finger just three days ago, proposing to her—for a second time—on the Santa Monica pier at sunset in front of a cheering crowd.

He'd been holding the ring when he did it, rendering Ava more speechless than the first time he'd asked. That was quite a feat, considering that first time had occurred when they were inducting each other into the Mile-High Club on Air Force One. When she'd finally found her voice on the pier and gawked at the ring, Ethan only slung back a smirk and said his sunshine could now wear the sun too.

"*Caramba*," she whispered. *Sergeant Archer, you're hell-bent on spoiling me.*

If only that musing didn't tangle the pit of her stomach in abject anxiety.

"You're talking to your ring again, aren't you?"

She jumped. Ethan had seemingly teleported across the room and now pressed up behind her. Just her luck; she'd fallen in love with a man who was half ninja. "No," she retorted. "It's ignoring me today, anyhow."

He wrapped his arms around her and rested his chin on her head. "Do you blame it? Engagement rings get inferiority complexes too."

The knot in her gut tightened. Something in his murmur told her he wasn't referring just to the ring anymore. "Ethan, I—"

"Ssshh. It's okay. If you don't like it—"

"No! *Ay dios mio*, I love it!"

"But...?"

She swallowed hard. His Dom tone, a low cadence of command, had entered the word with undeniable force. Despite his gentle hold, he expected an answer to his hard question.

His *really* hard question.

It was time to address the giant elephant in the room.

Ava stepped gingerly from him. There was a seat built into the window that offered views of the sweeping cliff and expanse of ocean. Right now, she was just grateful for its presence in helping her trembling knees.

As she lowered to the cushion, she tugged at her lip with her teeth. She doubled the pressure when Ethan settled next to her. She was seriously in trouble. The man took her breath away in normal circumstances. But here, with his eyes nearly matching the sea and his broad chest sheathed in a thick Irish sweater, he was male decadence—and Dominance—defined.

He reinforced the point by reaching and curling his hands around her wrists. He used the unconventional hold on purpose, sending an undeniable message. She was in his care now. Everything she said from her heart was safe. But he expected her to spill *everything* inside it.

After letting her wallow in silence for a minute, he quietly ordered, "Tell me."

Ugh. This sucked.

"I—" She huffed and stared out toward the sea.

"Ava." He tightened his hold. "This is me, remember?"

"Why don't I just refuse to talk? Then you can punish me and—"

"*Ava.*"

She fell into silence when he secured both her wrists in one of his hands and used the other to yank up her chin. As soon as the force of his cobalt blues hit, her resistance evaporated. Tears stung her eyes and seeped down her cheeks. "Ethan," she whispered, "I'm not sure I belong here."

His reaction was everything she expected. A scowl full of hurt and confusion. "What? Why?"

She tried to clear her senses with a breath. "That's my point."

"I don't under—"

"Of course you don't. Because you've probably stayed in this suite fifty times before."

"Well, it's better than staying at my parents' place when I go for visits." A grimace twisted his face. "Fuck. Talk about a place where you can't breathe."

Her brows jumped. "Your parents' house is swankier than this?"

Resignation took the place of his frown. "Mausoleums are swanky too, baby. Doesn't mean I'm comfortable in one."

His intention was to ease her nerves. She knew that and

wished she could confirm his success. Instead, her dread ballooned. She squirmed in his hold, suddenly afraid to let him see the enormity of it. As she broke down like an idiot, he released her wrists in order to pull her onto his lap.

"Baby," he soothed. "Ava, come on. I know you're nervous, okay? But—"

"Nervous?" she spat. "Why the hell would I be nervous? Just because I'm meeting your polo club parents in a dress I bought in a rush off the rack, at their dinner table that'll have thirty forks at each place setting, to talk about a wedding that'll cost more than I make in a year—"

He kissed her into silence. Tugged her face up to look at him again. "All they want to do is meet you," he murmured. "It'll be nice, just the four of us. And we'll probably talk about the weather and sports." His forehead furrowed. "And, uhhh, Mom's orchids."

She sniffed. "I like orchids."

His smile was dazzling. "There you have it."

Ava tilted up her chin in a little plea for another kiss. After Ethan obliged, she whispered, "Okay. I'll try not to embarrass the crap out of you."

He dug his long fingers into her hair and pulled hard. "There'll be no more talk like that, woman. You are my queen. You'll wear my diamonds, you'll walk at my side, you'll be amazing, and you'll *never embarrass the crap out of me*."

She carried those words with her through the next few hours, enjoying a walk with him on the beach before they returned to the suite to prepare for the first dinner she would have with her future in-laws. They warmed her as she showered, pampered, and dressed and even made her smile as she slipped into her dark-purple dress, cut in a classic wrap style and then finished with her favorite pair of strappy Prada heels. They girded her as Ethan drove up the winding driveway to his parents' home, which approached mansion status with its ornate, Tudor-style architecture, including a Shakespeare-inspired fountain in front. She held them in her heart as tightly as she clutched Ethan's arm when they approached the door, which was set beneath an archway of white English roses.

He knocked and they waited.

He turned and kissed her, surrounding her in his leather-pepper scent tinged with John Varvatos cologne and the luxurious wool of his black dress sweater. She gripped his silk tie and shirt as he openly adored her with his lips. His groan vibrated through her, thick with his desire. Best of all, his love enveloped her, warm and complete.

Okay, maybe she *could* do this.

She got to savor the thought for another ten seconds, right up to the moment the door opened, flooding them with light—and the grins from at least fifty unfamiliar faces. In front of them was a woman who looked so much like Ethan, Ava had no doubt about her identity. She beheld the beauty of Elle Archer for the first time.

"Surprise!" the woman exclaimed before pressing her lips to Ethan's cheek. "Happy engagement!"

CHAPTER TWO

Ninety minutes into the party, Ethan still couldn't figure out if this was the best thing Mom had ever done or the worst.

He exchanged a glance across the room with Dad, whose sympathetic shrug said he didn't have the answer either. Good thing they'd broken out the good Scotch. The amber liquid in his glass helped cut the edge in his nerves, though he paced himself with obsessive care. He wanted to be ready to get back in the car any second. Ready to drive Ava out of here if Mom had any more bombshells hiding up her dress's flowing sleeves.

Shit.

Did it suck major balls that he jumped to suspicions like that about his own mother? That would be a resounding *yes*. But had history given him every damn reason for the leap? That would be an even bigger *yes*.

Sure, he knew she loved him, but many times—*most times*—that depended on how far she could control him. When he'd signed up with the army, she'd treated the decision as the giant folly of his youth, something he'd grow out of before coming back to walk the Archer line—a line that would start with her orchestration of his fiancée selection and wedding. Although he'd dared to think otherwise, she had squelched his hope on the night he called to tell them Ava had accepted his proposal. Instead of asking to meet Ava, she'd muttered something to Dad about contacting her friend at the Atherton paper so they could compose an announcement that would make the occasion sound "halfway respectable."

Why couldn't he shake the suspicion that this was nothing but an extension of that PR campaign?

Fuck.

The word rumbled through his chest, making him realize he'd accidentally let it fly aloud. Fortunately, he had the wall to himself at the moment. He had no illusions the respite would last. It was hard to be the party's inconspicuous guy when the "Congratulations" loop on all three of the room's wide screens had your name on it.

Sure enough, a barrel of damn monkeys poured over him the next second. At least that was what the mix of buddies from his high school and college years felt like, trying to yell over each other as they dragged him outside. Though it was a chilly San Francisco night thanks to the soggy front spilling over from the South Bay, all the space heaters were blowing at full force around the glass-rock fire pit, which was also cranked to full force. The lights in the black-bottomed pool were on, and the landscape floods were making a valiant effort to impart an impression of the tropics in their fruit punch tones.

During the journey outside, Ava reappeared at his side, bearing the fresh Scotch she'd gone to get for him. She managed a sweet smile despite the discomfort clinging to her gaze. As several more girlfriends appeared on the arms of their guys, the expected *chings* of fingernails on wineglasses began, signaling that the couple of honor had to entertain the crowd with a kiss.

He eagerly jumped on the opportunity.

Even with the crowd surrounding them, he didn't waste the chance to lock their mouths hard. He didn't regret the choice. His woman always tasted good, but tonight...*wow*. The wine on her tongue, along with her natural essences of coconut and vanilla, pulled his tongue in deeper, deeper...

"Sheez, Archer. You demoing a tonsillectomy tonight?"

The question carried the unmistakable snark of Link Masters, who'd likely trademarked that tone by now. The guy had been one of Atherton High School's gods, with his café au lait skin, piercing green eyes, and entrepreneurial genius that made him a millionaire before he could legally drink. He'd grown up to be a cocky-ass Bay Area big shot, though his arrogance was balanced by his infectious humor, generosity to his staff, and unswerving loyalty as a friend.

The guy could also take the same crap he dealt, which meant Ethan didn't hesitate to drawl back, "Bite me, Linky Blinky."

That earned him a round of appreciative groans from all the guys. "Yo, Masters; it's almost Christmas," somebody called out. "Think we'll get a Linky Blinky reprise tonight?"

Ethan smirked toward his friend. "I double-dog dare you, man."

Link held up both hands. "No fucking way. I may own half the big city, but your mom will own *me* if I run through her party dressed in nothing but battery-operated Christmas lights."

Ethan chuffed. "Right. Like anyone's going to see anything."

"Pssshhh. Better than other people I know, damn near whipping their junk out and doing their woman in the backyard for the crowd's enjoyment."

He shared a secret look with Ava. Actually, that had almost happened last week in Seattle. Their scene in the main room at Bastille had gotten so hot, her ass turning such a gorgeous shade of red beneath his floggers, that he'd barely gotten her down from the St. Andrews cross and into a private room before spreading her wide and fucking her until they both collapsed.

That had been a *damn* good night.

Drawn by the indigo arousal in Ava's eyes, telling him her thoughts rode the exact same train, he braced her jaw with one hand and dragged her close, claiming her mouth with his again. For an instant, the world spun away. Her little mewl, barely audible except by him, vibrated down his throat and begged him for more. Yeah, more. That sounded so fucking good right now...

"Archer! *Shit.* Get a room!"

He pulled up, enduring the catcalls as Ava dabbed her lipstick off his jaw. "Have one, actually," he volleyed to his friend. "And you know, Blinky, that doesn't sound like a bad idea." He grabbed Ava's hand and started to rise. "You heard the man, sunshine. Back to the Four Seasons for us. Good night, every—"

As the crowd's roar of protest cut him off, Link pushed him back down. Parker North and Knox Redding, two of his best gamer buddies, helped. Both of them had women on their arms tonight as well, and that freaked him out. He'd kept up with both guys via in-game message boards through the years, and neither of them had ever mentioned a serious relationship interest. While Amy and Kamlyn seemed nice, he wondered if they'd been picked *by* his friends or *for* his friends.

"All right, spill." The demand was made by Troy Stearns, one of the few jocks who'd rolled with their crowd instead of his fellow sports stars. Tall as Ethan and built of honed muscle, Troy would've been a kickass Special Ops man, though his ability to wallop a baseball had taken him on a different path. He'd just signed a multi-year deal with the Giants and proposed to his college sweetheart during a seventh-inning stretch to commemorate the success. "Everyone knows how I popped the question," he elaborated, "but all of us know nothing about your story, Archer. Well, aside from the 'thwarting the terrorist plan' shit."

"That story was incredible." Troy's fiancée, a polished little blonde named Sarah who he'd met while attending Cal State Fullerton, pressed her hand against her heart. Ethan smirked and pulled Ava tighter onto his lap when she gasped quietly at the woman's egg-sized engagement ring. "Did you really have to chop off the president's hand to save his life?" Sarah continued. "And did he really let you?"

He gave her a small nod and then dipped his head at Ava. "And this kickass woman hauled it to the ambulance for us."

This time, the guys joined the women in their gasps. "That's what I'd call an unforgettable one-on-one with the leader of the free world," Link bantered.

"You mean besides the 'wanting to barf up everything in my stomach' part?" Ava returned.

Ethan joined his friends in giving her a raucous laugh at that—but the humor wasn't shared by the women around the circle. He wished he hadn't expected their reticence, but it came as no surprise. As good little girls of society, they'd all had the candidness bred out of them long ago. Now, none of them even realized it was missing. They looked at Ava like children barred from a candy store. Full of longing. And jealousy.

"Uh, wow," Sarah stammered. "That's so..."

"Unique," Kamlyn filled in. Or was it Amy? They were so alike in their beige sweater dresses and pearls that Ethan kept mixing them up.

"Yes, errrrm, unique." Sarah flipped her hair over one shoulder and flicked a little smile. "And refresh my memory, Ava. Why were you at the studio too?"

If Ava got any stiffer in his arms, he'd swear he was holding a doll instead of a woman. It was because she saw straight through Sarah's thin ice of courtesy. The woman's bullshit detector was one of the billion things he adored about her. Another was her ability to maintain her calm no matter how far other women brandished their cat claws.

"I work at the lot."

Ethan squeezed her waist in reassurance. He knew how much it chafed her to be sworn to secrecy on the details beyond that. She could never reveal the part about being held hostage in an empty dressing trailer after being knocked out with sleeping gas that was supposed to be illegal on American soil. She could never disclose that one of Hollywood's most beloved producers had actually been the traitor who'd led the whole operation, nor that California had been less than a minute away from becoming a nuclear wasteland.

He supported her by adding what he could, in a voice filled with pride. "She was the one who made it possible for the team to get inside the soundstage."

"Ohhh, that's right." One of the Amy/Kamlyn twins chirped in with it. "You're on the payroll for Ethan's ex, right?"

Sarah flashed her fake smirk again. "Oh, *that's* it. You... wash her hair or something, right?"

"She's Bella's stylist." Ethan showed no mercy with his tone now, grinding anger into each syllable. He saw that even Troy echoed his sentiment, looking at Sarah like she'd turned into a creature he didn't know. "Every thread of clothing and speck of makeup you see on Bella Lanza is designed by *this* woman, not Bella."

"Hmmm." The woman considered that, though it was clear the needle on her diplomacy dial hadn't been budged much. "So how come I haven't heard of you, then?"

When that caused a shocked glare even from Troy, Ethan was positive something wasn't right. Troy was a stand-up guy, meaning he wouldn't put a ring on it with any shallow bimbo, but every word out of Sarah's mouth said otherwise. That had to mean that the words weren't hers. They'd been manipulated by someone else. Someone who'd been damn good at artful suggestion and had given the impression of Ava as a Hollywood poser instead of a legitimate stylist.

He clenched his jaw until his whole skull felt locked in a vise. Without turning his head, he started scanning the inside of the house. *Where the fuck are you, Mother?*

Ava shifted on his lap before answering Sarah in an uncomfortable murmur, "I'm sorry? I'm not sure I understand."

"Why haven't I heard of you?" Sure enough, the Elle Archer influence was apparent in every nuance of Sarah's tone now. "You know, like Rachel Zoe or Kate Young?"

He felt the deep breath that Ava took and released. When she lifted her chin a little more at Sarah, her profile was as regal as a queen confronting an insolent courtier. He felt like borrowing some of Link's arrogance for himself now. *Eat shit and die, my friends. I get to marry the goddamn queen.*

"Rachel and Kate are good friends," Ava finally said, "so I'll pass along your regards the next time I see them. Some folks in our field don't mind keeping a high profile. I'm fond of privacy myself. Makes it easier to get through the grocery store line when I've had a bad day and want to stuff my face with Ding Dongs and potato chips—but I'm sure you wouldn't know anything about that, and that breakout on your chin is just due to stress or something." She used Sarah's gawking silence to push off his lap and get to her feet. "By the way, a honey and cinnamon mask will clear that up pretty fast. If the pimples spread, try some toothpaste." She shrugged. "Helps with morning breath too. You can wake up, lick your own face, and you're ready to go."

Only through supreme self-control did Ethan hold back his whoop of approval. He was glad he did, because when she turned back to him, it flipped a one-eighty back into unease. Despite the zinger with which she'd just nailed Sarah, her smile was forced at best. But her gaze was what scared him the most. The indigo depths no longer held even a glimmer of her normal verve. All he saw were shadows, dark with sadness... and defeat.

"Baby?" He mouthed it more than spoke it, letting her see the open question in his stare. And the fear too. He'd never seen Ava back down about anything, except the day at the studio when she'd waved the white flag on their relationship. The day she'd torn off the scars from her past and turned them into the open wounds of her present—and let all that blood cloud everything she trusted about him too.

"I'm done, Ethan." She pulled her fingers from his. "Take your time. Have fun. I'll be waiting in the car."

He barely heard the last part of her statement. His heart had started ramming his ribs at her first two words.

I'm done.

The implication extended way past the party, and she was delusional if she didn't think he'd get it. He let her have the dignity of her exit, but he'd be damned if she got all the way to the car. As he'd hoped, she got lost between the patio and the front drive and ended up in the middle of Dad's putting range. He found her stomping around in the dark, in the middle of the third green.

"Ava."

His growl was infused with enough command that she jarred to a stop—for two seconds. She huffed, coiled her arms tighter, and then restarted her pace as if he'd only tapped her Pause button.

"There's a damn miniature golf course in your backyard, Archer." She flung an arm out for emphasis. "Wait, I get it. The thing's another test, right? Part of some obstacle course people need to pass to get out of here? At least you could add some colored lights, a couple of windmills, and some clowns with trap door mouths."

Her sarcasm lifted a fraction of his anxiety. She was still reaching for humor, though it was in a voice that wobbled worse than her steps in those stilts she called shoes. But it proved she still cared, in her adorable, insane way. That, added to the mist forming a beautiful nimbus around her hair, made him yearn to close the gap between them, roll her to the ground, and give an awesome new meaning to the term *hole-in-one*.

Instead, with legs braced and hands jammed in his pockets, he returned, "It's not my backyard."

She sneered. "Close enough."

His answering snort was easy to summon. Maintaining the even keel on his tone was another story. "Ava, I lived here a *long* time ago. This place—for that matter, those people back there—represent nothing about me anymore." He scowled as she tromped across the fourth green and started poking her foot in its miniature sand trap. "What the hell are you—"

"Hmm." She deliberately cut him off. "It's got to be around here somewhere."

"What?"

"Your head. You've clearly found some sand in which to bury it, and this seemed the logical choice." Before he could think of a comeback to sputter, she marched back over to him. "*Caramba.* Don't you seriously see how *all* of this affects us, Ethan?"

He re-enforced his stance. "The only thing that affects 'us' *is us.*" He openly gritted his teeth when she reacted to that with a grimace. "Christ, Ava. I thought you'd understand that better than anyone. You know that city you work in? The one Rhett refers to as *Hollyweird*? The one where the clothes a person wears and the place where he lives don't define the scope of his character?"

"Of course I understand that." Every word was bitten out, as if she struggled for patience with a naughty puppy. "This—this is different."

"Different." Echoing the word acted like a key in the lock of his understanding. A key dipped in poison. "Different because it's me." He rocked his head back. "Because it's changed your view of me."

Her lips flattened. "Ethan, I love you. That hasn't changed. It *won't* change."

He straightened his head and squared his stance. "But...?"

"But now I'm also going to marry you."

He kicked up his left brow. "The two are usually inclusive of each other."

She flung out both arms this time. "This is your family, damn it. I'm going to become a member of your *family*, Ethan."

"And I'm going to become a member of yours. I still don't

understand the issue."

"I'm going to bear your name!"

"You want me to take yours instead?" He cocked his head, giving the idea some mental traction. "Ethan Chestain. That sounds pretty good."

She folded her arms back in and rolled her eyes. "Sure. Like your mother would ever speak to you again. Or your father, for that matter."

His instinct shot off its second flare of apprehension in as many minutes. It was official; she was dancing around another subject here—but his inability to discern its cause, though he scrutinized every inch of her actions for the remotest clue, made him feel like a blind rat in a maze. "Damn it, Ava. What's this really all about?"

The way his words made her stop confirmed he was right. She wobbled in her heels again, making him clench every muscle to hold back from rushing her and yanking the damn things off her feet. His frustration only increased as the mist turned into a light rain and she huddled against it, looking sad and nervous and small.

"Talk. To. Me."

She tugged on her lip with her teeth. When she looked back at him, her eyes were as big as twin moons. "Your—your family doesn't like me."

"My family doesn't *know* you." He slammed a fist against his thigh. "Thanks to this stunt of my mother's, none of them has had a chance to spend more than ten minutes with you." He openly scowled. "Though I think my cousin already has a crush on you."

She flashed her you're-full-of-shit glare, though her lips quirked a little. "The investments guy or the pharmaceutical mogul?"

"You think *I'm* going to say?"

That coaxed her into a full laugh. The moment was a blip of relief before she slouched again. "Maybe this was all for the best anyway. Maybe I'd have just made the night a giant *chingadera* by now." She shook her head. "And maybe..."

His trepidation needle hit the red zone again. Thank fuck for his training on the teams, which allowed him to approach her without revealing how thoroughly she scared him right now.

"Maybe what?"

He was going to flog himself for not leaving her silence alone, probably sooner than later. But her face, plastered with wet curls, was etched in such desperation. Her posture was bent in such defeat. Her grief was his call to action. He'd slay any enemy for her.

"Maybe I'm just not going to be good at this wife thing."

Any enemy. Except for when that foe was herself.

Her whisper, pitched high with its honesty, plummeted between them just before the heavier drops from above. Ethan stared hard at her through the rain, thankful for the leaden chill of it in contrast to the acid burn of helplessness in his veins.

Maybe this was all for the best.

It was, nearly word for word, what she'd said to save face when finding Bella Lanza parked on his lap during their covert operation in Hollywood. Oh, how graceful she'd been while totally backing out on him.

He'd let her get away with the retreat back then to preserve the integrity of the mission, but now he wasn't going to be so kind. Now the mission was *them.* The stakes were a hell of a lot higher. And he'd be damned if he let her get away with sneaky and graceful when they'd fought so fucking hard to find each other, to win the rarity of their love. He'd given her a custom engagement ring to signify that and told her so when they sat on the sand after his proposal, watching the stars rise over the ocean. She'd cried harder and curled into his lap, telling him how deeply he'd climbed into her soul.

He'd believed every word she whispered then and still did now. The woman loved him. It was still as real to him as the marrow in his bones.

But she was running from him. *Again.*

Why?

Frustration plowed through him. If they were anywhere but here, getting drenched by a rainstorm on the grounds of his parents' estate, he'd order her to strip, kneel, and start spilling. Reality was a harsh CO sometimes. Tonight, the bastard dictated patience. Luckily, he *could* be a patient man when he wanted to be.

"Ethan?"

Ava's apprehensive murmur yanked him out of his brooding. Perfect timing. He reached and took her hand as another affirmation pushed to the forefront of his mind—and the core of his cock.

Patience had its payback when it was funneled into a plan. Especially a daring, devious, and decadent one.

"Ethan?" she asked again. "Are—are you okay?"

"Never been better." He tugged her toward the path that led around the gazebo, toward the service gate where they'd be able to leave the grounds without anyone knowing. "I just happen to be done too. Let's get the fuck out of here."

CHAPTER THREE

Ava woke to a dim gray room and the sound of rain pounding the suite's bay window. During the night, the squall over San Francisco Bay had collided with a storm front from the ocean, temporarily turning the hotel and its grounds into a page out of *Wuthering Heights*.

Or perhaps the skies were just sending down empathy for her spirit.

Things with Ethan were still a mess, with most of the blame rightfully astride her shoulders. He'd wanted—*deserved*—honesty last night, and she'd all but broken into a tap dance to evade him. But the first hour of Elle's not-so-little "surprise party," complete with Ethan's country club friends everywhere but the rafters, had toppled what little calm she'd been able to maintain about the night. By the time she'd regained her equilibrium, the blonde on the patio dug into her like a rabid TMZ reporter, making it time to punch the Game Over button. Didn't take a course in rocket science to figure out why—but the psychological crap from her past wasn't a load to dump on her fiancé during a rainstorm in the middle of his dad's backyard golf resort as their engagement party was reaching warp speed.

So...she'd played conversational duck-and-run. And had honestly expected to catch hell for it—*sí*, perhaps even there in the rain during the party. In the end, Ethan saved her dignity by dragging her back to the car but had leveled another stunner by actually driving her all the way back to the hotel. His forced smile remained in place the entire time too. There wasn't another eyebrow raised in question, a probing glance from those piercing blue eyes, or a merciless upturn of those elegant lips. He gave her only surface courtesies, making her stomach wrench with the certainty that he was simply waiting for the privacy of their suite.

Once behind those doors, he'd unleash his darker methods of interrogating her...processes that would only start with his palm against her ass. The man was extremely inventive with found items, no matter where they were together. She'd actually squirmed in her seat as she thought about what plan was formulating in his devious mind, overtaken by a demented mix of fear and anticipation...

But here she stood, nearly eight hours later, without a single bruise on her backside. Or a defining soreness in her sex. Or a reminiscent ache *anywhere* on her body.

As soon as they'd gotten back to the suite, Ethan had kissed her softly, said he was beat, and taken a shower. Once done, he'd kissed her again, repeated the bullshit about being tired, and climbed into bed. She'd stood in the middle of the living room for another ten minutes, expecting him to emerge with a smug stare and the assertion that he was just kidding, when the light went out in the bedroom—and confusion turned up its glare in her mind. After the intensity of his focus back at the mansion, his about-face didn't make sense at all.

Now, as she woke up and found him nowhere in the suite, her perplexity grew. She shivered despite being covered to her knees in the gray battalion T-shirt that she'd permanently confiscated from his wardrobe.

What the hell was going on?

Her frown deepened when her gaze swung over to the dining nook. The table was set with a full breakfast spread. As she got closer, an array of savory smells made her stomach snarl and her interest spike. She openly groaned when pulling off the food covers. All her favorites were here: a Spanish omelet with chorizo and fresh guacamole, a huge bowl of fresh California berries, and Irish steel-cut oatmeal with her favorite toppings.

Propped against the full coffee pot was a notecard, filled out in Ethan's writing.

Sunshine,
Stretch before breakfast.
And eat all your protein.

There was nothing else on the card. Not his normal little doodle of a sun, not his name or even his initial. Her heart pinged in a wonderful, illicit way as she considered that. She bet if he *had* included it, the letter wouldn't be *E*. It would be *S*. For *Sir*. Wherever the man had scooted off this morning, she was certain it had been with a Dominant power in his stride. Now she couldn't wait for him to get back.

That brought back a new urgency to being totally ready when he did.

As she lowered herself into a runner's stretch, she put the card on the floor and reread it a dozen times. This was probably the first time she'd seen his authority exercised in print—and she was a little stunned by how deeply it reached into her system, mentally awakening her need for him. It didn't take long for the direct line between her brain and her body to spark up after that. By the time her muscles were limber, her pussy was warm and her vagina pulsing.

Dios, she hoped he returned soon.

While she ate, she tried distracting herself with the

weather. She laughed a little at the musing. Yep; she'd become more of a Southern Californian than she thought. From Santa Barbara to San Diego, even light showers were enough to lead the six o'clock news, so the blustery day outside the window was a fascinating panorama.

There were times, of course, when she missed Seattle... and home. The melancholy happened more frequently now that "home" meant Ethan. She knew he felt the same about her and LA—at least until last night.

Her arousal faded beneath the weight of new anxiety.

Mierda. Had the events at the party changed his feelings about things...about them? Despite his blatant gesture in having breakfast brought for her, including the note about protein that carried the subliminal message about needing her physical strength for the day, she wondered if this was just a prelude for more serious things he wanted to discuss. Maybe last night had been more of a revelation than what he originally expressed, showing him what a square peg she really was in the perfect round hole of his world. Their confrontation in the backyard had simply put a perfect cap on things, and now he wanted to break it to her. Could she blame him? He'd only be reaching conclusions that had come to her ten hours ago.

She shoveled the rest of her food in, not in the mood to enjoy it anymore. When she was done, she contemplated getting dressed, though she took lazy steps back to the bedroom, hoping Ethan would reappear with a plan that *didn't* involve clothes.

Once she turned the corner, her stare fell to the dresser—and the empty valet tray there. Ethan had put his watch there last night, along with the call ticket for the car. Both were missing now.

Her trepidation spiked higher. What the hell? Had he left the hotel completely?

Into the silence that continued as her answer, the phone pealed.

After she told her heart that the coronary was only a false alarm, she hurried to scoop up the phone. "Ummm...hello?"

"Good morning, Ms. Chestain. This is Seth at the valet stand. I hope I didn't wake you."

"Not at all. I was just finishing breakfast."

"Good, good. Mr. Archer thought that would be the case."

She felt her eyes widen. "So you've already spoken to Mr. Archer this morning?"

"Of course, when he had his car brought up. He left about an hour ago and instructed us to have the town car available for your own departure in thirty minutes."

New discovery: it was completely possible to choke on air. "Th-Thirty minutes?"

Poor Seth. She heard him grunt a little, like he'd accidentally stepped into an "accident" from one of the shih tzus carried around the hotel by eccentric biddies. "I trust that's still an acceptable time?"

"Uhhh, sure." She rushed into the bathroom with the intent of stripping for a shower as fast as she could. Half a minute had already gone by. Sergeant Archer had reached a new level of sadism in giving her only a half hour to get ready. Didn't he know she needed at least fifteen minutes just to pick out a decent outfit?

Perhaps he did.

And had handled that little issue too.

She flipped on the light to the bathroom to find a full outfit on the hook, in decadent red and black, already waiting for her. After assuring Seth she'd be down in a bit, she clicked the phone off and left it behind in order to flip over the note that also dangled from the hangar. Ethan's writing again filled the card.

Wear only what's here.

Put your hair up.

The hotel driver knows where you're meeting me.

Her nerve endings danced as her heart skittered through a few beats. *Caramba*, this man knew how to climb inside her soul and scoop out its naughtiest needs. To be summoned to meet him, wearing the clothing he'd picked and the hairstyle he'd instructed, made her feel things that most of the world might call weak. But in this moment, in her mind and heart, she felt nothing but wicked...and wanted. For these next few hours, she was going to be his plaything, his property. Simply *his*.

If she wasn't on such a tight deadline, she would have cried in gratitude. Maybe Ethan did know her, perhaps better than she knew herself. Knew her, understood her...and accepted her for it.

She couldn't wait to see him again. And thank him in person...in whatever manner he desired.

★ ★ ★ ★ ★

An hour later, her goal hadn't changed. She just wondered if Ethan's had.

"*Estas loco*, Archer?" she muttered as she slid down the town car's window and peered up...then up some more. The storm was still raging, and the rain sluiced down thirty floors' worth of flawless mirrored windows like a modern age waterfall. At ground level, embedded into a sculpture of chrome and glass, was an emblem that swirled an archery bow into a big letter *A*. The Archer Systems logo.

The door upon which she was leaning was pulled open. The hotel's driver stood there, suspending an umbrella for her. As the guy's gaze settled on her face, he frowned. "Is there a problem, Ms. Chestain?"

Except for the fact that she'd been summoned to a sterile corporate monolith tucked behind two security gates, instead of a discreet dungeon somewhere in the bohemian belly of San Francisco? No "problem" at all.

"I'm sorry, Brandon." She attempted a smile. "You're getting soaked because I can't stop being nervous."

"It's okay. Do you have everything you need?"

"I think so." She glanced inside her little red purse, which perfectly matched the shade of her dress, a simple but stunning D&G design with a fitted V neck and a flowing skirt. Yes, Ethan had picked the clutch for her as well. He'd even made sure to stock it with a mini tube of lube, which had done all sorts of things to her anticipation level about this "meeting."

Which now seemed like it was going to be a *real* meeting. She wondered if she'd needed to bring a pad and paper for taking minutes.

Way to orchestrate a buzz kill, Sergeant.

Brandon walked her to the vestibule of the building's entrance and then buzzed for the receptionist to receive her. Ava tried to take a few calming breaths. A few moments later, a curvy redhead who wore a dress that looked authentically vintage gave her a dazzling smile as she opened the door. "Good morning. You must be Ms. Chestain. I'm Ashley. It's so nice to meet you."

"It...is?" She couldn't hide her puzzlement. She'd expected a more glacial greeting from the receptionist *and* the building. Instead, Ashley's demeanor reflected the atmosphere of the lobby, understated yet warm.

Ashley chuckled. "Of course. Please come in. Mr. Archer's expecting you." She flashed a conspiratorial grin. "Eagerly, I would also say—although you didn't hear that from me."

"Of course not."

She didn't get a chance to exchange more than that with the woman, since the elevator dinged as soon as they got to it. "This is the express to the penthouse," the woman explained. Ava wished that news came as a surprise—or removed even one of the needles assaulting her nerves now. Instead, it added a thousand more.

She didn't feel any better once the doors opened at the end of the elevator's bullet-fast climb.

Another receptionist, a pixie with short black hair who also introduced herself as Ashley, was just as accommodating as Ashley the First as she led the way to a massive, industrial-style door inset with shards of polished glass. "Go on in," she instructed. "He's expecting you."

The words resounded in her head as she pushed open the door. Did everyone in the damn building know that Ethan was *expecting* her today? Even, as Lobby Ashley had asserted, "eagerly?"

Ethan turned as soon as she walked in. He stood in front of a floor-to-ceiling window next to a sprawling desk that was topped by a stunning slab of gray and black marble. In front of the desk were three ergonomic chairs with gray leather that looked soft enough to sleep in. Eight high-backed versions of the chairs were positioned around a spacious conference table with laptop drop spaces and charging portals for every electronic device on the planet.

All of it was nearly as beautiful as he was.

The deep-blue business suit was clearly custom, probably Isaia or Ralph Lauren, and turned his tall, muscled frame into a jaw-dropping business silhouette. His flawless white shirt and cobalt silk tie made his tanned skin stand out, though the contrast was helped by the fact that he'd bypassed his morning shave, giving his jaw more definition with cliffs of scruff. Before she could stop it, her imagination took over, thinking about what those coarse hairs would feel like against her lips as she worked her way along the base of his face in eager nips and kisses...

As her gaze rose to the rest of his face, her fantasy halted. Then shattered.

Lobby Ashley had overstretched with her assessment. He was "eagerly" expecting her? There was nothing "eager" about the smooth smirk that came and went across his lips. And the unflinching concentration in his deep-blue gaze? It wasn't eagerness by the longest shot in the book. Even the angle of his head was defined by serene command.

Once more, her senses downed a shot of pure arousal—with an anxiety chaser. Did this trip to the clouds mean she was about to experience paradise or judgment day?

"Hi there. Welcome to Archer Systems." His tone was as composed as his stance.

"Thank you," she murmured. After trying a couple more steps, she stopped. He'd selected a stunning pair of Jimmy Choos for her, but the things weren't great about supporting knees of jelly.

"You look incredible."

She didn't know how to respond to that. He said it as if he could've been standing there with a spreadsheet in hand, commenting on random numbers. "Thank you," she repeated, feeling ridiculous. After trying to recover with a shrug, she blurted, "Now that we've got *that* out of the way—"

"Did you wear everything I laid out for you?"

His emphasis on *everything* left her no doubt about his meaning this time—and had her battling another wave of frustration. The only items left to discuss about her ensemble were the black thigh-high fishnet stockings accompanied by a red and black garter belt. The logical completion pieces for the lingerie, panties and a bra, had both been missing. Despite the burning temptation to level a zinger at him for that, she pulled in a steady breath and replied, "Of course...Sir."

"Let me see."

The spreadsheet voice again. His CEO pose continued too. Keeping her eyes locked on his chest but letting him see her exasperated grimace, she set down her purse and shirked her coat. His utter stillness betrayed how intently he watched each of her moves, causing her sex to pulse and her breasts to tauten. Her stiff nipples pushed at the dress's soft fabric, more than proclaiming her lack of a bra. So much for having to elaborate on that one.

"Beautiful," he commented. "What about the rest?"

She let him see her squirm. "I followed your directions, Ethan. I—"

"Then let me see." He broadened his posture and cleared his throat. "Lift your skirt, Ava, and let me see."

Spreadsheet voice was gone. Dominant voice had replaced it. Which, of course, made every cell in her pussy wetter and hotter as soon as she pulled up her skirt to let him confirm her obedience. "Satisfied?" she snapped.

"Quite. Thank you."

As she let the fabric fall, her cheeks flamed with heat. Unable to contain her vexation anymore, she slammed her hands to her hips and glared straight at his face. "What the *hell* is going on, Ethan? Why are we here? And why are you acting like...that?" *Because I'm caught between being completely creeped out and completely turned-on right now, and I'll crawl out of my skin if a decision isn't made soon.*

He came closer by two measured steps. A shrug actually slid across his shoulders. "I just figured one good wall deserved another."

She turned her gaze down again. Shook her head. He didn't elucidate on it because he didn't have to. They both knew what he meant. "You went through all this trouble, put *me* through all this trouble, to talk about my *walls*?"

"I yanked us both out of our comfort zones." He pounded out every word with the confidence of Thor throwing his hammer. "You can't tear down walls without shaking up the foundations."

She gulped. He'd hurled the hammer, broken up the concrete, and it all landed in the center of her chest. "Okay, listen. I didn't intentionally keep you out last night. It was—"

"I know what it was. And for last night, it was okay. Emotional survival isn't a crime. But this is a new day. And all of this"—he swept a hand to indicate the scope of the room— "might be a lot of my days, in a few years. I won't be humping a ruck, hurling out of planes, and sneaking up on the bad guys forever, sunshine. One day, my way of giving back to the world might be from this office. You're going to have to be okay with that." He moved close enough to touch her now, and he did.

With his hand tugging up on her chin, he uttered, "We're here to get to the bottom of things and make it okay."

Ava tried to pull back, at least a little. The potency of his gaze was too much now, going too deep, and recognizing too much of the territory in her soul that it observed. "Fine," she retorted. "It's all okay, and I'm okay with it. It's not even happening yet, so can't we just move on?"

"No." His fingers tightened around the tip of her chin. "We can't."

"Damn it—"

"Look at me, Ava." He shocked her by suddenly releasing her. Just as vehemently, he shot away and spread his arms. "Look. At. Me!" His breath pushed in and out of his chest in harsh surges. After a second, he shook his head. "Yeah. Just what I thought. You glare at this suit and tie the same way you once did my uniform and dog tags. Pulling out your preset labels about the image, along with the mental walls to stick them on, just like you did in LA back in June."

"Then stop me." It was half-snarled retaliation, half-shouted plea. She jammed her arms down to her sides. "Stop me like you did then. Make me tear off the labels and rip them up. Make me see." She raised one of her fists, her muscles trembling from resisting the urge to pummel him with it. "*You* summoned me here, dressed in the clothes *you* specified, to this building, to this room *you* completely control. It doesn't get any better than this, Archer. You want to shake up my foundations? Make my *walls fall?*" She put those two words into mocking air quotes. "Then do it. *Sir.*"

Wind rushed the window, a wild contrast to the unnerving silence that he returned to her rant. She'd pushed something in the man, though. The midnight shadows that crept into his gaze, along with the tight line that was now his mouth, told her as much.

She supposed she should have been scared, but that shit was hard to scrape up when fury still reigned in her blood. Did he think he'd get her to open up about everything just by dictating her wardrobe, pulling the big, bad CEO card, and teasing about the pleasure she'd get if she was a *good girl*? She was a long way from twelve years old. Sitting in the principal's office didn't make her tremble anymore. If he wanted her attention, he was going to have to—

Take control.

Exactly like he did now.

Oh *cielos*, how he did...

One even step forward. A subtle tilt to his head. A new squaring of his shoulders. Innocuous little moves, yet within a handful of seconds, they lent the outward enforcement of a powerful aura that now flowed off him like smoke from a rocket on countdown. His entire face smoldered with that same smoke. His stance widened with its latent power. And he lifted one of his hands with its elegant command, curling one finger at her in wordless bidding.

Like that finger was a damn sheep hook, Ava was helpless in his thrall. By the time she stepped within arm's distance of him again, the mush in her knees had spread upward. Her thighs ached, her sex clenched, her pussy trickled anew. Like a magnet that recognized its polar pull, every inch of her body identified its need for his...every corner of her soul acknowledged its match to his.

"Take off the dress."

She didn't argue. She barely hesitated. Her resistance and anger slipped away as easily as the dress, left behind in the

WILD

crimson puddle at her feet. She dropped her head, taking quiet delight in the low, approving rumble from his chest. The only sound she gave in return was a high sigh as Ethan brushed his knuckles across both her breasts, coaxing their tips to stand up higher for him. *Yes. Yes...*

"Say it," he growled, as if his mind had a window into hers. "You want me to do it? You want me to topple your walls, Ava? Then tell me—and make it count."

Ruthless man. Incredible Master.

He knew how to bring her heart and spirit home, beneath his rule, willingly merging her will with his. "Yes." Desperation turned it more into a gasp than a word. "*Sí. Mi maestro. Sí.*"

She raised her head a little, wanting him to kiss her. *Dios,* needing the command of his mouth on hers. Ethan pressed closer, letting her nude flesh feel how close he was, filling her senses with his scent, a masculine mix of rain and pepper and arousal. She let her lips part a little, her balance swaying as she anticipated the heady invasion of his tongue on hers.

It didn't come.

He swiped one of his thumbs across her mouth instead. The stroke was a rough precursor to the push he gave the digit all the way in, making her moan from the salty taste of his skin. Ethan's graveled growl harmonized with her as he pumped his flesh in and then back out, a primal emulation of what she hoped he planned on doing to other parts of her body...with other parts of his.

"Come here," he finally directed. He left his thumb in her mouth while clasping the back of her head with his other hand and pulled her back to the conference table. The treatment was feral and brutal, a collar and leash short of yanking her like a naughty pet—and she loved every moment of it.

Ruthless man. Incredible Master.

Only Ethan could do this for her. He knew when she needed things harsh, as well as the perfect limits to which he could push without going over. Sometimes she wondered if the man possessed a secret mental drone that he sent into her mind on recon missions when she was sleeping, taking pictures of all her secret sexual fantasies. If that was the case, then she officially gave him clearance for more flights.

There was a chair at the head of the conference table, styled in the same fashion as the others only bigger and statelier. It might as well have had *Commander* etched into its leather back, since that was blatantly its purpose.

He let her go in order to pull the chair out and settle into it, his legs braced apart, both hands sprawled around the armrest ends. He was a warrior of Wall Street crossed with a starship captain, making her more achingly aware of how she stood before him, naked except for her fishnets and wanting him in about five hundred ways. Craving to do things for him... if he'd only let her...

"Kneel."

Starting with that.

She lowered as gracefully as she could until she was on both knees before him. When he widened his thighs, she looked up, grateful to see a whirlwind in his eyes that urged her closer. *Mierda.* With the midnight intent of his gaze, the tension working beneath the scruff along his jaw, and the thick hair falling over his forehead, he was pure carnality poured into human form. She couldn't stop staring, and she was glad he let her.

He kept her gaze bound to his as he lowered his hands to the fly of his pants. The clink of his belt and the grind of the zipper made physical imprints on her senses, making her shiver as violently as if he'd reached down and stroked her trembling clit. She didn't even try to hide her gasping reaction. As if she'd want to. The moment she sighed, it unleashed more signs of desire on his face, twining the ribbons of connection tighter between them, inciting one pleading word to her lips.

"More."

Ethan's face hardened in all the most perfect ways. As he scythed into her with the power of his gaze, he sliced out a hand into her hair and around her nape. He pulled hard, guiding her down, undaunted in his command—

Giving her exactly what she needed.

As the beautiful bulge in his underwear grew beneath her gaze, he growled one more perfect order. "Take it."

Ruthless man. Incredible Master.

All hers. Hot. Hard. Delicious.

CHAPTER FOUR

He'd gone to heaven.

Ethan pushed out a weak laugh. That had to be the most shallow, stupid, *guy* kind of thing to think. But he'd be hard-pressed to remember—yeah, he really *was* going there—any other moment in his life when he yearned to stop the clock for a very *long* time.

She'd always been so fucking good to him with her mouth, but now...it was like Ava had never tasted him before today. With every thrust of her mouth on his cock, she pulled and sucked and licked with serious care, as if trying to memorize every inch of his penis via her throat. He felt adored, even worshipped. He was warmed in ways that went beyond biology. There was music beyond her sweet little hums, vibrating through the sensitive mushroom at his tip until he had to clench his thighs to hold his climax back. And he swore there was magic in her fingertips as she tunneled beneath his pants and clutched his hips, gripping for purchase as he controlled her pace with his hold on her ponytail.

Control. Wasn't that the ironic word of the day? He was fast losing his, falling spellbound to this woman, who awed him with her sincere need to please, with how her desire seemed to mount in proportion to his.

On a tight grunt, he finally pulled her back. Ava moaned in protest, but he secured her head tighter. "Eyes up here," he directed—though when she complied, exposing him to the depths of her gaze, he almost regretted the instruction. Her indigo irises belonged on a she-cat, radiating nothing but raw animal need. "Damn," he grated. "You're really hungry for this, aren't you, sunshine?"

Like the feline she so potently evoked, she gave him a little nod. "Oh yes, Sir."

He arched one brow at her in a deliberate taunt. "Even though we're in the penthouse office, and I'm in this suit, and the kitchen will probably be bringing us lobster tails for lunch?"

She dipped back down, attempting a little lick at his dark-red crown. "Lobster's not what I want in my mouth right now."

He'd been saving a teasing grin to give her along with the brow. It faded as his cock twitched, instantly telling him whose side *it* was on here. "I should seriously fill your throat with come for that."

Her pupils dilated. "*Sí*. You should."

He rebuked her with a thick growl. She'd deliberately stressed her accent for the comeback, which made his dick respond with another aching jerk. While they both watched, it sprouted a huge drop of precome. Ava stared as if his erection had turned into a bar of fucking Godiva.

"Go ahead," he said, "but enjoy it well. I've got other plans for how you're going to take my cock inside you today."

He loved watching the color that flared to her cheeks as she bent her lips to his erection one more time. With her eyes still lifted to his, she rolled her tongue several times around the base of his glans, spurring a harsh hiss from between his teeth. Finally she moved back to his head, sipping off the liquid there with a needy moan. Holy *fuck*...

"All right." He had to push the syllables out as he forced

his cock back into his pants and feverishly zipped up. He didn't bother with his belt, though. Very soon, it was going to come in handy for other purposes.

The same comprehension crossed Ava's face while she watched him begin to pull the leather free from its moorings. As she emitted a breathy Spanish expletive, he let out a chuckle. This was one of his favorite parts about being the woman's Dominant...these moments where he pulled an action that stunned her enough that she let go of herself, allowing him to play with her thoughts. Though real apprehension bolted itself on her features, he also watched her nipples bead harder and her tongue dart across her lips. A little fear went a long way when it came to moistening this woman's pussy.

He rose but left her kneeling in front of his chair. She knew better than to move, but he also anticipated her stealing glances at him as he took the long way around the large conference table. In this case, he actually counted on it. He wanted her to see him picking up her purse from where she'd left it on the table and reaching in to retrieve the lube he'd stocked there—along with the tube of red lipstick she'd also tucked inside.

A grin sneaked across his lips as he watched the puzzlement that pursed hers.

After striding back around to the head of the table, he braced himself in front of Ava again. She kept her head down now, exhibiting a flawless submissive's pose, stirring him to stroke the top of her head in appreciation. He sifted the tips of his fingers through the cascading curls of her ponytail. They were as curvy, silken, and perfect as the rest of her. That lush beauty, along with the generosity of her heart and the loyalty of her spirit, blew him away every day. How the hell could she ever lose sight of her own worth...not see the splendor that he did every time he beheld her?

He vowed to make her see that more clearly.

"Up," he bade softly, using one hand to help her stand. With the other, he pushed a couple of buttons in the table. Two holes flipped open, clearly meant as cup holders, on the left and right of the big boss laptop bay. He eyed the distance between the circles and nodded, pleased with himself. This would be perfect.

Ava's mind, which sometimes trumped his in the arena of kinky possibility, snapped to its own conclusion a second later. "*Caramba.*"

He smirked. "You know that shit only encourages me, baby." Though he seriously wanted to fuck with her head a little more, keeping her off guard was the higher priority. Without preamble, he grasped both sides of her waist and swung her up, placing her ass perfectly in the laptop bay. Since that naturally hiked up her thighs, he slid his grip down to both her legs and then spread her wide. When he reached her feet, he shot her a teasing mope while easing off her heels. "Take a memo, Ms. Chestain. The next time we order a conference table, the cup holders need to accommodate high heels."

"Of course, Mr. Archer." Her breath chopped out of her in quaking spurts as he took off her other shoe and positioned her heel into that cup holder. She supported herself on her elbows, watching him with fervent focus as he glided both hands back up her legs...approaching the flower that was now spread and ready for him. "W-Will that b-be all, Mr. Archer?"

He took his time about shaking his head, instilling salacious intent to every inch of it. "Not by a fucking longshot, Ms. Chestain."

"I s-see. All right, then. Wh-What else can I get f-for

you?" She went on battling for breath as he traced his fingers up the seams between her pussy and her thighs. Christ, she was glistening for him. Her clit peeked from between the wet folds, begging for him to take a taste. "Coffee? Tea? Me?"

"Wrists," he returned. As much as he longed to dive his face into her sex and devour her through the first of many orgasms, he stuck to his plan. That began with finishing pulling off his belt as she lay back on the table and dutifully held up her arms. She made him ten times harder as she emitted adorable little mewls while he wrapped the leather strap several times around her wrists. He finished off the bondage by leaving a sizable lead off the end. It always made sense to have a few ways of guiding one's subbie, and he found the tongue useful right away, letting him yank her close for a tender but teasing assault with his lips on hers.

"*Ay dios mio*," she rasped when he was done. Her gaze was hooded, her cheeks flushed, and her lips full with blood from kissing him...and sucking him. Ethan ran his tongue along the seam, sneaking in another taste along her smooth teeth.

"You taste like lust, sunshine. And come."

"I want more," she entreated. "Please, Sir?"

He pulled away reluctantly. "Lie back, Ava. We have a little lesson to go through first."

She scowled, openly disgruntled—and suspicious. "Last time I looked, this was an executive office, not the training room."

"Hush," he admonished, straightening to stand upright between her legs again. "Extend your arms over your head." As he trailed the tips of his fingers along her inner thighs, he emphasized, "You are open to me now, Ava. You are open *for* me. Tell me you understand."

She let out another quivering sigh. She loved it when he caressed the insides of her legs, and they both knew it. "I—I understand, Sir. Ohhh, thank you, Sir."

"You're welcome, sunshine." He invoked the words slowly, giving them all the force of three other words that resounded in his heart. *I love you. I do, Ava. So much.* "Does this make you feel good?"

Her skin shivered and pebbled as he explored around her kneecaps and down her shins. "Ahhh, yes. Really good."

"And beautiful?"

"Yes...yes."

"And special?"

"Yes. Always. With you, Sir...always."

He stopped and clamped hard into her lower thighs. "No. Not always." As her muscles tensed, he persisted. "Not last night. You were with me last night, and yet you fell prey to people who wanted to tear you down. And you let them."

Her eyes closed. She turned her head, clearly trying to hide from him, which was impossible with her arms stretched out. "Last night was about a lot of things, okay?"

"I know that, baby." He eased on his grip. After a second, he skated his hands up to her waist and tenderly held her there. "I know we had a massive curve ball thrown at us—"

She cut him off with a huff. "Try a whole inning's worth."

"That's fair," he conceded. "But it's also life. It's going to be *our* life, whether it's my mother, or my job, or *your* job. You remember the first day we saw each other again, on the set? When Bella hijacked your day by sending you to the villa to coordinate her party?"

She realigned her head and opened her gaze back up to him. "How could I forget?"

"We managed to turn *that* curve ball into a homerun, right?"

"Hmmm." She giggled. "Right."

A smile rolled over her lips, breathtaking and bright. Its beauty spread to the rest of her face. She took his breath away when she looked like this, her dimples deep and her eyes alive, but telling her that wasn't going to sink the lesson in. Making *her* see it, not just in her mind but in front of her face, was the only way to make it stick.

He could absolutely arrange that.

As he pushed his hands up to her breasts before slowly teasing her nipples, he gave her a new command. "Tell me how you feel right now."

At first, she flashed him a saucy version of her are-you-fucking-serious glower. But when she looked harder and understood his deeper context, she visibly tamped her frustration. "You're not making it easy to focus on that answer, Sir. Not when you...touch me like that..."

"I strongly beg to differ." He let her see how the curves of her body made his teeth clench and his nostrils flare. He let her feel it by sliding his fly against her pussy, stimulating her with the hump of his straining cock. "Besides hot, horny, wet, and wanting, how do you feel right now?" He scraped his thumbs across the gorgeous red tips of her nipples, tormenting her, adoring her.

"Ohhhh! Mmmmm..."

"Lovely." He squeezed her tips harder. Nudged his hips tighter inside hers. "But not answers. I'm waiting, Ava."

"All—all right!" she retorted. As the storm howled harder at the window, her voice dipped into a raindrop-soft rasp. "You—you make me feel...treasured."

"Treasured," he echoed. "That's good." He kissed her softly in thanks. "Very good."

"Thank you, S—what the hell?"

Her protest came too late. Not that he would've let it halt him. As he'd planned, her deep-red lipstick made an ideal marker for writing the word diagonally across her torso. From her right hipbone to her left breast, she was now branded: *T-R-E-A-S-U-R-E-D*.

"What else?" he prompted her again. Damn. Forming the words was harder than he thought—but so was his cock. Gazing at his writing across her body brought a surge of possessive lust he hadn't anticipated but sure as hell wasn't going to deny.

The change in his tone wasn't missed by Ava. Her smile got wider, her tone huskier, as she supplied, "Desired."

He rumbled his approval before writing the word up the inside of her left thigh. Ava lifted her head to watch him do it this time. Her eyes glittered, betraying her own decadent delight in his branding job. "How about *bonita*?"

He smiled and nodded. The Spanish word for "beautiful" was a perfect choice—and a great excuse to give his letters some fancy flourishes as he inscribed it to her opposite thigh. Ava rewarded his creativity with some throaty laughs, along with a little gyration of her hips that tempted his thinning self-control.

He didn't help that effort by letting the lipstick continue a few inches past his finish point...until he started tickling the edge of her labia with it. Her breath hitched, acting like a thread around his cock. He must have been insane for worsening the pressure as he bent and inhaled the heady scent of her desire, but once he was that close to her essence, he couldn't stop.

"*Mui bonita*," he murmured while leaning in to kiss her

tender tissues. "*Te adoro*, Ava. *Me excites mucho.*"

"Ethan!" All the muscles beneath his lips clenched. The aluminum cup holders clinked in their casings as she writhed. "*Dios*, please tell me we're almost done with the vocabulary lesson."

He made her endure a roguish chuckle as he nudged aside her labia with his tongue and then gently licked the hard ridge of her clit. "But why? You're giving me so many interesting new words for the list, baby."

Her thighs quivered as her pussy flowed. "Like *exasperated*? And *frustrated*?"

"Hmmm. More like *lubricated.*"

As he rose, he tossed aside the lipstick and opened his pants once more. He let out a ragged snarl as soon as his cock broke free, punching against her outer folds with throbbing insistence.

"And lathered," he added. Dear fuck, wasn't that the case. No matter how hard he fought it, her channel sucked his erection nearer with its hot, tight temptation. He was already an inch inside her by the time he grabbed for the lead on his belt, hauling her back up against him with one brutal pull.

"Perhaps...lewd," he said with a wolf's sneer, kissing her hard.

"And lickable." He shoved his way into her mouth tongue first, jamming it along hers in time to the lunges of his cock into her sweet cunt.

"And loved."

It spilled from him as he reached home deep inside her, the head of his cock welcomed by her deepest cave. He withdrew and plunged again. Ava screamed and let her head roll back. "Loved," he repeated before jerking her close again, marking her neck with the force of his vow. "I love you so much, Ava."

Every thrust took him in deeper, even as the climbing pressure in his shaft incited him to drive faster. He felt the lipstick smearing onto his own thighs, and as Ava tore off his jacket and then his tie, he knew the shit was getting on his clothes too. He welcomed the stains. He wanted them. In sharing them, he committed himself to the bond of their bloodlike color...pledged that for the rest of her life, this amazing woman would always feel branded by his desire and adoration, would always know how deeply he treasured her, how thoroughly he loved her.

"*Te amo, Maestro,*" she cried to him in return. *I love you, Master.*

"Then come for me, sunshine." He swooped the lead over his head so her bound wrists were locked around his neck. "Come *with* me." With his hands cupping her ass, he was able to slide her body tighter against his. He locked his stare to hers as he grinded her pussy harder on his hot, pounding length.

"Yes, Sir," she said in a sweet whisper. "Oh yes, Sir. Oh... yessss...ohhhhh!"

As her mouth fell open and her climax washed over her, Ethan detonated too. He released his moan into her mouth as he jetted his seed into her body, the white-hot ecstasy claiming every inch of his skin, every tendon in his limbs. Her lipstick was everywhere on his clothes and body, her scent was everywhere in his head, and his deepened love for her was everywhere in his soul.

After their breathing evened, he reached back and unfastened his belt so she could move. He tenderly pulled her legs down too. As he helped her climb off the table, he cracked, "Well, I know who won't be keeping a straight look on his face for any future meetings in here."

She slapped his chest lightly, making him chortle. Though she snickered a little too, her features quickly sobered. "Are they really bringing lobster up for us? Because it looks like I tried to make you over or murder you and failed miserably at both."

He gathered her back against him, savoring the feel of her body as he brushed tendrils of hair from her face. He'd only asked the kitchen to be on standby for lunch today because he honestly had no idea how open she was really going to be to his plan for their little "open and honest" summit. Since Ava had astounded him once again—and he hoped to God she never stopped for the lifetime he'd spend loving her—he decided to take another risk with their plans for the day. A pretty huge one this time.

"I have a better idea for lunch."

She instantly picked up on the enigmatic underline in his tone. "Oh?" Her response was playful and light, almost injecting him with a frisson of guilt.

Almost.

He kissed the tip of her nose. "You trust me?"

"With my body, heart, and soul."

Okay, *now* he felt guilty. But he also knew he was right. No matter how much she'd wish her lipstick was really his blood in another hour, this was the lunch she needed. The healing *they* needed.

CHAPTER FIVE

This was his "better idea"?

Ava held nothing back from her glare as Ethan drove the car through the private gates that led to his parents' residential community.

She'd readily agreed to "sneak out the back" with him at the office, even though that plan included a chilly ride in the building's freight elevator and getting curious looks from the workers at the loading dock. But after discovering that they all had genuine affection for Ethan and were less concerned by her lipstick all over him than by the joy of meeting her, it was fun to hang out and listen to him trade quick life updates with them.

After a few minutes, Ethan pulled her off to the car, that mysterious smirk still in place on his face. Yeah, the same one she wanted to slap clean off him now.

As he pulled the car around to what looked like a back entrance to the mansion, she intensified her glower. "You ever heard of a little something called *too soon*?"

He turned, resting his forearm atop the steering wheel, his dark cobalts pinning straight to her. "Sunshine, listen—"

"*Dios mio*. Are you really trying that again?" She jerked her head to indicate the chilled mist, rain, and wind that was pretty nasty, even for Central California. "Best as I can tell, there's no sunshine around here for miles. Give up on the explanations, Sergeant."

His gaze narrowed and his lips compressed. "Fine. If that's the way you want it, no explanations." He paused for a moment, releasing a measured breath, giving Ava a ray of optimism in thinking he might just restart the car and take her back to the hotel. But that was the moment she forgot he was a stubborn, unrelenting, I-*always*-achieve-my-goal member of the First Special Forces Group. "You know that leaves me no choice but to pull the command card instead."

She angled her head back against the headrest. "Yeah, I know."

Another breath left him, this time as a huff. "Ava, I'm not going to haul you bodily out of the car. The choice *is* ultimately yours. But I'm due back at base day after tomorrow, which means I'll be on a plane for somewhere by the end of the week. Getting onto that bird will be a hell of a lot easier if I'm assured that you and my parents haven't started off on the completely wrong foot." He reached for her hand, wrapping his warm, long fingers around hers. "It was *their* wrong foot to begin with, but nonetheless—"

"All right, all right." She yanked her hand back so she could use it to smack his shoulder. "You had to play the deployment card, didn't you?"

His answering chuckle made the car feel like a little bungalow of warmth against the storm. She followed the line of his shoulder, so strong and formidable, back up to his face, which was alive with his brilliant eyes and deep-dimpled cheeks. *Dios*, how she adored this man. He really *was* her haven in life's storm, asking her for so little. She owed it to him to try to make a go of it with his parents, even if it would never be what she'd ultimately hoped for.

"Creativity's my middle name," he bantered, "remember?

The US Army has trained me well."

"*Cabrons*," she muttered. *Bastards.* She shoved the car door open as he laughed again. "Fine. Let's just get this over with. And *you* get to explain the stains all over your shirt."

"Not necessary." To her surprise, he walked around the front of the car, scooped her hand into his, and kept walking— away from the main mansion. After passing by a large greenhouse, probably filled with his mother's prized orchids, they arrived at a little stone cottage, situated off a quaint path off the back of the pool deck. "We can clean up in here," he explained, "and nobody will bother us."

"What is it?" She looked around in curiosity after he unlocked the door, flipped on the lights, and let her walk in ahead of him. It seemed like a clubhouse, with a small seating area, a couple of changing booths, and a lot of expansive shelves that were now empty. On the wall were posters of rock bands from fifteen years ago. An ancient video game system sat dusty in front of an older model TV monitor. "*Mierda.*" She giggled. "Am I actually in the Ethan Archer teen-man cave?"

"Guilty, I guess," he answered. "This place became my retreat for years. It's supposed to be a showering and changing hut for pool party guests, though it wasn't so convenient after Dad and Mom added the newer one closer to the house. There's a shower in the bathroom, and I'm sure I've got an old sweatshirt or two hanging out in the credenza too."

Ava seized the opportunity to turn arched brows on him. "Your retreat, huh? Where a lot of your old clothes just happen to be left behind?"

He rolled his eyes. "Yeah, yeah. Full disclosure time. So we may find a few other...presents lying around."

"Shiny pretty ones?" she jibed. "In cute little foil packets?"

He gave a cavalier shrug but walked back toward her with a hint of awkwardness in his step. "I've liked girls for a long time, baby. You know that. At least we were always safe." As he planted himself and drew her close with a flirtatious smile, Ava emitted another giggle.

"I think I have the visual now. A midnight swim under the stars, a promise to show her the rest of your tattoo in the pool house..."

"Back that cart up. What kind of a wild child do you think I was? My parents would've killed me if I had my toe tattooed, let alone my leg." He slapped his right thigh. "The ink didn't come until a year and a half ago, after I nearly lost this thing to a ground rocket attack."

She wound her fingers into his to silently thank him for the revelation about the tattoo. He'd never told her much about it beyond how the interlocking symbols were the Chinese word for *gratitude*. A bit more of him made sense to her now, making it somehow easier for her to conjure him as a gangly sixteen-year-old, sweet-talking a girl beneath the summer stars.

But even though the image was endearing, it again underscored how different their backgrounds had been, especially after *Mamá* had died. Ava chuckled because of it. "Changing hut, huh? Where I come from, the 'changing hut' was the back of Andrea's mom's van, where we took turns holding the towels up for each other and hoped the boys didn't come back early from surfing."

Ethan's eyes lit up. "That sounds like a blast."

"It was cold and frantic and meant half the beach came home in my panties." She finished with a grin. "But yeah, it was a blast." Her stomach did a teenage-style flip in response to how his eyes intensified when she mentioned underwear.

"Guess I should be glad our paths didn't cross," she murmured. "For you, I might've dropped the towel."

"And for you, I would've cut surfing short." He tugged her chin up and concluded it with a kiss, which fast turned into a hot tangle of tongues. And then another. And another. Within minutes, he had her pinned to the wall as they necked like feverish kids who'd newly discovered the magic of French kissing.

The rain came down harder on the little cottage's roof, adding to the illusion that they were all alone, locked in a secret haven with nothing but time and passion to burn. Ethan moaned into her mouth while tucking a hand beneath her skirt and palming her ass. Ava answered his quest with a high mewl and a desperate grind, needing more of the bulge that now throbbed against her naked pussy. "Oh, Ethan," she rasped, lost to the magic of his strength and the desires from every touch. "Ethan...Ethan..."

"Yeah, baby." His words were like steel shavings in her ear, demanding as the cock that pounded at the zipper fitted to her core. "I know. I know."

"Ethan?"

They froze together. The strident call hadn't come from her. It was outside, from somewhere in the rain. And it was female.

"Ethan, are you out here, honey?"

And it was getting closer.

"Shit," he spat—right before the door swung in to reveal Elle Archer in a sleek white rain trench with a matching umbrella and rubber boots. Well, the boots didn't match exactly. They had little interlocking cherries all over them. What the hell did cherries have to do with dodging rain puddles?

"Well, here you are!" Wearing an overly bright smile, the woman clearly tried to look everywhere except the obvious: the spot where Ethan still had his hand rammed beneath Ava's dress. "I was talking to Ashley at the office, and she said you'd been in but then had disappeared before lunch. Then I thought I might've heard your car on the back driveway, not that I could hear a thing through all this rain..."

Ava barely held back a snort. Of *course* she couldn't hear a thing. Or wasn't watching that damn driveway like a she-falcon hoping for a mouse to drop in for lunch.

"...so have you dropped in for lunch?"

Ethan straightened and let Ava do the same. "*We* thought it might be a good idea to come by," he responded, "since last night was such a zoo."

Elle gave a preening sigh. "Oh, but *what* a zoo! I think we'll make the city news page with it, not just the society column. If it's a slow news week in San Francisco, they might carry a little piece on it. Didn't everyone look terrific? I'm sure Avery Reed wore that suede number just to catch your eye, E. You always told her you liked her in brown, and—"

"I'm partial to red these days."

He bit out every word as he wrapped a possessive hand into Ava's. She hated admitting that it felt better to have him holding her like this, but it did. *Mierda*, what was wrong with her? She dealt with lunatic attention seekers every day of the week. Hell, she worked for a woman who chewed up women like Elle Archer for breakfast. *But you don't want to marry Bella Lanza's son.*

And there was no time like now to suck up her fears and make that fact known.

Plastering on a brave smile, she scooted forward and said, "There's nothing wrong with brown, either. It's a wonderful neutral. I have lots of it in my own closet."

Elle blinked at her like she'd just spoken every word in Martian. Once more, Ethan's grip came as the reassurance she needed, though the new tension to his presence was disconcerting. Or maybe "tension" was putting it diplomatically. A peek up at his profile confirmed her suspicion. His lips were a board-straight line, as taut as the glare he bolted into his mother.

"Sunshine," he uttered, "you're shivering. The bathroom's through that door. Why don't you grab a quick shower?"

She gave in to the instinct to squeeze *his* hand now. "Sure."

His mother huffed and waved a dismissive hand. "That isn't necessary. She can shower up at the main house." Her face pinched. "Dear heavens, Ethan Aaron, it looks like you need to, as well. Is that...lipstick?"

Like a scene from some superhero cartoon, Ethan pulled up on his posture, seeming to grow a foot in the process. "She'll shower here."

Elle rolled her eyes. "You're being ridicul—"

"Get in the shower, Ava. Please. Now."

She didn't waste any time scurrying toward the door— though unbelievably, she actually felt a twinge of concern for Elle. She knew Ethan would never physically lay a hand on his *madre*, but the dark smoke invading his gaze and the pulse that hammered in his jaw were enough to make her throw the shower on but leave the stall empty. She went back to the bathroom door and cracked it open just enough to get a peek at what was going on.

"Is that really lipstick on your shirt, E? What happened?

It's everywhere. Which is definitely where you *weren't* last night. I barely saw you after Daddy gave his toast."

"Mother." His broad shadow shifted, and there was the sound of him taking a heavy step.

"Somebody said you left early, but I'm sure they were just—"

"*Mother.*"

"What?"

"I'm only going to say this once, so sit your ass down and listen."

Ava pressed a hand over her mouth to muffle her gasp. Elle wasn't so diplomatic. "I beg your pardon, young man?"

"I left 'young' behind a while ago, Mom. That doesn't mean I don't love you." His hands appeared, reaching for hers. "If there's one thing the army has taught me well, it's just how much I *do* love you and Dad, how grateful I am for you both." He pulled in an audible breath. "But my heart has grown big enough to love another. Ava's my soulmate, Mom. No amount of parading my exes out at your parties or pretending this is something I'm going to get over, like Batman or Buffy the Vampire Slayer, is going to change it. I proposed. She said yes. And I've never been so happy."

There was a significant silence now. A thick sniff. "Just like that, then?"

There was a smile in Ethan's reply. "Yeah. Sometimes you get lucky, and—"

"Luck has nothing to do with it, Ethan!" A chair scraped before the cherry boots took some furious stomps. "She's... what...a Hollywood hair person or something?"

"She's a respected stylist and designer for one of the biggest stars in the industry. Her looks are on the red carpet, and—"

"Stop. *Stop.* I can't listen anymore. Do you know how many years I spent as you were growing up, cultivating the appropriate relationships for you? Watching all the right girls for you?"

"*Ava's* the right girl for me. The right *woman.* And you know how I know that? She reminds me a lot of you, when you drop all this society bitch stuff, and you're simply a passionate, joyous person." There was a rush of energy as he stepped back over to her. "She wants a mom. She hasn't had one since she was nine. She cries about it in her sleep, and it breaks my damn heart."

Ava swallowed hard. Tears stung, sudden and sharp and sweet. How the hell had he put all of that together? And knew it with such perfect clarity?

"You're with her when she sleeps?"

He actually got out a laugh. "Yeah, Mom. Sometimes I am. But even if I wasn't, I'd know one thing for certain. All she wants to do is be a great daughter for you. She wants to get to know you, damn it, so yank down your walls and let her!"

Elle squirmed and fumed through a very long pause. "Since it's you asking—"

"I'm not asking."

She *psshed* at him. "Don't be insolent."

"Mom, I'm the guy who cut off the president's hand to accomplish shit. I'm. Not. Asking."

She didn't bristle at him this time. For a second, Ava wondered if the woman even breathed. She wasn't sure *her* lungs were cooperating beneath the weight of her astonishment.

And the love that had just grown a thousand times over for her incredible sergeant.

At last, Elle yanked her trench shut again and swept toward the door, readying her umbrella for another tromp through the deluge. "I'll fix some sandwiches from the party leftovers," she offered breezily. "Both of you come up to the house when you're ready, and we'll have a good visit. Maybe you can help set up the Christmas tree while I get to know your fiancée a little better."

Ethan pulled his mother into a tight hug. "I'd like that. And I know she will too."

She pulled back and gave his clothes another long scrutiny. "Can I request that you take off the cosmetics counter before you step foot in my kitchen?"

Ethan threw his head back on a laugh. "Yes, Mom. You can. And I will."

Ava bit her lip, new tears burgeoning, as she watched Elle lean up and kiss her son's cheek with real affection this time. But as soon as the woman was gone, she couldn't wait to get her own hands on the man once more.

"Oof!" Ethan caught her and chuckled as she launched herself against him. "Wha—"

She cut him short by mashing her lips to his, drenching him in kisses she couldn't make passionate enough or long enough. "I'm going to burst with it," she finally confessed with gasping fervor.

"What, baby?"

"My love for you." She cupped his beautiful face, gazing deep into the cobalt eyes that had always aroused her sex and stirred her heart...but now captivated her soul too. "And yours for me. And your belief in me. And the way"—she choked on a tight wad of emotion—"you watch over me when I sleep, and keep my secrets safe, and—"

He cut her off with a reproving growl. "You were supposed to be in the shower."

She popped her stare in feigned innocence. "Ohhh, yeah." With a teasing finger, she motioned backward toward the bathroom. "About that..."

Ethan shot up a brow. "Go on."

Mierda, she was pushing it but couldn't help an impish tilt of her head. "I need to know something first. Did you really have a crush on Buffy the Vampire Slayer?"

"*Ava.* The shower?"

"Wellll..." She was her own interloper now, letting out a high gasp as his hands found their way beneath her skirt again. "Ummm...it's...it's nice and heated up now, Sir."

Ethan suckled her neck as he reached from behind to finger the folds of her pussy. "Sure as hell seems that way."

She sighed and pulled off the dress as he tromped into the bathroom, carrying her by her thighs. As rain drenched the world outside, they drowned together inside, awash in the torrent of their passion, the flood of their desire. As Ava let her sergeant fill her with his body and submerge her in his love, her soul confirmed a beautiful, undeniable truth.

She never wanted to come up for air again.

GLACIER GIRL

Wyatt and Josie Hawkins

CHAPTER ONE

"You've got to be kidding me."

Josie Hawkins *wasn't* kidding about the accusation directed at the woman who'd snagged the heart of her favorite nephew, Garrett, but Sage had obviously lost her mind. That had to be the only excuse for why she now stood there, looking like a runway model for snow accessories and fluffy boots, proposing they go inside the little studio tucked off a cute courtyard in Des Moines' East Village—and shed everything they wore for a photographer.

"Come on, Jo." Sage's seafoam eyes sparkled. "It'll be fun. Valentine's Day is around the corner. This kind of thing is better than chocolate for guys like ours."

"Valentine's Day is not 'around the corner.' It's months away. And Wyatt loves my chocolate brownies."

"He'll love a raunchy picture of you more."

She huffed. "I'm not getting naked for a total stranger."

"Like you've never done the same thing for strangers at a kink club."

Josie compressed her lips. She and Sage had been through enough together to know very personal things about each other, like the erotic domination they both enjoyed from their loving but hot-blooded husbands. But Sage had traveled a lot of the world and now lived near Seattle and its robust kink scene, whereas the cultural excitement of Josie's life involved driving thirty minutes through corn fields to get to

Des Moines, where she could pull "inspiration" from antique stores, vintage-clothing boutiques, and homewares displays. And these days, she was too busy even for that. Running into town consisted of stops for the essentials and nothing else.

No. Not running. Trudging. She saved the running for the marathon of keeping up with Violet Charlotte Hawkins, twenty pounds of feisty energy, who'd now discovered her legs were good for lots of things besides kicking during diaper changes. Her daughter had been the hugest blessing ever from the Almighty; the timing on the delivery had just been a little late. She and Wyatt were the walking, talking, exhausted ad campaign for the highs—*and* lows—of parenthood in one's forties.

But it also wasn't like life had allowed them a choice.

Another correction. It wasn't like a three-way marriage had allowed them that choice—especially when the third arm of the triangle was known to the rest of the world as the US Army's Special Forces. But she had no place boo-hooing about that fact. She'd willingly agreed to the circumstances. Sort of. She'd fallen so instantly in love with Wyatt Hawkins, all those years ago on that snowy Chicago street, that the man could've walked up in a clown suit and she'd have giddily run away with him and the circus.

Sometimes, being married to an SOF soldier felt that way, anyway.

More crying in your milk about this, Josie? Well, suck it up, Mrs. Hawkins, and get on with being a good friend to the other *Mrs. Hawkins around here.*

"Sage. Sweetie." She quirked her mouth into an indulgent smile while patting her niece-in-law's hand. "In case you can't tell, in these parts, 'kink' refers to a knot in a garden hose, and 'club' is where the Assistance League hens play bingo on Friday nights."

Sage frowned. "But you and Wyatt haven't always just played convert-the-barn every time you want to play, right?"

"No." But she hedged with the answer and was clear about it. She didn't want to get into this here and now—not because it was Sage but because it did no good to mourn a life she'd never have again. Those post-PTSD, pre-Violet days filled with heart-halting anticipation, when Wyatt would tell her he was knocking off early to head off with her to Chicago for the weekend...

Chicago.

Yesssss.

Which also meant Dreamland.

Funniest name in the world for a BDSM club, but also the most fitting. There, in the stylish public and private play rooms, she and Wyatt had carved out a magical new identity for their relationship, as man and woman and Dominant and submissive. The lifestyle roles gave them permission to step outside themselves and deal with the challenge of a couple finding their way back to each other after multiple deployments and a lot of time spent more apart than with each other.

But life also moved on. And Vi had happened. Then her fortieth birthday. Then Wyatt's involvement with various "off-books" missions helping Garrett, Zeke, John Franzen, and God knew who else beat bad guys who probably made the Taliban seem like the Golden Girls. Yes, he'd been paid well to take those risks—but more importantly, she knew he *needed* the gigs. The rush. The exhilaration. The danger. The adrenaline.

The stuff she couldn't give him anymore.

"So, I repeat..." Sage added a tapping foot for emphasis.

"What's the difference between getting naked for an hour now as opposed to shucking it all in a club for your man? Ohhhh, wait." She stabbed a finger up. "There *is* a difference. After *this*, you'll have some cool pictures..."

"No." Josie folded her arms. "I won't."

"...that'll have your Master drooling..."

"No."

"...and wanting to reward his good little girl..."

"I said *no*, Sage." She shook her head, only to be poked by guilt at her friend's crestfallen face. "But I'll hang out and cheer *you* on, okay?"

Sage jammed her hands into her parka pockets and kicked at a stubborn patch of snow at the edge of the patio. "Nah. Forget it. Won't be any fun without a friend."

"Aw, it's okay. I bet Garrett will still want to spank your sexy ass, even if you don't dress it up with makeup and glam filters."

"Sugar, I'm six months postpartum."

"And *sugar*, I'm a full year ahead of that."

"Which is why our asses would love us for a little rouge and airbrushing!"

Josie chuffed at the woman's last-ditch effort at persuasion. "Which is why I'll be happy to lend you my killer brownie recipe." Another snort emerged. "Oh, stop pouting, goofy girl."

"Whatever you say, glacier girl."

The guilt set in again—but only for a moment. Jo treated the feeling with the same efficiency she gave a lot of emotions these days—by wadding it, ramming it into the trash compactor of her mind, and then firmly pushing the On button.

There. All done. No fuss, no muss. Damn good thing, since

she needed the mental compactor open and freed by the time they got back to the farm—and she had to deal, yet again, with everything she felt when seeing Wyatt's mission go bag waiting on the credenza in the mud room.

Like the urge to hurl the whole damn thing into the combine along with the corn.

Like the blazing curiosity about what he'd do if she did.

Like the way her pussy clenched, hoping there would be a harsh and epic punishment for it.

Yeah. She was damn glad her compactor was wide open and ready to go now.

CHAPTER TWO

The girls returned from their trip into town as Wyatt and Garrett rolled in from checking some broken sections in the back fence. Everyone was chilled and hungry—and in the case of the two newest Hawkins family members, restless as hell. Vi and Racer hadn't been fond of spending the last hour strapped in carriers on their fathers' backs, and they now rolled, crawled, and squealed together on the den floor, incited even more by the fruit salad dancing on TV.

"Well, hello there, beautiful." Wyatt strolled into the kitchen after hanging up his jacket and toeing off his boots, beating an instant path to his wife. Though she was busy transferring groceries into the pantry, he leaned in to kiss her cheek. Her skin was still stained a rosy hue from the cold, translating to his immediate hard-on. He liked turning other "cheeks" that color too...

"Hey. How's the fence?" Clearly, her mind wasn't in the same zip code. He clamped down his frustration—a recurring theme lately—choosing instead to help her restock the cabinet. After all, restocking was what they did best. Their daughter loved to snack often, though she burned off the calories as fast as she consumed them. Her energy hadn't been so easy for Josie to handle lately. On heavy snow days, these walls had to become Violet's world. The girl did *not* like walls.

"You first," he said amicably. "How was the trip to town?"

"Fine. Uneventful." She shrugged, making her cowl-neck

sweater slide off a shoulder. Wyatt moved in before she could correct the angle, dipping a soft kiss to the top of her shoulder. She had gorgeous shoulders, especially when they trembled like this...because of his touch...

That recognition alone tightened everything in his pants—and this time, Wyatt didn't fight it. He pushed in behind his wife, making sure she couldn't fight it either. It had been too damn long since they had interacted with each other as Master Wyatt and his sweet girl. Not that she hadn't been "sweet" in other ways, but giving him sexual pleasure was entirely different than submitting to his direction as her Dom and honoring that extraordinary connection they had when in those roles. Funnily enough, Josie had been the one to first suggest they explore Total Power Exchange and had saved sanity because of it. Now, she was the one needing an exfil back to her right mind, but he wasn't sure how to get her there...

Because every time he tried, she reacted just like she did now. One spark of all the right attraction cut short by an ice storm of efficiency and resiliency. Like the ice queen from Violet's favorite movie, alone in an ice tower, where she could be sheltered and safe.

From what?

The shitty—and ironic—thing was, *he* already knew that answer. Correction: the *answers*. Just like Jo had been able to open the window inside him, pinpointing how lost and anxious he'd felt after that last official mission for the Big Green Machine, he was the one with the magic glass cutter now, punching a hole into her psyche. She was a forty-year-old mother of an eighteen-month-old dynamo, living in the middle of corn fields and cow pastures, having to deal with a husband who still needed to go play G.I. Joe from time to time.

No wonder she didn't want to come out of her ice castle.

But now he at least knew it—and was trying to melt those walls, even if he had to do it one icicle at a time.

"You and Sage buy anything fun?"

One icicle at a time, even if he had to do it with this pretense of casualness, seeing if she'd crack about the naughty nudes photo session. Yeah, he knew about that—because he'd been the one to enlist Sage to suggest it. Maybe if Jo first loosened up during a frivolous girls' afternoon, she'd be ready to approach submissiveness again...

"Hmmm. Sage bought a couple of new outfits for Racer. And *oh*"—her face lit up, making Wyatt push away from the counter—"you remember that special flagstone we were looking at, for widening the front path? It just went on sale at that cool masonry place. Sale's on until Monday, but they said if you call, they'll hold an order until Wednesday."

"Great." He ordered his smile to stay lifted though was certain none of it reached his eyes—not that Jo was paying attention. "So...anything else?"

But as he issued it, Garrett and Sage reentered the kitchen in time for Sage to throw a secret twitch of a head shake at him. The tiny move provided his answer three seconds before Josie did.

"Nothing beyond the usual, honey. I got everything on the essentials list then filled up the truck and the generator fuel cans. If that low-pressure front moves in after you take off for Afghanistan, we'll be set until the plows can get this far in."

"Afghanistan?" Garrett swung a stare around, eyebrows hiked. "What the hell are you—"

"Bah," Wyatt volleyed. "Don't play prissy and shocked, boy. You know privately hired teams are used all the time for the messy minor shit. Snake eaters can't be everywhere at once. We both know that."

Garrett shrugged like he'd been told to eat his peas. "Yeah, but I thought you were done with messy."

"Not when messy pays this well."

"And it's only for a week." Jo's quiet affirmation came with an upsweep of her toffee-colored gaze. The message in the look, exclusively from her to him, was evident. *Promise me you'll be back in a week.*

Wyatt didn't falter in sending her an unblinking affirmation. He also let her see his deep breath in, conveying so many things he couldn't with words. How did you tell a woman, out loud, that you were racing back into a war zone by choice— and that the money was only the first part of that decision? That there was other shit tied into your resolve, like feeling you were doing something significant to make the world safer for your family? And then there was the uncomfortable stuff— like admitting you needed the rush purely for your masculine identity. An identity that wasn't getting fed any other way lately...

And maybe that was totally jacked up.

Maybe it was time for him to clean up the mess he had at home before shipping out to do it in another country.

"But before I leave, I think I need a little time alone with my wife."

Garrett joined his wife in a chuckle. "Sounds like a damn good plan to me, Uncle."

Sage added a mischievous grin. "Me too."

Josie got on board with adding her own laugh to the mix, though her mirth was cautious, tagged by lifting her to-do list. "As long as that plan lets me finish all this too, then plan away, sir."

With speed he'd perfected a long time ago, Wyatt snagged the paper from her fingers, stuffed it into his back pocket, and yanked his wife close, savoring the subtle but sudden melt of her icepack. How much more of her could he dissolve with a long, lusty kiss? What would she do if he redefined "global warming" with a savoring squeeze of her gorgeous ass? Garrett and Sage wouldn't mind. Hell, they'd probably applaud.

Yeah. He was going for it...

Until a pair of children's screams all but stripped the paint off the walls.

"Bay-uh!" came Vi's zealous shriek. "Mama. Racah steal Bay-uh!"

Everything Josie had just revealed for him was zipped back into the mama ice queen veneer. "Annnnd the battle for stuffed-animal possession begins," she muttered wearily—though Wyatt had instincts about this kind of shit too, and they all ordered him not to give up without at least one more push for triumph.

"Jo." He caught her by an elbow, making her stop just as Vi's fourth bellow shattered the air. "Garrett and Sage can handle it." He tucked his other hand beneath her chin, forcing her to confront his stare—and the glass cutter he still wielded.

She drew in a long breath.

So did he.

Her caramel gaze melted a little more—clearly wanting to heed him.

Silently, he willed her to.

"Mamaaaaa!"

And up went the woman's frozen fortress again. Josie's features closed off, revealing exactly that. "Garrett, throw on some water to boil for mac 'n' cheese," she charged before jabbing a finger at Wyatt. "And if that doesn't calm the banshee, I'll need your help with a Plan B, Daddy-o." With one hand on the swinging door that led out into the living room, she turned and eyed Sage. "Ready to do this, Mama Hawk?"

Sage's grin was game enough to someone who wasn't looking for more. "One sec. Let me grab Racer's backup pacifier just in case."

"Roger that."

Sage's grin stayed glued in place, even after Jo pushed out into the chaos. Her eyes now betrayed the extra element Wyatt had sensed before—a combination of *holy shit* and *what the hell.* All of it resonated in her voice as she repeated in a subversive mumble, "Daddy-o?"

Garrett pursed his lips to mute his snicker. "Have to admit, Uncle, I thought you preferred *Sir.*"

"I do, goddamnit."

"Then what the hell?"

Wyatt snapped a glare at Sage. "Were you even able to suggest going for the erotic photography?"

Garrett pulled the plug on the laughter. "E-Erotic... photography? Whaaaa?"

"Wyatt thought it might be a good way to relax Jo a bit," Sage explained. "We were going to do it together and surprise you guys with the results."

"I'm surprised," Garrett said, and pleasantly so, judging by the goofy grin spreading his mouth wide. Sage bumped him a little, rubbing her head in as if to relay she'd make up for his loss, before punching her attention back at Wyatt.

"I went at her from a few different angles, too," she revealed then. "I even called her 'glacier girl.'"

"Damn." Garrett's tone was full of admiration.

Wyatt scrubbed his jaw with one hand. It beat punching the wall. "What'd she say to that?"

Sage shook her head, inserting a quiet tsk, before replying. "Turned around and told me she'd forgotten batteries and dog food and we had to go back for them."

"Shit," Garrett muttered.

"*Fuck*," Wyatt growled.

Sage crossed to her purse hanging from a hook near the door and started fishing through an outer pocket. "If you ask me, she's shutting down on purpose. It's not postpartum depression, though." She turned, pacifier in hand, to trade a meaningful glance with her husband. "I have a little experience with that one. And this..." She tilted her head. "Well, this feels different. Like she's activated a survival instinct but now made it her norm."

"Which hasn't been helped by me running off to play soldier boy every few months." Wyatt finished it off by gritting the F-word again, which was received with a few long moments of pensive silence.

"What do we do now?" Sage finally murmured.

"You mean what do *I* do now." Wyatt braced into a determined stance. "And the answer is, I handle it—with drastic measures if need be. But I'll need your help."

Garrett clapped him on the shoulder. "Whatever you need, Uncle."

Sage added her open smile and nodded. "From both of us."

Wyatt gave them his gratitude with some quick hugs, not able to extend the mushfest beyond that. His mind was already spinning with what needed to happen next—with the steps required of him to make things right with his woman. The wife who'd given him a child. The submissive who'd given him his balance. The person who'd set him free to find his purpose and connection...but, right now, at the sacrifice of her own.

It was time to make that shit right.

Even if it meant ordering her to do so.

CHAPTER THREE

This was weird.

Rarely could Josie wake up to Wyatt's empty pillow and be happy about it, but today was an exception. She needed a few minutes to get out her mental packing tape and fix the frayed edges on the boxes in her head.

And her heart.

Especially the one with her husband's name on it.

It wasn't like the thing didn't have a few layers of fix-its on it already. Wyatt's box was a big one and even had subdivisions inside. She'd gotten everything so organized in the damn thing—until yesterday.

She'd gotten a little wet just thinking about posing nude for him.

She'd gotten even wetter when the man got all growly with her in the kitchen.

But there was nothing like a farm to run and a tantrum-throwing kid to surrender a twitching pussy to sheer exhaustion.

She'd fallen into bed, acknowledging Wyatt's arrival between the sheets with a happy sigh, especially when he'd moved in for some tender spooning. And yes, she'd felt his throbbing erection at her ass. And no, she hadn't possessed a shred of energy to wake up and do something about it.

Though now was a different story.

Six hours of sleep later, she was ready to show her man

exactly how much she'd miss him once the guys from the team showed up to haul his gorgeous ass off on this new mission. How much she missed him every second of *every* damn mission. Thank God their sexual chemistry had persisted past Violet's birth, even if the magic of their D/s dynamic seemed a thing of the past now. If she couldn't ensure the man would miss her as a submissive, at least she could remind him how thoroughly his cock enjoyed her pussy.

What time were the guys coming to get him, anyway? Was it seven or eight a.m.? She hoped for the later call time so they wouldn't have to rush and she could make herself halfway presentab—

"Jimmy fucking Carter on a corncob!"

She lurched out of bed, though her gape at the clock on the nightstand never wavered. The display *had* to be wrong— though a backup check on her phone confirmed what the clock's readout said.

She'd *not* just slept in by a few minutes.

It had been a few *hours*.

"What the hell?"

The room answered her with nothing but silence as she jammed both feet into her faded slippers and all but threw on her robe over her sleep tank and baggy bottoms. There was no logic to this. She had the alarm clock set for six every morning, including weekends, with her phone's alarm as a safety net in case of a power outage. Never had they both failed her.

"What the *hell*?"

The last of it squeaked out before she got halfway down the stairs. The second she laid eyes on the open door to the mud room, she froze in place, feet on two different steps, instantly grasping the instinct that assaulted her brain.

Something was wrong.

But there was the next rub. Her logic rallied for the rest of her instincts to kick in and confirm that wrongness—and got stuck for a long minute on that weird hamster wheel. Her heartbeat wasn't kicking into double-time. Her blood was its normal temperature, not the fearful fix of flames and frost.

Because she *wasn't* afraid.

Just confused.

"Really confused," she confirmed to herself, trying to add up the details she could gather so far.

The mud room door was open—which meant Wyatt hadn't yet left for the mission, because the man *always* closed and locked that door when he left to fight the bad guys. It was symbolic for him, to ensure her that nothing "messy" would ever get into their home while he was away.

But if he hadn't left, why was his go bag missing from its normal spot? And what was *her* overnight bag doing in its place? And while she was on a roll with the strange questions, why were cartoons playing in the den at a reasonable decibel level? And why wasn't her little girl shouting her usual nonstop commentary?

"What...is...going...on?" Every word corresponded to a new stair she now cleared, arriving in the entryway as a painful scowl scrunched her face.

The expression didn't ease when a familiar scent tickled her senses, fresh as wind but naughty as leather, just before her husband's presence filled the foyer from behind. She had a chance to break into half a needy moan before Wyatt stepped over to consume every millimeter of her personal space as well, caressing the fronts of her thighs and teething the side of her neck.

"Good morning, Sleeping Beauty." He growled through his long inhalation at her skin. "And I do mean *Beauty*."

So *now* her heart revved to Mach Five. "Is it?" she managed to respond, even making it breezy and bold despite longing to melt fully back into him. "I'm not sure everyone around here agrees with that, Mr. Hawkins."

Wyatt didn't wait for her to melt. He shifted forward, bracketing his legs against the outsides of hers. "That so, Mrs. Hawkins?"

Another growl unfurled from him, deep and savoring, as he worked his body around hers like storm clouds rolling in around a helpless tree. And God, did Josie feel helpless. And God, did she love every second. When she drew in another breath, her lungs were only able to claim it in short, choppy spurts. "I...I overslept."

"I know."

"By a lot."

"I know."

"Because you turned off both my alarms?"

"That I did."

"*Damn it*, Wyatt." Somehow, perhaps with some kind of divine intervention, she shoved away from him. As she spun back around, a shiver overtook her. Her traitorous body always knew the difference between the heated paradise next to him and the cold tundra in trying to resist him. But most frustratingly, her husband knew the exact same thing— sharpening the bite beneath her new charge. "You know I have a thousand things to do today!"

In contrast, his own expression was full of frightening calm. *Hell.* She hadn't seen that expression on his face for a long time now. She used to love it and hate it in the same moment—usually when she'd been cuffed and stationed at the man's feet, waiting for him to decide what wicked treatment he was going to mete on her trembling body.

And *that* was not *now*.

This situation was different.

Very, *very* different.

"Did you hear me?" She pushed a huff onto the end of it, folding her arms.

Wyatt's jaw jutted. "Loud and clear, my girl."

Jo swallowed. *My girl*. The bastard knew what *that* did to every cell of her bloodstream too. At least he hadn't said my *sweet* girl. But he knew better than that, on a day like this, when so many things had to be handled...

"And you're still proud as a rooster strutting the hen house about letting me oversleep by *three* hours?"

He quirked the corner of his mouth. "Roger every drop of that, my love." Now the other corner. The resulting smirk, a look that always turned her belly to goo and her pussy to mush, grew in confidence as he moved back in, backing Josie into the foyer corner between the mud and dining rooms. "As a matter of fact, I'd encourage you to aim for a little nap this afternoon." He pushed in a little more, angling his face over hers and dropping his voice to a sandpaper grate. "Your stamina is not a negotiable item for our agenda tonight. It is required, Josephine Eliza, and I *will* have your *full* cooperation on that."

For a long second, Jo didn't speak. During the next one, she had to bite her lip to rein in a high laugh. Some of the reaction emerged anyway, tittering out of her as she stared in candid wonder. "What the *hell* have you been smoking, Wyatt? And why didn't you share some with me? Ohhhh, wait. Maybe you did last night, and that's why I don't remember anything after my head hit the pillow...?"

More laughter echoed through the foyer—though she wasn't taking the fall for it this time, and Wyatt was nowhere close to humor, with his grin faded. She looked over as Sage and Garrett appeared, with Sage carrying Racer and Vi riding on Garrett's back. Her daughter's fingers were sticky, with a tiny marshmallow crown still stuck to a thumb. Ah-ha. Princess Puffs cereal worked its kid-silencing sorcery every time.

"Looks like we timed our entrance perfectly," Garrett quipped.

"Yeah." Sage giggled. "Just in time to save Jo's backside from paying for her wiseassery."

Josie scowled. "That's not a word. And even if it was...little ears?"

Garrett grinned. "So maybe *Sage's* backside needs a reminder about wisdom and its applications."

Before Sage could form a comeback, Wyatt grunted and pulled away from the corner, keeping Josie tight against him with one steel girder of an arm. "You two can throw down about all that after we get back."

Garrett ticked two fingers over his right eyebrow. "Acknowledged. We got your six. You kids go have fun."

"Okay, *whoa*." Josie finally got free, slicing both arms wide in the air. "'After we get back'?" she accused Wyatt. "'Go have fun'?" she flung at Garrett. "And in case you're not aware, we're not kids anymore. And I'm still in my ever-loving pajamas!" In a disbelieving mutter, she added, "At ten in the damn morning. On a day *you* shouldn't even be here." She stabbed a finger into Wyatt's chest. "I'd say I'm dreaming, but my dreams aren't this insane. Okay, then. This is just an alternate reality. Hogwarts goes to Iowa. The Upside Down without the creepy viny stuff.

The Matrix minus bending spoons..."

"How about just...Dreamland?"

For moments after Wyatt murmured the sultry suggestion in her ear, she could do nothing but blink. Then stammer. "D-Dreamland?"

He kept his lips angled in at her ear. "Our flight leaves for Chicago in a few hours. I just checked us in online."

"A...few..."

"And you're all packed. Sage helped me grab your essentials—including the corset dress still hanging in your closet with the tags on it."

"The...corset dress..." Okay, now it was official. She truly had to be dreaming, because she'd resigned herself to simply staring at that fantasy outfit for the rest of her life. The window for actually getting to wear it somewhere appropriate had surely passed her life by...

But no. This *was* her life, rushing and real, confirmed by her daughter's happy squeal as Garrett lowered Violet so she could run back to the den for her favorite plush toy of the week. When Vi ran back in, Garrett stooped to remind her and the stuffed snail that Mommy and Daddy were going out for a sleepover just with each other, but she was going to the "big kids' sleepover" at their home for the night. Vi was so pumped, she stopped long enough for wet kisses to her parents before running off to set up a celebratory tea party for Racer, the stuffed snail, and a dozen dolls.

Sage was recruited as the tea-party assistant while Garrett headed upstairs to prep Racer for his morning nap, meaning the foyer was suddenly empty again. But just in one sense. Josie could swear her astonishment had become a real creature dancing along the walls around her and the man who'd just bashed in the gates of her psyche with one hell of a ramrod.

Shockingly, a few cells of logic had stuck out the attack and now prodded logical thoughts back. Because of that, she twisted in Wyatt's embrace, hooking a couple of fingers into the collar of his crisp white shirt. But just a couple. She didn't want to mar the perfection of him, which she now had a chance to fully take in. The button-down shirt was tucked into slacks that were mostly charcoal, save for their subtle white pinstripes. Dress shoes would've been the traditional choice for a finisher, but Wyatt had opted for trendy boots instead. Dark-gray lace-ups with an industrial flair. The look was rugged but polished and perfect for him.

No. Beyond perfect.

Just like every second of this day so far.

She stared up at her husband, for once not even thinking about masking what she felt. Happy amazement. Awed surprise. And yes, blatant shock. All of it led to her truly curious query. "How long have you been planning this?"

"Hmmm." Wyatt bit his bottom lip, turning his face into devastating deviousness. "I'd say...about eighteen hours?"

She felt her eyes try to jump from their sockets. "Liar." She tried to laugh out the accusation but soon recognized it was a no-go. Wyatt Nathan Hawkins had been custom-wired for a lifetime in Spec Ops and covert missions. He liked clear-cut plans and tons of details with which to execute them, meaning last-minute surprises and "make it up as you go" were the stuff that gave him hives, even if he was the one doling out the fun.

"You know that normally I'd own that," he replied with too much ease. "But on my entire stack of Bolt saga manga, I swear this all came together only after you got home with Sage yesterday."

She did a double-take. His favorite super hero had just been invoked. Okay, he *was* serious—as well as telling the truth. "Well, damn." Another double-take. "And hold the hell on. After Sage and I—" She stepped free, folding her arms in obvious indictment. "Wait a damn second. She...she told you, didn't she?" Just a few seconds of his fish-needing-water gape, and she had her answer. "She *told you* about how I refused to do that dumb naked photography stuff with her. *That's* what this is about. Now you think I'm repressing shit, so you canceled out on an entire mission to make new arrangements for us in Chicago instead. Shit. *Shit.*"

Wyatt let her pace out the ire for two and a half steps before sliding back into her path and circling her waist. For two seconds, she struggled but realized she had no chance against his rigid grip. Once she softened, he compelled her even closer. They both moaned as he worked his heated touch beneath her robe, gripping her hard enough to leave indents on her hips.

"This is about us burning away all the ice castles, Jo. *Not* just yours. Those walls are my doing too. And just as much my fault."

She got down a painful swallow. His confession was everything she'd been longing *and* dreading to hear. While she missed the intense connection to her lover and Dominant, it was also terrifying to consider a return path to that dynamic with him. What if they couldn't find the path anymore? What if fate had just given them the path for a little while to navigate a darker part of the forest in their life's journey? What if paths didn't get given out to parents, and their life was doomed to just be a massive meadow in which their routes crossed once in a while and the rest was a spread of sunshine in the spring, a coat of frost in the winter, and a lot of boredom in between?

They could live with boredom, couldn't they? It wasn't all *that* bad. It sure as hell beat the cliff where she and Wyatt had once been—memories that caused her to fight shudders even now. No, they'd *never* be there again. And maybe the meadow was what they settled for in its place.

But he was offering more than the meadow.

He wanted to go find the path. And he wanted to do it with her. He'd stepped way outside his comfort zone to prove it. Canceled out on a mission. Planned a trip to Dreamland at the last minute. Packed *her* bag too. She was stunned the man wasn't visibly twitching by now.

So why was it so hard for her to even think of shaving down a part of her glacier, to show the man she hadn't frozen through all the way? To give him just a peek at what lay so deeply hidden in her ice caverns. The woman who still longed to be his obedient little girl...his perfect, beautiful submissive?

Because she didn't feel so perfect anymore.

Or beautiful.

But maybe that was where she needed to start—no matter how scary it was.

She got a shaky breath in and pushed it out with equal jitters. Finally, softly, she confessed to him, "I'm...I'm scared."

A deep rumble came from Wyatt's chest. Its vibrations still hummed in his muscles as he gathered her tight and close, kissing his way through her hair.

"That's all right," he murmured. "Scared is all right, my love. Sometimes, scared is even good."

She sent a wry laugh into the middle of his broad, beautiful chest. "Oh? That so?"

"Damn right." His voice was a dark but steady growl now. "The fear reminds you how important the mission really is."

Josie absorbed that, really hearing his solemnity as she inhaled his clean but rugged scent, before rejoining, "So... you're scared too?"

He gave his reply at once—though the words walked the same unsteady ground as hers had.

"Terrified, baby. Terrified."

CHAPTER FOUR

In a number of ways, Wyatt had almost kicked himself for allowing Jo to go ahead and change her clothes before they got on the road to the airport. She'd looked so fucking breathtaking after flying out of bed this morning, a sexy mess in her pajamas and slippers and then her shock and delight, that he'd almost ordered her to just stay that way until they got to Chicago. It wasn't like Des Moines was a central hub of the commercial airplane world, but he hadn't enjoyed the idea of anyone gawking at his woman and entertaining the same thoughts he did.

The thoughts giving his imagination a *very* fun show right this moment.

And yeah, nearly half of them inspired by the wardrobe change he'd almost forbidden.

Thank fuck, at least for a few seconds, he'd chosen to think with his better sense instead of his idiot dick.

But just for a few seconds.

Definitely not *these* seconds.

He was back to prioritizing every move and action according to the aching flesh between his thighs, especially as he obsessed over the sight of the woman in the airplane seat beside his. The way her ebony hair contrasted with the creamy rose of her cheek. The eager attention in her gaze, lending golden glints to her bronze irises as she stared out the plane's window while they ascended and broke free of the clouds. The way the sunlight angled in and across her lush body, clad in a wraparound black dress and fishnet stockings, finished off with a pair of kickass black suede boots.

Those suede boots.

The ones she'd been wearing the night they first met. When the snow had sparkled in her hair like tiny stars in a silken galaxy. When they'd laughed about stuff so stupid, he couldn't remember a damn thing about the subject matter and absolutely everything about her giggles.

So many things.

He remembered *so* many things about that night...

But most of all, the way she'd looked up at him with such hope and happiness, delighting in nothing else but the moment...nothing else but him.

Just like she gazed at him now.

But now was also when that narrative changed a little. The woman knew him better—*much* better—than she had during that first wintery wonderland of a first-date-that-wasn't-a-first-date. She proved it by notching her head to the side and lifting a tiny, incisive smile before teasing, "Okay, hotshot. Penny for your thoughts. Or do you have to charge me more because this is first class?"

Another switch-up in the plot. On that first night in Chicago, Wyatt would have overreacted with a belly laugh. Now he chose to lean over, letting his desire rise to his eyes, and tell her in a low growl, "I'm thinking that you wore *those* boots."

Her stare turned the color of hammered copper. "Well, you liked them in the middle of that snowfall."

"No. I *loved* them." He slid his flute of champagne into the holder at his side, needing to fill his hand with the curve of her cheek instead. "Just as I knew I loved you, Josephine...damn near from the first moment I ever saw you."

He listened as her breath caught. Watched as her lips trembled. Then tensed as she forced back her emotion, downing half the contents of her own flute as a blatant diversion from the emotions he was dredging up from her, whether she liked it or not. Right now, he'd have bet all the money he dropped on this flight on the *or not* option.

"Ohhhh, goodness. That's very good stuff." She smiled and rubbed at her nose, probably dealing with all the bubbles she'd just downed. "I'm not even going to bust out the pointy fingers at you for splurging on first-class seats."

Yep. She was clearly steering back toward frothy subjects and safe conversation—though Wyatt saw the acknowledgment, deep in her constantly averted gaze, that the piper was coming to her for payment soon. He and Josie hadn't ever wasted time with a frothy and safe phase. That was never their connection, nor would it ever be. Steel needed fire. Blood needed a cut. Dominance needed its submissive.

He needed her.

More than she would ever know.

More than he'd been taking time to tell her lately.

But for right now, he'd let her have her fizzy fun. "We're not hurting for money, Jo," he assured. "The last few missions have paid well." And had come with the pube-splitting clusterfucks for it too, but she didn't need to know that. "So now, let's just celebrate." He accepted another split of champagne from the attendant and swiftly topped off both their glasses. "To all the best parts of the night that started everything, as well as the best parts of our new chapter."

A mesmerizing smile tugged at the bow of her mouth.

"Hmmm. I like that." She raised her glass. "To an awesome new chapter, husband."

"To a new chapter...my sweet girl."

He extended the emphasis on those last three words while tilting his glass forward. As they tapped the flutes and then drank the bubbly, he leaned his head over as well...ending the quest with his mouth firmly on hers. Josie moaned like a needy kitten as he traced the seam of her lips with the tip of his tongue, accentuating the tingle from the champagne for them both, until she finally surrendered and let him plunge all the way inside.

Wyatt joined his low groan with hers, letting his tongue swirl hungrily against hers, reveling in the buzzworthy taste of her. Dear *God*, he had to have more of her. But not right here and now...

Wait.

Why *not* right here and now?

Readily, he concluded that his cock was ready to fuck her in twelve different positions—but that was only because his mind had already shifted firmly into the domination lane, where the fulfillment of controlling *her* lust was even better than his own orgasm. It was the very reason he'd made so many calls ahead to Chicago, planning what was going to be the most incredible night of submission she'd ever know—but who said they had to wait for that part for the fun of this adventure to begin? Maybe a little preview was exactly what she needed...

With that thought emboldening him, he took out one of the complimentary blankets that came with one of these first-class thrones and spread it across her lap.

"Oh, *my*," Josie cooed, stroking the soft cover. "This is lovely, Mr. Hawkins. Thank you."

Wyatt smoothed the fabric a little higher, until it was nearly tucked beneath her breasts. Holy fuck, did that dress do all the right things for her cleavage. The pregnancy had given her three extra cup sizes, but so far she'd gone back down by only one, a cause for his own private national holiday right about now. Just the thought of what he wanted to do to them tonight emboldened him to say, "Correct yourself, girl. Don't you mean, this is lovely, *Sir*?"

Her gaze flared. Her lips parted. A longing little sigh poured out of them. "Of course," she conceded quietly. "I meant exactly that." Her stare dropped into her lap. "And thank you...Sir."

"Very good." He modulated his own voice lower, directing the words close to her ear once more. "And now, I'd like you to put that champagne back into the holder. You can have the rest of it in a little bit...when you're finished pleasing me."

He saw more of the whites of her eyes, though she obeyed his dictate. "I'm not sure...I understand. Pleasing you? Here, in these seats?" Revelation flashed across her face then lilted her voice. "Ohhhh. Maybe I should follow you to the bathroom? Errrrm...will we have enough room to—?"

He halted her with another kiss, though this time, he didn't tease his way into her mouth. He crashed his way in, ordering her tongue to make way for him, toppling a good deal of her body's resistance in the same forceful sweep. That was a *very* good thing, because he took command of her hand too... guiding it beneath the blanket and between her legs.

From the outside, they probably looked like a lovesick couple in a passionate mackdown. On the other side of the aisle, a guy in rocker denims with Stryper-worthy hair even mumbled, "Lucky bastard." Wyatt couldn't say he disagreed.

His woman's mouth was honey and champagne and lust. Her body, now confined under the blanket, was writhing warmth and trembling desire.

Perfect.

She was absolutely perfect.

"W-Wyatt— *Sir*," she stuttered, the moment he gave her enough room to even speak. Her sibilance sent wisps of warmth across his lips, weaving a spell through his senses. "Wh-Why... Wh-What..."

"I'm letting you in on the theme for our fieldtrip, my girl." He spoke it directly against her lips, ensuring nobody else would hear him over the drone of the engines and the constant *bong bong*s of the attendant call bells. There was yet *another* perk of flying first class. "By the time we leave Dreamland, you're going to *know* never to hide your needs from me again."

She gasped, having the gumption to look truly outraged. "I— I do *not* hide—"

"No," Wyatt volleyed. "You don't hide things. You only deep-freeze them." He almost laughed. Fuck, she was cute when she was cheeky. But there'd be time for sharing a few chuckles later. Right now, he was after her full and complete attention—achieved by dipping in and biting his way along her neck and then all the way around the curve of her ear. "And now, it's time you learned how to melt again."

As he worked his tongue and lips at all the sensitive skin around her ear, her breaths puffed at a disco beat against his own neck. The heat worked its way under his shirt before zipping to his beltline and then below, making him lift the armrest and slide closer to her, pressing his aching cock against her blanket-covered thigh.

"Oh." Josie's high-pitched rasp vibrated along the

underside of his jaw. She shifted as if to bring her hand up and cling to him, but Wyatt cinched his hold tighter around her forearm, keeping it locked beneath the cover. "I'm...I'm melting, okay? It's...it's working."

He snarled against her neck. "Not enough."

"Wh-What?"

"It's not working enough." He pushed on her arm, directing her hand toward the creamy juncture of her thighs. "I want you in a puddle, girl."

"I...I don't understand..."

"Rub it."

"Rub...what?"

"You know what." He worked his grip down to her wrist, guiding her toward the heated triangle at her center. "You're shielded by the blanket and by me. Nobody's going to see and nobody's going to know, except me—and I'm the only one who matters anyway. And now, I'm the one ordering you to do this, Josephine. Slide your fingers into your pussy, find your perfect little clit, and massage it until I tell you not to anymore."

Her breathing snagged. Her muscles tensed. "Are you out of your fucking mind?"

"No, but I want you out of yours." He dragged away far enough to confront her by a few inches, turning his gaze to pure command and his jaw to hard steel. "Get to work on getting yourself off, baby girl, or I'll get on that pretty pussy for you." He let a knowing smirk show itself in his eyes. "And believe me, I know *all* the spots that make you scream the loudest."

She went all kitten on him again—if said kitten had just been dunked in a rain barrel. But even though her teeth were gritted and her eyes were ablaze, she pushed her hand free from his grip and started little circling motions at the center of her body.

Wyatt dropped the smile from his stare. He watched, smoke now invading his senses, for all the outward signs of her arousal. "You're stunning," he praised in a whisper. "Look at you, my Josie. So fucking sexy." He leaned in again, inhaling deep at her cleavage. "I can smell the arousal from your hot cunt. Are your nipples hard under your bra?"

She shivered a little. "Y-Yes."

He arched a brow. "Yes *what*?"

"Y-Yes, Sir," she grated.

"Ah. Good. Very good. And are your thighs tense? Is your ass clenching?"

"Yes, Sir."

"Are you stroking yourself through your panties?"

She swallowed.

For a second, he saw her consider a fib as her reply until she realized he probably already knew the answer. And he did.

Her voice dipping with resignation, she answered, "Yes, Sir."

"Then push them aside." He lifted up again, observing her intently. "Put your fingers directly on your clit."

From the moment she did, he knew it. That sensitive strip of nerves, now stimulated directly, put her entire body on high alert. Her teeth sucked in her whole bottom lip, struggling to keep her shrieks from breaking free. As if her cause was really being served. The energy flowing from her was like a power station about to overload, a tangible warp on the air itself.

"Holy God," Wyatt rasped, wondering if he'd blow a wad simply from the effect of her heat between their bodies. "You're brilliant, my gorgeous girl. Astounding." He took her lips, intending to go gently but finding himself nearly devoured by her answering lunges. "When was the last time you did this for yourself?"

Josie jerked her head back and forth. "D-D-Don't...rem-m-m-ember."

"Then that's too long," he growled softly. "And now, you'll rub harder and make it happen."

"Oh, God." Her gasps were hot and desperate against his mouth. The blanket shook from the force of her frantic effort. "*Oh...God...*"

"Harder," Wyatt dictated in a whisper.

"It's..." She pushed up, biting his lip. "I'm..."

"Faster."

"I'm going to scream."

"No." After tugging the blanket high enough to cover her chest, he reached inside her dress and squeezed one of her nipples. "You're going to come."

What a perfect, obedient girl she could be.

What an unspeakable, unforgettable sight her orgasm was.

He helped her, absorbing the burst on her lips with the pressure of his own, though he didn't shut his eyes during a single second of the contact. He couldn't. He had to watch as her body coiled and clenched from the effort of not surging out of her seat. He had to feel as wave after wave of her sexual fulfillment rolled over and inside and around her and then pulsed into him.

Then he had to plan...timing exactly the right moment to issue his next order to her.

Not yet...

Her breathing evened. Her body eased back into the seat. Her tremors slowed.

Not yet...

She rocked her head back. Released a soft sigh.

But he didn't let her get too far.

With their mouths still just inches apart, he gauged the rhythm of her exhalations. Not too fast, not too slow. She was on the downside of her high but not at the bottom yet.

Now.

"Give me another, Josie."

She jolted, but he was close enough to stop her, enforcing his dictate with the direct pressure of his mouth. Though she groaned in protest, he kept up the harsh kiss, working her lips with his until she relented, letting him conquer her soft recesses with demanding stabs of his tongue and gnashes of his teeth. By the time he was through, the sounds in her throat were twined with conflict. Her logic was locked in a duel with her lust.

The look was sexy as fucking hell.

He soaked it in with sinful, selfish appraisal—almost wondering if he didn't want to just stop her at this precipice and make her wait for more tonight. But he'd already given her the command, and now the follow-through was necessary.

Besides, there *were* the fringe benefits to consider.

He still had a hand on one of her breasts. Playing with her erect tip provided a damn good alternative to thinking about his own.

He smelled her pussy even stronger now. The scent was an aphrodisiac all its own.

Best of all, he could use this opportunity to prime her a little for tonight.

"Another," he repeated, adding a growling undertone for emphasis. "Grind your fingers on your clit, gorgeous girl. Play with yourself until you come for me again. You have no idea how much I enjoy watching your pleasure, Josie."

His confession pulled her into the realm of at least trying to obey—though her teeth sneaked over her bottom lip, and her brow furrowed in blatant discomfort. "Sir," she whispered. "I don't know if I can."

"You can." He brushed his lips across hers. "You *will*."

"But I'm... It's still...so sensitive..."

Wyatt used his free hand to adjust the blanket's coverage. He also angled his body more directly over hers, shielding her more from any curious eyes in the aisle. "Then use your other hand to help," he instructed. "Fuck yourself with them, as deep into your cunt as you can go, while stroking your clit with the other one." He waited, looking on like a hawk, as she maneuvered both her hands into position. "Do it, Josephine," he stressed as she hesitated with a flush extending to the roots of her hair. "This is your test, girl. I have things planned for your pleasure tonight, but they'll rely on your exact and perfect obedience of your Master. If you can't comply with what I ask now..."

His deliberate trail-off was unfair but necessarily so. Sometimes a man could melt a glacier; other times he had to take a buzz saw to it.

And when the buzz saw worked, he got to watch the stunning results.

The mesmerizing miracle...

The gradual parting of her lips as she penetrated herself with rhythmic intensity.

The poetic flutters of her lashes against her cheeks as she grinded and pumped and stroked.

The burst of awareness across her face as the certainty

of her orgasm built. And built. And pushed. And crashed. And punched her psyche right out of this plane, over the clouds outside, into the stars beyond, and through the cosmos beyond *that*...

"Kiss me again, Sir." Her voice was a high, heartrending squeak. "I'm going to explode for you again."

And fuck, how she did—forcing *her* mouth into *his* now, thrusting her heat and life and submission into him, not just giving him her orgasm but *gifting* him with it. Not just meeting his requirements but exceeding every damn one of his expectations.

Not just obeying him.

Submitting to him.

And never had she taken his breath away more fully.

Never had he been more certain of the plans he'd made for them at Dreamland tonight.

Never was he surer that when they flew back out of Chicago tomorrow afternoon, his glacier girl would be completely liquefied.

He couldn't fucking wait.

CHAPTER FIVE

Interesting piece of trivia. It *was* possible to feel like the prettiest princess at the ball, even sitting at a BDSM club's bar, nursing an iced tea.

Key ingredient number one, get lucky enough to land the world's most amazing Dom, who wouldn't take no in giving a girl her first orgasm of the getaway trip before the plane had even landed. Just thinking of what Wyatt had made her do was an instant blush inducer, no doubt lending to her overall glow.

Ingredient two? When the same ruthless Dom turned back into the world's most indulgent husband, insisting they hit Michigan Avenue for some shopping before their luggage was even delivered to their room on the top floor of the Peninsula. The boots on her feet now, as well as her glam eyelashes with the sparkly tips, were a product of that three-hour spree.

Ingredients three and four inadvertently came as a package. When a girl had been through all that shopping and then told to get her ass to the hotel's spa for her scheduled Healthy Glow facial, that little break was bound to turn into an hour-long nap in the spa's quiet room.

And yes, there was one more ingredient—and it wasn't the corset dress, which she counted simply as the icing atop the delicious cake to which all the other fixings had contributed.

The last ingredient—but also the most important.

Wyatt.

Ohhhh, wow. Her Wyatt.

The way he'd reached inside her psyche and seen exactly what her sanity needed. The way he'd been able to step outside of both of *them* and seen how frayed their connection was really getting.

The way he'd beheld his glacier girl and known she needed a little melting.

All right, a lot of melting.

The way he knew exactly what kind of heat she needed for that, too.

Though right now, she had to admit she felt pretty damn resplendent in her own regard. Maybe not grab-your-shades-suckahs-because-I'm-slammin'-smokin' time, but decent enough to hold her own on a barstool with a pair of giggling ingénue to her left and an eager pair of Doms eyeing the girls to her right. She was glad she didn't have to unsheathe her mama bear claws on behalf of the girls, though. The dungeon monitor, apparently a nice guy once one got over the fact he dressed and sounded like Lurch from *The Addams Family*, obviously had the situation parked in the middle of his radar.

The Doms ordered the subbies a couple of rum and cokes.

The subbies accepted the drinks with shy glances and batting eyelashes.

Jo sipped her iced tea and thanked the dear Lord above, along with every angel in his posse, that she'd never have to worry about the dungeon dating scene. Even with her collar left behind in their room, at Wyatt's request, she knew she wouldn't have to worry about any random Doms sliding up with sleazy pick-up lines. As glowy-princess as she felt in her custom black leather and lace, it was still clear she wasn't on the lookout for a play partner. Not enough of her breasts, ass, or desperation were hanging out to broadcast *that* message...

An assumption she should've known better than to make.

As soon as she rested with that conclusion as a comfortable truth, a massive masculine presence scooted onto the barstool between her and the ingénues. Not Wyatt but radiating the same kind of aura. The kind of man who wasn't just physically formidable but exuded dominance without even thinking about it. Even without the club's ambient lighting, dark marble columns, and pulsing erotic soundtrack, he'd have detonated a thousand charges of submissive awakening inside Josie. The reaction didn't mean she wanted to sleep with him—hell, she didn't even *know* him—it only meant that certain men called to women like her.

And made them want to fall to their knees.

And say "Yes, Sir" as naughty things were done to them...

Holy *shit*, she couldn't wait for Wyatt to get back from checking them into their private room for the night.

She sipped her tea again. And, for the first time, wished Wyatt had instructed her not to order anything stronger. At the time, with his eyes darkened with the promise of making up for lost time when they got to their private play room, she'd gladly agreed to the mandate. Right now, with Dominance on Two Feet parked next door, she wished to numb her nerves with the help of Señor Tequila.

Yep. He had two feet, all right. Clad in a pair of oh-my-God-hot shitkickers, leading to a pair of oh-my-God-even-hotter leathers covering two of the longest, finest, most well-hewn legs she'd seen beyond her own husband's. She vowed not to gawk at anything beyond that, but then the man spread a hand against one of his massive thighs, making it impossible not to notice the ink on his forearm. The tattoo depicted a dragon straddling a brick, with a length of rope flowing from its mouth into both its talons. At once, Josie identified the design. It was custom and distinct, belonging to a dungeon she and Wyatt had stopped in to when visiting Garrett and Sage in Seattle. The club, Bastille, was co-owned by Garrett's CO, John Franzen, along with a Dom she'd never be able to forget.

Max Brickham.

Amendment. She doubted *anyone*, Dominant or submissive, was capable of forgetting the man after a first introduction. Brick was Bastille's version of a statesman, gadfly, and security team all in one. He flirted, fucked, and fought with the same shameless intensity, apologizing to none but also taking care that he didn't have to. There wasn't a visitor to Bastille who didn't want to be around him—and here, thousands of miles from Seattle, the same phenomenon was proving true. Both groups at the bar, women and men alike, had eyed Brick's arrival with keen interest.

Actually, most of them were giving the dark-haired, blue-eyed hulk everything but their phone numbers on napkins—except for Josie.

Which made the next moment, in which she finally noticed *his* open appraisal of *her*, almost a comedy in its absurdity.

Nevertheless, Jo straightened her posture, hyperaware of needing to be Wyatt's composed emissary, despite how he'd instructed her neck be left bare of her submissive's collar tonight. The absence of the steel against her neck now made her feel weirdly naked, making her glad for the ability to turn herself into a human ice cube. Sometimes, freeze-drying one's emotions really *was* a good thing—

Unless those sensibilities were assaulted by the hunk of a Dom on the next barstool.

"Excuse me." His voice was every bit as smooth and

confident as she recalled. "Don't I know you?"

Josie turned and lifted a cordial smile—allowing herself to a small inward preen at the two girls behind him, not at all delicate about assessing what she had and they didn't. Funny how things can just change in twenty-four hours sometimes. This time yesterday, she wanted everything *they* had. Youth. Freedom. Sleep. Why was the grass always greener for everyone else?

Though right now she didn't feel at all like Brick's grass. More like the house cat in the grass, being eyed by the industrial-strength lawnmower in the next yard over. Well, the next bar stool over. His attention on her was like being sliced with an unerring blade.

"You have a good memory," she replied, surprising herself with the evenness. "I've been to your club, Bastille, in Seattle before. My name is Josephine, but everyone calls me Josie."

She dipped her head in respect, keeping both hands on the bar. Wyatt had never demanded high submissive protocol from her, but she was still glad about knowing a few of the key moves—though that didn't stop Brick from stepping over, latching one of her hands beneath his own, and lifting it to his lips. Damn it if Jo's body didn't go into instinctual overdrive, blood clamoring and heart racing, as he managed to turn the courtly move into something with slightly more meaning.

"Your eyes," he murmured. "Christ, they're like lie-detector probes."

Well. Talk about a line to make a girl go still. "I'm not certain whether to thank you or slap you."

"Neither." He shrugged, though on those massive shoulders, even that casual action resembled Mount Shasta about to erupt. "Or both, I guess." He wielded new blades on her with the pure blue force of his eyes. "It just means I can't lie to you." He pushed off his stool to push in closer to her. "Which means I have to confess...I already knew who you were when I sat down." He rested an elbow on the bar, leaning in a little closer. "And I haven't forgotten you since your visit to the club."

Her breath clutched. "Now I really don't know what to do with you."

Brick threw his head back, barking a laugh. "Oh, little one...I think the better question is what *I* want to do with *you*."

Okay, *whoa*.

And *no*.

She hopped off her own stool, waving an explanatory hand along the front of her dress. "Okay, for starters, *not* such a 'little one' here—but I got a gorgeous daughter out of the deal, so no apologies either."

"None needed." Brick's gaze turned heavy. "You're stunning..."

She planted her hands on both hips. "Second, you *do* remember that I played at your club with my Sir, right? The man who is also my *husband*?"

A strange snicker played at his lips. "Oh, yeah. *That* bastard. I remember him vaguely."

Josie's hands went slack. So did her jaw. Deluxe Version Dominant or not, she was going to claw the man's eyes from his skull. "Excuse the *hell* out of me?"

She was held back from her final advance by shackle-strength hands at her elbows. Wyatt's usual scent was given an extra dose of sexy because of the fitted leathers he wore, similar in cut and color to Brick's, now bracing at both sides of her legs—and aligning the bulge of his crotch against the top of her ass.

"Better save up the excuses you ask him for right now, baby. Who knows when you might need them later?"

Brick pushed off the bar and sauntered over with an ease that unsettled Jo's mind...and shot all her blood straight to the apex of her thighs. Despite the men's good-natured exchange, she went ahead and spat again, "Excuse the hell out of me, Sir?"

Behind her, Wyatt chuckled.

In front of her, Brick chuckled harder. "Hmmm," he mused, stepping closer to smooth his fingertips along the slopes at the sides of her neck. He kept going, though...trailing both hands right down into her cleavage. *While Wyatt watched.* "You have quite a little spitfire, Hawkins."

"*Not* little," Josie grumbled.

"And usually not so fiery, either." Wyatt molded himself in even tighter from behind, tucking his mouth against her ear. "But I warmed her up a little on the plane ride out here."

"Nice work." Brick softly tucked his fingertips around the top of her corset, running his touch along the tops of her breasts. "And we're here tonight to make sure the glacier gets melted the rest of the way."

"Exactly."

One word...she'd probably heard her husband utter a thousand times before.

One word...suddenly making everything different.

One word, daggering to the deepest parts of her body, arousing magma that truly had been dormant and frozen for so long...

Now awakened and alive...

And terrified.

Holy. Shit.

Wyatt had called Brick, asking him to fly all the way out here for this.

For her.

Her incredible hero of a husband was really this serious about getting rid of all her ice castles. He wanted her back without a speck of frost, in all her passion and fire and force, even with the extra mama bear rolls on her body and all the demands that turned her into life's bitch instead of the other way around. But when all of that nonsense was pushed back and melted away, the essence of *them* hadn't changed. The strength of *them* was still here, a mighty and magnificent fortress of its own. Under all the ice, Sir Wyatt and his sweet submissive were really still here.

They just needed help finding it.

And Wyatt hadn't been too proud to ask for that help.

Even if it meant giving her to another man. A Dom he'd already been watching with her as far back as their trip to that club in Seattle—where Brick had affected her precisely as he did now. Shaking her reserve. Rattling her composure. Cracking her ice.

A Dom now determined to turn those cracks into a full fissure.

Funny how fissures started with the tiniest of rifts.

And how a man could simply grasp her fingertips, as Brick did now, and split open her senses with unfightable awareness.

He's going to break you. Beautifully. Brutally.

And holy hell you're going to thank him for it.

"Our room's ready." Wyatt directed the information to Brick as he swept around, taking hold of her other hand.

"Perfect," their guest answered, his gaze a cutting cobalt beneath that stark skull cut. "Then shall we?"

Josie took a deep breath, compelling her feet to move as she left the bar between the two men. Their path took them right past the two young women still nursing their martinis— and now throwing her looks of open envy. Somehow, she swallowed the urge to laugh.

Be careful what you wish for, girls. Very, very careful.

CHAPTER SIX

"Are you sure you're ready for this?"

Wyatt looked down at his wife's angular features. He had her braced by both shoulders. She was unable to hide from him even if she wanted, but aversion seemed to be the last thing on her mind anyway. She met his gaze directly and boldly and even smiled. In return, he stared into her, *through her*, adoring what he beheld. It had been too damn long since they'd looked at each other like this. He was pissed it had taken a flight to Chicago and a night in a dungeon to make them stop long enough to do it, but he swore the next time wouldn't be so... negotiated. So tense.

Because tense *was* what he felt as Brick emerged from the Dominants' prep room on the other side of the private play room. Physically, he was an equal to the man. Brickham was around his age, early- to midforties, with a defined torso covered in scars that gave away his years of life in jungles, trenches, and desert village alleys. His legs, roughly the size of construction pipes, bulged against his leathers. All in all, he wasn't a man to be taken lightly, in or out of the dungeon.

And he was going to dominate Josie as no one but Wyatt ever had.

The knowledge caused a strange rockslide inside of him, like an avalanche caused by a controlled explosion. Certain pressures were relieved in some areas though multiplied in others. This step was necessary. Josie knew too many tricks to hide from him, too many ways to bend his sympathy. Brick wouldn't be allowing that bullshit.

That much was evident by the apparatus set up by Dreamland, per Wyatt's specific orders, after consulting with Brick about a session best suited for the theme of the night. Defrosting his beautiful little brick of ice.

Now, Josie fully studied all the equipment, as if needing to as proper preparation for answering Wyatt's question. He didn't miss the heavy gulp she got down while doing so. It almost resembled some mad scientist's experimental lab, with a flat steel table outfitted with leather straps beside a tank of glowing blue water. Different levers apparently operated interaction between the two. Nearby, the room's leather-covered bed was set up with a full cart of impact play toys, along with a stack of blankets and pillows for aftercare.

They were a *long* way from aftercare.

But if all of Wyatt's instincts were firing right, his woman was going to need a hell of a lot of it.

Fuck.

For a split second, he was tempted to order Brick out and call all this off. Josie wasn't going to like parts of this. Maybe *all* of this. He hated the idea of her being uncomfortable or in pain—at least not the kind he hadn't brought for her ultimate pleasure. But wasn't that Brick's end goal too? To get her through the crucible, so she was stronger and happier on the other side? To break her down so he could build her up? To bust open her ice so she could finally see the sun again?

Or was he just feeding himself the boot camp bullshit in order to feel better about the hugest mistake he'd made in their relationship?

"I am." Josie's declaration snapped his focus back—onto

her, where it belonged. "I *am* ready for this, Sir. I trust in what you both want to do here." She took both his hands in hers, squeezing him in reassurance, doubling his self-doubting pangs. How amazing she was. How strong. His beautiful girl...

"I love you, Josephine." He spoke it from every depth of his heart, dropping his head to meld his lips to hers.

"And I love you, Master." Her whisper fisted his whole chest.

"Touching." Brick strolled past them, quipping the words with dry efficiency. "Now let him go, sweetheart. He won't be far, and he's still your ultimate control here. He knows your safe word and your limits better than me, so you call that fucker out if you need to stop during any of this, all right?"

"Yes, Sir. Of course." Josie finished it with a subtle shiver and a hot flush. Strangely, it didn't bother Wyatt to witness either. Brick's acquiescence to his ultimate authority here, along with the knowledge that he was allowing the man only temporary access to his girl, brought a rush of new sensation to him. *Empowerment.* Brick may be the mad scientist here...but *he* was the boss with his finger on the ultimate control panel.

Let the experiment begin.

"Strip," Brick commanded her, not breaking his stride toward the steel stairs leading to the raised platform with the bondage table. "Then bring your pretty naked self up here to me, girl."

Resisting the urge to help her, Wyatt walked to a leather loveseat positioned on another raised dais, just high enough to view all the fun across the way. As he sat down, the room filled with background music. Brick liked lots of guitars and a fuck-me-hard beat for his D/s scenes. The man's head bobbed in time to the music as he checked various gauges and knobs connected to the glowing blue tank. Not that Wyatt was paying much attention to him, as his woman carefully stripped out of her clothes. Inch by incredible inch, she revealed more of her perfect nudity, captivating Wyatt's gaze—and dick. He grabbed his length through his leathers, acknowledging the ache that hadn't fully gone away since her mind-blowing orgasms during the flight, riveted on the proud puckers of her areolas, the gentle flair of her hips, the entrancing cream of her thighs...and the beautiful slit at their center.

She shivered as her foot hit the stairway's first step, but the proud angle of her head never faltered. Once she stood on the platform behind Brick, he turned and studied her, head to toe and then back again. With his next perusal, he let his hands follow, boldly feeling her everywhere, until Josie bit her lip to keep from gasping. But she failed even at that when Brick cupped her mound and slipped a finger up her tunnel. Then a second.

"Oh!" she finally cried out. "*Oh!*" Then louder, as Brick used his hand to smack her pussy instead.

"You'll speak only when spoken to, subbie. Understood?"

She released a stuttering breath but nodded and rasped, "Yes, Sir."

Brick nodded as well, satisfied, but stepped back with his arms folded. "I was right, back in the bar, you know. You *are* stunning." When Josie communicated thanks only by lowering her gaze, Brick smiled. The sentiment didn't find its way into his words. "Your pussy is also sweet and wet and hot. I was surprised by that, since your Dom informed me that you've taken great pride in being an ice princess lately. He said you even seemed *proud* of that."

Again, Josie said nothing, though her head descended an

inch lower. Wyatt could all but see the gears spinning in her mind, trying to predict Brick's end game with the reasoning.

Wisely, Brick didn't leave her alone for too long with all those thoughts. They were part of the underpinnings of her ice palaces, a truth evident to anyone who truly knew her.

"Up on the table," he directed with a clinical chill. "On your back, with hands over your head." As Josie complied, he continued, "I'm going to help you feel what being a glacier *really* feels like, sweetheart." He secured her feet to the table first, her legs spread, and then her hands high over her head. Two straps across her middle, one at her waist and one across her thighs, followed.

Wyatt was transfixed. From where he sat, he could see how Brick's stark treatment affected Jo. Her clenching thighs and glistening pussy were proof of her raging arousal. But what had he planned now? The whirring of gears and motors beneath the platform started up as Brick pushed some buttons and threw a lever. The steel bed beneath her shook.

Then lifted.

Then slowly flipped over.

Until Josie, strapped to the platform, was poised facedown over the glowing blue tank. After two seconds like that, she visibly shivered. Clearly, Brick didn't plan on treating her to a nice dip in a hot tub.

"Everything okay?" Brick inquired. "Nothing too loose or tight?"

"N-N-No, Sir." She trembled again, harder this time. "I-I mean, yes, Sir. I'm f-f-fine."

Wyatt couldn't believe how strongly she turned him on. Her bravery in doing this, even knowing it wasn't going to be pleasant, reached to a place of primal satisfaction inside him.

She was doing this for him. For *them*.

"Perfect," Brick confirmed, his voice a knowing growl. "Then into the glacier you go, subbie."

There was a slight splash as the brackets on the platform unhitched, sending all of Jo's naked form all the way into the blue water. At once, Wyatt watched as she fought and writhed from the impact. This was a woman who watched the annual polar bear plunge television coverage and called everyone in the group a damn fool.

It was over in less than three seconds. Brick wrenched the lever back over, reengaging the hitches and pulling her out. Josie, soaked and sputtering and gasping, whipped a furious gaze his way.

"Bastard!"

To his credit, Brick only chuckled. "Having fun, glacier girl?"

"What the *fuck* do you think?"

"Well." He dipped his head, admiring her dripping form. "I think you look goddamn gorgeous with all that water dripping off your beautiful body. And I *know* your Master agrees with me. He's over there stroking his cock like he wants to get it inside you right now."

"D-D-Damn g-g-good idea. Why d-d-don't we d-d-do that?"

A *smack* cracked the air.

Josie's scream followed it.

"What the *fucking* hell?" she blasted at Brick, who had just struck an open palm across her pussy.

"Talking out of turn, subbie," he scolded. "I let it slide, knowing you were getting used to your first dunk, but now I'll thank you to stay your tongue."

"Wait." Josie blurted it as if only half his message had registered. Judging from the shock on her face, perhaps that was the case. "What? My— My *first* dunk? *Owwww!*"

"For that, a swat after each dunk now, subbie." Brick's jaw now emulated his name. "Want to try for two?"

Technically, it was a question. Pointedly, Josie ignored it. She stared down at the water, grimly determined to take the treatment without earning any more of the Dom's sadistic swats.

But Brick delivered on what he did promise. Unflinchingly. Unerringly.

Splash.

Smack.

Splash.

Smack.

A total of ten splashes.

A total of nine smacks to Josie's dripping pussy.

An endurance test for Wyatt just as much as her. His cock was a screaming torment in his leathers even as he stroked it with force, battling to alleviate some of the pressure from watching his soaked, nude beauty struggling at her bonds every time she emerged from her glowing blue hell. Brick's sharp spanks were another layer of erotic anguish. Wyatt knew what that kind of treatment did to his girl's naughty pussy. The bites of pain would be just enough to reheat her tunnel, only to be refrozen with yet another dip into the tank.

But now, after that tenth dunk, Brick wasn't back with the crop. He held something else, a device Wyatt couldn't identify. The curiosity came as a relief. For a few blissful seconds, he wasn't even concerned about the duress in his dick. The bulge in his friend's leathers betrayed Brick's own rising lust. Was there anything more stimulating to a Dom than a submissive pushing past her fear and discomfort for his pleasure? The struggle was real, and maybe Brick was about to let them all have a break.

But he'd forgotten exactly who this Dom was. Max fucking Brickham. Best friend to John Franzen. Co-owner of Bastille dungeon. A connoisseur of every BDSM flavor there was. The guy probably trolled ice cream stores just to get kinky inspirations for those names too...

A thought that couldn't be more appropriate for Brick's next ruthless deviation.

"You look pretty as an ice cream cone, sweetheart." He tilted his head in, checking Jo's hands and feet for proper circulation. Apparently satisfied she wasn't turning blue in the wrong places, he went on, "So maybe I should just turn you into one."

What the hell?

The words flared through Wyatt's brain like a kinky version of the Northern Lights. Even his wildest guesses about the contraption in Brick's grip didn't come close to the crazy reality of the thing.

"A DJ friend turned me on to these." Brick boosted his matter-of-fact tone to carry across to Wyatt as well. "Cryo gun. Instantly freezes shit you get it close to—like sexy drippings off a subbie's sweet body."

"Holy fuck." Wyatt returned his hand to his crotch.

"Happening soon," Brick promised. "But first..."

Josie's high cry punched the air as he lowered the cone-shaped nozzle over one of her breasts and pulled the trigger. There was a hollow *shoosh* and a spray of what looked like fog—but when he pulled the cone away from her breast, a long icicle had been formed off her nipple. It gleamed in the dungeon's lights, as did the formation Brick created from the other breast.

Wyatt jolted to his feet. With hands fisted at his sides, he called across to Brick.

"Do it to her pussy."

CHAPTER SEVEN

Oh God. Oh God. Oh God.

Josie's senses exploded with no other words—forget the possibility of thought. She wasn't sure she'd ever be warm again and, at this point, wasn't sure she cared. Her body and brain, stripped of all feeling with every new dunk into the hideous blue tank, were now nothing but trembling cold...and blissful numbness.

She'd even been able to tolerate the bastard—that was Brick's name now, just *Bastard*—turning her nipples into icicles. Even in her half-lidded gaze, they were kind of pretty. The frozen peaks gleamed in the dungeon's lights like sculptures at a winter festival...

That was before he got ordered to do the same thing to her sex.

Commanded by the man who was supposed to be looking out for her. The man who'd always let up on her at a point like this in the play room. He'd never push her like this. Would never order the resident bastard in the room to—

"Ohhhhh!"

To do exactly *that*. Making her scream as loud as she could, consequences be damned, as his evil gun fast-froze every drop of water still caught in her pubic hair. One blast, changing everything down there. It hurt. It throbbed. It stung.

She wanted to be done with this.

Damn it, she needed to be done.

But though the sobs echoed in her mind, none of them spilled out. *Overcome and endure. Shove it all down. Freeze it all back.* It was what she had to do, even now. It was what she'd always done.

How much more could they do to her, anyhow?

She allowed herself a relieved gulp when the answer seemed to come right away. The platform started rising and turning again, soon returned to its original position on the dais. Though she still couldn't stop shivering, it was clear her hell in the blue tank was over.

But that didn't mean *all* hell was over.

She held true to the thought, and its dread, when Brick approached again. Though he unbuckled the two middle straps, he made no move to unlock her from the wrist and ankle straps. She still lay there, exposed to his piercing blue gaze, as the ice mounds on her body began to drip and tease her chilled flesh.

"You know, glacier girl, you're pretty damn beautiful like this."

She only glared. She knew better than to say anything unless he asked it of her directly.

"So tell me. Do you enjoy being made of ice?"

She had to inhale in order to form words. "No, Sir."

"Not fun? Despite being utterly stunning?" As he spoke, he started stroking one of her nipple icicles. The column wasn't very thick, making it break off in his hand after a few swipes. Josie gasped and then sighed as her newly exposed tip hit the warmer air—but not for long. With the small spear of ice in hand, he kept her areola hard and puckered with taunting, frozen circles.

"N-No," Josie repeated. "Not fun."

"So you want to be warmed back up again?"

"Yes, Sir."

"To finally melt for me? And for your Master?"

"Yes, Sir." Now she couldn't get it out fast enough. The feeling had started tingling again in her fingertips and toes, and it was incredible. A miracle. Her gratitude was so complete, it threatened to flood the dams of her control again. She repeated, on the brink of revealing the tears so close to her edges, "Yes, please."

"Good." Brick's tone was practically professional, which intensified the jolt as he flipped the latches free on her remaining restraints and then dragged her to the bottom edge of the table until her legs hung over. "Because I've been wanting to do this since the moment I first saw you tonight."

"Th-This?"

But she'd barely stammered the question before the big Dom had his leathers unsnapped, his erection pulled out, and a condom halfway slipped on. Jo had all of three more seconds to glance down and gasp—holy shit, the man's penis was magnificent, with a steel ring pierced into the head—before he grabbed her thighs, pulled them far apart, and thrust himself into her as far as he could go.

"Oh!" Josie gasped.

"Fuck," Brick gritted. He withdrew, rolled his hips so his piercing nudged all the sensitive tissues just inside her entrance, and then clenched his hips and lunged back in even deeper than before. "Hawkins," he yelled. "You did *not* tell me how incredible her cunt is."

"Just as much a heaven as her mouth."

Wyatt's comeback was obviously as much a surprise to Brick as it was to her. Neither of them had heard him crossing from the other dais. But the sight of his beloved face and rugged bare torso made Josie burst with a sigh of pure joy. Normally her exclamation would bring out a gentle kiss or cheek stroke from her husband, but Wyatt had clearly been sipping on the special Brick cocktail tonight. Every plane of his face was stamped with the same rigid ferocity defining Brick's features.

"But why take my word for it?" he commented while unlatching his own leathers. Josie, with her head already turned, watched in ravenous wonder as Wyatt revealed his swollen cock and straining balls. It had been too damn long since she'd gotten to say hello to them like this, and that was a shame. Her husband's penis was a work of art, even without a piercing. He was about the same length as Brick, but his head always turned the most perfect shade of purple and his balls thrummed with such life, she was certain they shook from the force of his clamoring come. "You know what to do, girl," he drilled, pushing in just as a bead of white appeared in the slit of his crown. "Show our guest how well you can suck me."

Josie opened wide, letting him fill her mouth and throat to the fullest. Both men groaned at the sight, and it wasn't long before her own needy mewls joined their soundtrack. As they heated her from the inside with their cocks, they caressed her on the outside with their bodies, hands, and tongues. All the water that had turned her into an ice cube before now formed warm, splattering rain through the cracks in the steel table, only adding to the erotic symphony of their wet suckles, *thwop*ping thrusts, and harsh, heated kisses.

"Damn," Brick growled.

"Yeah," Wyatt snarled back.

Josie examined them both. While lust laced both comments, it wasn't the full definition of their comments.

They traded tight glances, as if they'd discussed a benchmark that needed to happen by now and hadn't.

What the *hell* was going on?

"Time to turn on all the burners," Brick declared.

"Ten-four." Wyatt's tone was gruff with approval, though he stepped away from the table and allowed Brick to do the same. But perplexity really busted in when they both pulled *her* off the table, each taking one of her hands.

"Wh-What's wrong?" She darted a worried stare between them—but her only answer came from Wyatt, who moved in to scoop her off her feet as Brick turned and descended from the dais ahead of them.

"Come on, sweet one."

"Sir. *Master*," she revised when that didn't fully pull his attention. "Why are we..."

She let it fade as Wyatt carried her toward the bondage bed. Somehow, perhaps using some crazy Dom superpower, Brick had already cleared the distance to the bed, shucked his leathers, and scooted to the middle of the vast surface. He lay there with his head propped against the headboard, his condom-covered cock still shiny with her juices, its length still erect and breathtaking.

Though Wyatt set her down gently on the leather, his voice violated the air with harsh command. "You know what to do with *that* cock too, don't you?"

Her heart flipped over. Wyatt was rarely this ruthless with her, but she loved every second when he was. "Yes, Sir." She bowed her head, pausing for just a moment to savor this moment. Was this even her reality? Twenty-four hours ago, she'd been folding laundry and preparing the farmhands' paychecks. Now, she was only worried about all the pleasure she could give these two erotic gods, their gazes agleam with lust, their cocks erect with need.

She had to be the luckiest girl on the damn planet.

"Good girl." The praise was thick and gruff in her husband's throat. "Now get on and ride him well, baby. I'm going to be watching."

If her channel wasn't thoroughly ready for all this before, the last part of his command took care of that doubt. *Holy shit.* She was really going to do this. Wrap her body around another man's cock—while her husband looked on with adoration and approval.

She wasn't just lucky.

She was blessed.

Every inch of her pussy raced and pulsed before she even straddled Brick all the way. As she sank down, the gorgeous Dom jacked his dark head back. Her moaning gasp filled the air between them. Gravity was working its wonders, angling even more of Brick's dick deep into her tunnel. The man himself aided the effort, anchoring her hips with fierce holds, ramming her pussy onto his length with stabbing lunges.

And yes...Wyatt watched.

At first in steam-quiet silence...but soon, with sounds that began to match Brick's feral grunts and sexual moans. He'd never put his dick back into his leathers and began to stroke himself with defined rhythm, heavily slicking its beautiful bounty. *Thwick, thwick, thwick.* The sound of his pleasure inundated the air—

And bewildered Josie.

That was a lot of lubricant, even for the precome she knew her husband was capable of producing.

She glanced over to see that he'd indeed gotten some help.

ANGEL PAYNE

His cock was red and swollen...and greased from the lube he poured on it with his free hand.

"Fuck," Brick groaned from beneath her. "Oh, fuck *me*. Hawkins, you ready to do this? This breathtaking cunt wants my come, man."

The hot—*hot*—effect of his words aside, Josie dashed an intense stare between the two men. "Is...is he ready...for what?"

Wyatt didn't deny her the answer. He just waited until he'd climbed on the bed with them, then knelt behind her to spread her ass cheeks, before speaking it.

"To be melted, my sweet girl. By both our cocks fucking you at once."

CHAPTER EIGHT

As Wyatt expected, she tensed.

As he also expected—or hoped—she slackened into compliance again. His girl wasn't some silly brat. She'd agreed to this scene tonight, complete with Brick's involvement, and had to know that double domination might mean they'd try to fuck her at the same time. She also had to know that the odds of it happening doubled every minute she waited to give him what he really wanted from her tonight.

She was holding it back.

Her complete meltdown.

The total surrender he needed.

Sometimes—like in the pauses between each of her icy dunks—she'd come damn close. But she had sucked it all back up and in, too damn afraid to show him the emotions in her heart and fears in her soul.

And now, she'd have no choice about the matter.

He wasn't giving up until he had it.

"Relax, sweet girl." He gave her the direction while pushing out the perfect spheres of her ass, baring the tiny hole of her naughtiest entrance to his hot gaze. "You know what to do. I've been here before."

"But *he* hasn't." It was a gritted seethe, making Brick chuckle a little. The guy stopped himself on a hiss as the lube Wyatt gave her ass crack dribbled down over his balls.

"Your Master is right," the big Dom said, helping Wyatt

out in the ass-prep duties. The man's long fingers looked like long vines along her skin, pulling her little hole wider. "Breathe into it like you've done before, and push your muscles out as he seats his cock in. You can do this, little one."

Josie let out a fuming huff. "Says the guy *not* being stuffed with two cocks."

Brick glanced around at Wyatt. "She should be spanked for that."

"No." Wyatt lined up his throbbing head at her tiny entrance. "She should be fucked for that."

In two determined thrusts, he was fully seated inside her ass.

She groaned hard.

Brick groaned even harder.

Wyatt made no sound at all. The bliss was too good. Her body was too perfectly puckered and tight, gripping his dick with a hundred rings of muscle, a thousand charges of heat. None of it let up as both he and Brick penetrated her, shuttling into her pussy and ass with callous force, making the woman moan and swear and cry out, her body hovering on the brink of orgasm like a storm hanging over the horizon, waiting for one good ion in the air to bust it all loose on the land.

Her hesitance ruthlessly teased his resistance. How much longer could he hold out? "Fuck," he finally snarled. "Jesus *fuck*, girl."

Had he and Brick really resolved they wouldn't come until they'd broken her? And if so, who the *hell* had dictated that stupid rule?

Oh, yeah. It'd been him.

Because no matter how badly he longed to explode inside her, even right now, no orgasm was worth the sacrifice of the true burst he needed. The true breakthrough he'd flown her here to get.

The eruption Josie finally, *finally* gave to them, as her climax slammed into her with sudden brutality. The speed of that apex and its unrelenting force shocked the hell out of her body and the rest of the resistance out of her composure.

She was quicksand.

She was surrender.

She was tears and sorrow and unending release.

And, as he and Brick burst too, pouring their heat and seed and passion into her, she was melted.

This time, for good.

ANGEL PAYNE

CHAPTER NINE

Valentine's Day was never one of those do-or-die things for Josie. She always figured that if she and Wyatt needed a day to show their love for each other, something was seriously wrong. Besides, a million times a day, the man gave her moments that were so much better than a preprinted card and a bouquet of flowers. The times when he made Vi laugh during their daddy-daughter tea parties. The breathtaking sight of his shirtless body at work in the field or barn. The new darkness in his eyes, telling her how he intended on kissing her deeply...

Dark facets just like the ones invading his gaze now.

Her breathing turned shallow as he moved in over her naked body, his fingers skating over her flesh before his lips hovered just inches from hers...

But not descending.

"Wyatt," she pleaded, only to correct herself. "Sir. *Please.*"

The dusk in his stare turned to midnight. He pursed his lips, edging his expression on a smile. "Please...what?"

"Kiss me." She undulated, offering up her mouth like a piece of fruit. "You're driving me insane..."

She hitched a little higher.

He moved off, shaking his head with sultry slowness. "I'll smudge your lipstick, love."

"Fuck my lipstick." She yearned for the man to move in and make a giant red murder scene of her lipstick—preferably, up and down the length of his cock.

"Just a few more shots."

Enough command underscored the response that Jo knew he was serious too. Yeah, she'd had to go and get real about Valentine's Day this year. She had to tell him she still wanted him to have glam naked pictures of her as a gift—but that she wanted *him* to take them.

She had to go and tell him that the idea of *him* as her photographer made her hot.

And melty.

It'd be fun, she'd told herself.

Probably even arousing, she'd told herself further.

A silly and sexy hour in the barn, she'd reasoned, letting her husband snap some dirty pictures of her with his phone.

Before she'd learned that the man had gone and paid off the boudoir photographer in Des Moines so they could use this studio all afternoon. Before Wyatt had made her change outfits three times—and hairstyles twice that much—before finally getting to the naughty naked pictures she'd wanted to *start* with.

Now, she'd been totally unclothed for an hour and the man wanted to click off a few more?

But as Wyatt returned to the camera on the tripod and adjusted the aperture settings, a devious idea took hold.

"You...want me to stay on the couch?" she asked him softly. "Right here?"

"Yeah." Wyatt's voice was distracted. He fiddled some more with the camera—

All the way to the part where Josie fiddled with *herself*.

"Errrrmmm....Josephine?" His breath halted as she flung one leg up to the back of the couch, spreading the petals at her center so the camera—and he—had all her actions in focus. As she threw her head back and rolled her hips, wantonly stroking her labia and clit, he demanded, "Josie? What the hell are you..."

"Melting." She dropped her voice to a husk. "For you, Wyatt Hawkins. Completely. Totally. Always. Forever."

At last, the man stepped away from the damn camera.

And approached her with dark eyes, a wolfish smile, a surging crotch...and a bursting heart.

"You just said exactly the right thing, glacier girl."

MOONRISE

Tait Bommer, Luna Lawrence, and Kellan Rush

CHAPTER ONE

"Hey there, flower."

Tait Bommer greeted her the same way he always did, following those two words by pressing a single red rosebud into her hand. One day, he vowed, she'd answer him by wrapping her fingers around the flower. After that, she'd open her eyes. And from there, he'd work with the doctors to bring her back to life.

He had no illusions about what kind of a life it would be for a while. Today marked the one hundred and ninetieth day she'd been in this coma, brought on by the trauma when she'd saved the West Coast of the United States from nuclear disaster by disposing of a self-detonating missile launcher by herself. Her body and brain had been resting for over six months. There would be therapy and setbacks, more therapy and then some progress, even more therapy...and then success. President Nichols had told the FBI not to spare any expense on her care.

Tait would spare no energy on loving her through every minute of the journey.

He settled into his typical chair next to her bed, on the side not consumed by the ventilator and other equipment keeping her alive. He left the rose on the mattress next to her hand before placing an iPod next to it, which blasted the newest Imagine Dragons album.

"This is good shit." He referred to the music as if she sat

there actively listening to it with him. He reached and stroked her forearm while adding, "I think you'll really like it. Hey, I just found out they'll be coming through Seattle next year on tour. If you wake up today, there's a chance we can catch them."

He considered those statements his carrots. He dangled at least a couple of them at her each day he visited, which hadn't been a lot lately due to the fact that terrorists couldn't leave the world alone, and he was on a team of special terrorist squashers. But now, she was too. The woman had saved millions of people who'd never know what she did. Who'd never realize that the woman in bed 222 at the SeaTac Special Care Nursing Facility was really the heroine who made it possible for them to be alive today, putting up tinsel and bells, anticipating their holidays...living their lives in joyous oblivion.

A nurse walked by in the hall, humming "The Little Drummer Boy." Tait swallowed on the heavy ache in his chest and stroked the tips of her motionless fingers. "That kid with the drum was a lot like you, flower. Didn't have much to give, but he gave his all—and he made a king smile."

He watched his hand tighten around her frail arm.

He watched his tears spatter on her pale skin.

"Come play your drum for the world again, flower. Come back to us, Luna. Please...come back to me."

CHAPTER TWO

Fog. Lots of fog. She was used to the stuff, but this was so much thicker, quieter, and calmer than what she was used to. It was nice to simply float in. Really nice. But it wasn't right. An ache nagged at her brain, telling her that. And so did the voice.

The voice. Yes. His *voice.*

Whose? Name? Brings music. Yes. Loves me? Yes! Brightens the fog.

Who?

*Want...want...*need *his name.*

He knew hers. He called to her all the time. *Luna, come back to me.* He lifted the fog with it. Lifted the fog and lighted her way...

So she could go back.

Back. Right. Need to push. Need to. But why? Just need to. Keep...pushing.

"Nancy! Come here! Did you see that?"

"Caroline, you're always seeing things that don't—oh, my God. Did her eyes just twitch?"

"I think they did."

"Oh! She just did it again!"

"I'll page Dr. Henkin."

"And get Sergeant Bommer, stat. Is he here?"

Bommer. Yes! Bommer. T-Bomb. T for...? Can't remember. Need to remember. Push...push...

"He's at the base for his own follow-up from the accident.

He said he'd be back in a few hours."

"Try him on his cell after you talk to Dr. Henkin."

"Of course."

Just beyond the fog, lights began to flash. *No. Too much. Too bright. Want peace. Want silence. Need to float...please.*

She let the dark mist wrap around her once more. Rest. *Yes.* Nothingness. *Nice.*

"Luna!"

He was here again. But he didn't lift the fog this time. He sliced it.

Hurts. Stop.

Don't stop. Need you.

"Luna, please try!"

I am *trying. Shit, Tait. Can't you see that I—*

A blare of understanding. A rip in the fog that would never be fixed.

Tait. His name is Tait, and he loves me.

He loved her. Had believed in her when nobody else did. Had chased her when she had Lor's exploding smart pad, and she was trying to carry it away so he wouldn't get hurt, because the world needed him, and because—

Because she loved him too.

"Tay-yay...Tay...Tay..."

Damn, it hurt.

"Yes. *Yes!* I'm Tait. I'm here, flower. I'm here."

She hated that nickname. She loved that nickname. She wanted to give him shit about it, but pushing even those few sounds out had drained everything from her.

Hurts. Rest now. Peace now.

He woke her up all too soon.

"Luna! Goddamnit, you have to try harder than that!"

"Sergeant, do you remember what I told you? This is a process. You have to be patient."

"Doc, it's been three days."

"And she's mumbled full sentences during them. She's even off the ventilator. Considering how long she was in the coma, I'm close to calling this a miracle."

Somebody gave a heavy sigh in response to that. Without a doubt, she knew it was Tait's. *Please don't hurt anymore. Please.*

Amazement blasted in when she heard her voice actually sending the words into the air. She didn't seem to be the only one.

"Wh-What? What'd she say?"

There was a man's laugh. Not Tait this time. "Why don't you ask *her?*"

No. That guy definitely wasn't Tait. He wasn't bad on the eyes in a Clark Kent kind of way, but—

Wait. Wasn't bad on the eyes? On *her* eyes? Wow. She was...awake. Sort of. Maybe more than that, if the dagger driving through her skull carried any weight in the matter. She winced from the invasion on her consciousness, hoping every blink would soon stop feeling like sandpaper on her vision. Still, the fog swathed the back of her consciousness, muffling a lot of the world to her—

Except Tait.

He was a brilliant overlay on top of everything else, with his golden eyes and wind-blown hair. And dear God, his smile... It was still so beautifully disarming because of the tilt to one of his front teeth, seizing her heart so tight one of the bedside monitors started beeping faster. She smiled back, and it made him laugh, exposing the shiny tracks down his cheeks. Shit.

There were a lot of them. Despite the joy of seeing him again, she winced at the pull they caused in her chest. This hurt. In bad *and* good ways.

"Are you...bawling?" Her voice was hoarse. It felt distant too. She realized her brain had sent a thought to form the words, but her senses were snapped off from everything except him. As if she were only awake because of him. After he laughed at her accusation though never answered it, he swept up her hand and crushed his lips to her fingers. She peered in curiosity. How'd those red rose petals make it into the bed with her?

Clark Kent said something. She blinked at him, but he looked and sounded like he was underwater. Blurry. Muted. Tait remained her only clarity.

"Hi," he finally said. His voice was soft yet deep. And perfect...so perfect. "How are you?"

She studied every inch of him. She didn't know why it was important, but it was. He was in civilian clothes, a dark-blue sweater and some baggy khaki pants, with his watch on one wrist...and burn scars that ran from beneath it. She didn't ask where the damage had come from. She simply knew. He'd raced after her that day, was right behind her until Ethan had tried to hold him back. Those seconds had saved his life, but he'd likely gotten close enough to have hands that would look like that forever. She'd managed to throw the thing into a dumpster behind the soundstage before it went off. And then—

Then Mom and Dad had been there—which was really weird since they'd both drowned in a ferry accident on the Puget Sound. How had they traveled over a thousand miles and twenty years to get to her? She'd wanted to ask them. More desperately, she'd wanted to go to them. To feel their embraces again. To tell them she loved them. But the fog had sucked her down instead.

She grimaced against the pain in her heart, which deepened the torture in her head. "I don't know." She gave him the answer with bare honesty. "I'm not sure...I'm really here."

"You are." Tait leaned closer. He smelled really good, like cedar and spiced apples, but the connection made her ache more. *Don't connect. Don't attach.* But it was too late, wasn't it? "You're here. It's a fucking miracle. And I'm so happy." He looked up then, through the watery wall between them and Clark Kent, and nodded at something the man said. "Okay, Doc. We understand."

"We understand what?"

Tait gave her a tolerant smirk. "You heard the man, beautiful. Time to rest."

That made her clutch him by the sleeves. No. She *hadn't* heard. "Tait—"

"Ssshhh, flower. It'll be okay. Time to rest."

She curled her fingers in tighter, compelled by the instinct that shot a sudden chill through her. The rest of her monitors started to blare, warbled because of the mental jelly in which she was still encased, but she didn't let go of him. Her head pounded harder as full understanding glared brighter. Tears began to run down her damn face now.

"Weasley, time has...never exactly been our friend."

She didn't try to hide the slow sadness from it. Still Tait retorted, "Well, that fucker's gonna have to fall in line now. He's stolen six months from us, and I'm demanding payback with interest."

She forced her face to rise toward his. Unfurled a hand from one of his sleeves and lifted it to the strong edge of his jaw. The dagger carved its way into new parts of her head. Her chest hurt. Getting breath felt like shoveling boulders with a spoon. Her arms and legs ached from the effort. "*We* were the ones borrowing it, Tait. I think...even this...is a goodwill loan."

His gaze left her for one second—a pause that told her everything. Disbelief and anger rolled over his face as her machines broke into full alarms. "What the fuck?"

She cried from the pain as he pulled her into his lap and against his chest. Along the way, she grabbed some rose petals and struggled to smell them to ease her agony. The effort made her even dizzier. Her throat was parched and her lungs struggled to make it from one second to the next. She dropped the petals and gripped his face now, needing his warmth and strength.

Despite her physical torment, her soul was suspended in a soft breeze of peace. Being here, in his arms...it was right. It was perfect. This moment was the reason she'd fought her way back. *He* was the reason. The fog was gone now, and she saw everything clearly. Felt the perfection of it in the depths of her heart.

Too bad her voice couldn't sound as sure of itself. "B-Borrowed time," she got out in a rasp. "It's—it's been our b-blessing and our curse, Weasley. Guess we should be g-glad that fate has a soft spot for true love."

His eyes, which had been liquid with grief, burst into flares of rage as he snarled at someone trying to pull him away from her. An army had invaded the room, racing around, yelling for things "stat" and screaming about a code blue. "Luna." He swallowed hard. His lips went into bitter twists. "Damn it, what are you talking about?"

She watched her fingers shake against his skin. Salty

wetness warmed their tips. "Ssshhh." It came out in quivering spurts. "Listen to m-me. You—you know I do love you, right?"

"And I love you." His lips shook as he lowered them to hers. "I've loved you more and more every day. Every hour."

"I know. I heard you. I heard all the music you b-brought in."

"You did?"

It was torture to meet his stare, but she forced herself to do it. The fog had started to thin. It was burned away by the light. Silver-white and spectral, edging out the sight of him. *No. Please. I still have to tell him. It's why I fought to come back. I need to tell him...*

"Tait, y-you *have* to listen to me. This is imp-p-portant." She watched him struggle not to negate her, but even then he pushed his fingers against her lips for a second, his grief-filled eyes begging her not to go on...not to seal the truth neither of them could fight now. She weakly swatted his hand away. "We g-got this moment as a g-gift. The Creator d-doesn't like it when people sh-shit on His gifts."

He cradled her closer. His twisted face tore at her heart. The capacity he had for love was a rarer gold than that in his eyes, a more beautiful sunshine than his smile. But nobody had ever told him that. He'd spent so much of his life in a lonely, hard place. His ability to see the loneliness in *her* soul had proven that.

She needed to tell him.

Then she needed to set him free.

"Luna." His whisper was also a plea. "Oh, God. Luna..."

The light grew stronger. "Not much t-time." She shook her head when he answered that with a vicious sob. "No. Stop. No more grief, Weasley. You're g-going to live, and love, and f-fight the b-bad guys, okay? You're g-going to be the g-good guy for me. You're g-going to be happy again...for me. Please!"

It was harder to breathe now. The light wanted her. It strengthened, making even Tait start to fade, and because of that, forms sharpened inside of it. In those forms, there were faces. *Mommy? Daddy?* They nodded and stretched out their arms toward her.

"This isn't...fucking...fair!"

Tait's roar whipped her back down into the pain. She untangled her fingers from his hair and reached out to her parents. "I'll b-be there in a m-minute, okay?" She pushed her head against his chest. "I—I love him. This is a little hard." She gave them a smile of appreciation as they nodded their understanding.

She listened to Tait's breath, sawing hard in his chest. To his heart, throbbing with all the life and love he had yet to experience before the light beamed on him. When it came time for that, she hoped she'd get to be one of the faces that appeared for him and offer her arms to help him in.

"Who're you talking to?" he grated. But she felt him answer his own question with another violent sob. He was a member of Special Forces. He'd seen enough buddies go toward the light to recognize what was happening to her.

"Weasley. D-Don't you d-dare be sad."

"Then don't you dare fucking leave me. Luna...please... fight harder. Fight harder!"

"It's n-not my ch-choice."

"No. *No*. No, damn it!"

"I h-have to go. That...was the d-deal."

"Noooo! Luna!"

She lifted her head and pulled him down for a soft, sweet

kiss. His tears soaked her face and hers mingled with them, hot and aching and full of love...taking the last of her life with them.

CHAPTER THREE

Kellan Rush didn't have a single good feeling about this.

He tried blaming his unease on the sauna-level humidity that the Indonesians fondly called their "dry" season, as well as the three-hour jeep ride to this village that had given "bumper car" a new definition. And oh yeah, there was also the mystery meat he'd eaten for breakfast, which would've been bad form to refuse from their Indonesian Spec Ops friends but had made him hurl for an hour. Otherwise, he was just dandy, thank you for asking.

No matter what, his A game was a requirement today. Intel had been received and validated, and they were ready to roll on it. An extremist group had infiltrated the village starting with the police department, who'd been extorting the merchants for protection money. Within the last week, the bastards had instigated phase two of their control, enforcing radical Sharia law to the point that girls were being sent home from school. The main road in town had been transformed into a sea of burkas. According to their partners with the Indonesian Special Forces, this place was a happy and bustling place as little as three months ago. Now, the village's vibe was subdued and depressed.

He was seriously ready to help change that.

He just wished he could be sure his partner was on the same page.

Okay, so Tait wasn't returning to active duty as the guy

he used to be. Kell had been told to expect that. Perhaps the smartass I've-got-a-one-liner-for-that soldier might return someday, perhaps not. *Nothing can be set in stone.* That was how the shrinks-on-high had phrased it. They'd also attested that Tait was going stir-crazy at his desk assignment at Lewis-McChord and that getting back into action might be the "best medicine" for the guy.

Kell grunted, thinking he should've pushed the idiots for a definition on that. Best medicine? For who and what, exactly? Tait's brain had been scrambled eggs for a full year, following the explosion in LA that put Luna in a coma. The eggs became a full-on omelet six months ago, when the ordeal ended with the woman finally gaining consciousness, only to die in Tait's arms an hour later.

So to put it succinctly, he had no idea what kind of soldier he was working with today. He and T-Bomb had run a solid month of training drills already at base, but there was a big difference between training and the real thing—usually about a gallon more adrenaline and a shitload more bad guys.

Today, that pot was even more crowded. The target was a parasite named Bayu Sharif, who'd appointed himself the village's Chief of Police two months ago. If they took him out, the force would be thrown into chaos. The best place to do that was at the entrance of the police station, which faced the town's main square. Though their partners with Indonesian Spec Ops would try to clear the plaza as much as possible, there was no guarantee they'd be completely successful. That meant every bullet out of his rifle had to be accurate enough to slay a lice egg on a monkey's head.

That meant the guy who spotted that lice better know exactly what he was doing.

Fuck. He hated himself for harboring this doubt about Tait. Less than a year ago, T-Bomb was his balls-to-the-walls wingman. They had each other's backs, be it in the mud of a jungle or the floor of a bar, eyeing the dangers of life and love for the other, literally risking their lives for each other. Tait's passion for control, along with his obsession for detail, made him the perfect storm to balance Kell's talents on the trigger. The battalion had taken to calling them the "bullet ninjas" because of the mission catchphrase they'd created together. *Six-five-four, bastard hits the floor; three-two-one, we're out and then we're done.* The ninjas were unstoppable. They were about to prove that to the world at the International Sniper Competition when their trip to Los Angeles, and Tait's fixation with that woman, had changed everything.

Women. *Fuck.* Nice as diversions. Truly shitty as fixations.

Now, though the ninjas were back together physically, Kellan had no idea if they'd synch up again in other ways. They were holding position in a bell tower located four hundred yards up the hill from the town square. Though some ops like this were harder than others, Kell had been looking forward to taking out Sharif since tagging along on the recon team's patrol last night and witnessing the man beating and raping one of his lieutenant's wives. Apparently, the asshole thought nothing of targeting the older daughters in town as well.

He voiced his opinion of that out loud. "It's damn time to put this monster out of everyone's misery." When a contemplative silence was his only answer from Tait, he went on. "Once Sharif's out, local Special Ops will lead the charge inside. It'll be a cluster and a half, but Rhett and Rebel should have no trouble doubling back up here to grab us before anyone figures out where the shot came from."

Tait did answer that one, barely moving from his stomach-down position behind his scope. "I was at the mission run-down too, Kell. And despite what you may think, I was paying attention."

"Cool." It was likely as close as he'd come to an apology. Sure, he had regrets, tons of them; it was just expressing the fuckers where his own mental omelets got made. He hoped Tait recalled that much.

The guy gave him hope by throwing over a smirk. A trace of the old T-Bomb peeked through as he drawled, "You look tense, Slash-aroo." Using Kell's call-sign in his unique way was another good sign. "You need to go let the snake in your pants do a little dance for a few minutes downstairs? I can watch the kid for you." He nodded at Kellan's brand-new Remington precision rifle.

"Bommer, I think you'd give BJs to half the battalion to get a few rounds with my new baby." He sent a gloating grin. "But I'm the only bastard who touches her right now."

"*Pffft*. That's just because she doesn't know any better."

"Hey, when it's right, it's right. Nobody can control true love."

The statement was like spilled neon paint. Once it was out, the damage was done—and impossible to ignore. Just like that, Tait's face tightened and darkened, all traces of his sarcasm swept beneath the mask of loss that had defined it for so damn long. "That's one nasty fucker of a truth, Sergeant Rush."

Kell blew out hard air while screwing his lips together with equal frustration. "T...man, I didn't mean to—"

"Of course you didn't. Forget it." But everything about his guttural tone said he hadn't and wouldn't. Nevertheless,

Tait was back to strict business the next second, opening up the radio line to state, "This is T-Bomb. I have eyes on the target. Local police jeep approaching from the southwest at approximately forty-five KPH with the chief riding shotgun. Additional occupants are the driver plus one bandit in back, accompanied by a female who appears to be a local." After a second, he muttered in a voice only Kellan could hear, "Christ, look at all that long black hair."

In the best of all possible worlds, Kellan would have the chance to roll over and whack the back of the man's helmet. Right after that, he'd growl at Tait to keep his sights on their black-hearted target instead of his black-haired companion, who was more than likely a prisoner instead of a passenger. But setting up a four-hundred-yard shot required complete control of one's breathing, voice, muscles, and emotions. He was successful at doing just that, drawing in slow air as he refocused his scope on the entrance steps of the police station. As he released the air in a steady stream, he said, "You wanna keep your eyes on the front seat of that jeep, Sergeant Bommer, instead of the back?"

Tait wielded another long silence as retaliation to that. And yeah, this time, it *was* retaliation. Kell knew T-Bomb better than a brother. To Tait, being called openly on his shit was like having his nose rubbed in it. But sometimes rubbing a creature's nose in its dung was the only way to teach the thing. Even then, it might take a few good nostrils full of crap to learn—and taking that time wasn't a luxury they had at this point. Kell had no choice but to trust that Tait's glance at that woman was just that. *No trips to the intersection of Memory Lane and Luna Street today, buddy.*

"Sniper ninjas, this is yellow team." The voice was thick

with an Indonesian accent. "We copy and confirm your visual. The jeep has passed by us at the south gate of town. Four heads inside the vehicle. Repeat, four heads."

"Slash." Tait's mutter had a strange, almost conspiratorial undertone to it. "Hey...we're only targeting Sharif on this hit, right?"

He inhaled again, deep and slow, imagining focus and control coming in and his mounting vexation with Tait getting blown out. "That's the plan, man." Honest to fuck, he felt like a character in a bad reenactment of *Dr. Jekyll and Mr. Hyde*. He had no idea, from one second to the next, which personality Tait was going to unleash on him. He just had to stay the course and maintain a Zen concentration, no matter which mutant finally showed. "But we're not going to accomplish the plan without your eyes. You feeling me?"

Tait's response, if it could be called that, was an updated announcement to everyone on radio. "The jeep's proceeding as planned." Okay, so it was Jekyll right now, returning with clinical severity. "Without any stops, estimated ETA at the station is less than five mikes."

"Copy that, T-Bomb." The voice belonged to Zeke, who was keeping watch over everything from the apartments over a bakery that overlooked the square. "Everything's normal here, at least as far as those asshats will see. Some villagers have chosen to stay and help us maintain the illusion that everything's hunky-dory in Sharia-ville."

"Outstanding." The declaration came from Captain Franzen this time. He was positioned in the alley behind the station and would lead the Indonesian troops as soon as Sharif was down.

"Blue team reporting." It was another Indonesian soldier.

"Sharif's jeep just passed us. They're on final approach to the main square now."

"Affirmative," said Zeke. "We've got visual too."

"Making final adjustments." Tait spoke it for both of them, letting Kell funnel his attention on dialing in the final increments on his Remington. Luckily, the guy's Doc J side was holding. "Ninjas on the hill are going silent until the fire order."

"Roger that, T-Bomb," Franzen confirmed.

Kell heard Tait's surreptitious rustlings. His elbows and knees scraped the cement as he moved around, focusing his scope. The sounds were comforting to him, the familiar cadence of his partner performing the sniper team version of a COA—*covering our asses*. "We've got a little breeze, Kell," he murmured. "Adjust trajectory by two degrees."

Kell dialed in the new settings.

"The jeep has stopped," Zeke reported. "Driver's exiting and helping Sharif's little lady friend out."

"Damn."

Tait barely lifted the word above a breath, though Kell was sure every guy who could see her had repeated the word in his own way. The woman's long black hair wasn't visible anymore because she'd wrapped a full sheath over her head—but there was nothing that could stop any of them from seeing her eyes in the little window. Both of them had been bludgeoned into slits, surrounded by severe tissue damage that was colored from bright blue to deep purple. Thanks to the power of Kellan's scope, he also saw the misery that glittered in the dark eyes beneath the damage.

And he knew Tait could see the same thing. *Goddamnit.*

The man's fury formed a palpable energy in the confines

of the tiny tower. Kell was no official shrink, but even he connected the wires on this one. It made no difference that the woman didn't physically evoke Luna beyond her hair. To Tait, it had been enough to throw out the desperate emotional ties, which included the horrified backlash upon seeing the evidence of Sharif's abuse. Just like that, the omelet between the guy's ears was officially ready for plate-up again.

Kell didn't lift his eye from the rifle's scope. "T, goddamnit, not now."

"That filthy, fucking, shit-covered maggot."

"Tait!"

"Blow his head off, Kell. Take it the fuck off!"

"Trying, man." His shoulders rose and fell from the sudden spike in his tension level. *Not good.* "But T-Bomb, this isn't called a team effort for—"

"Ninjas!" Franzen barked the demand. "You guys okay up there?"

Kellan gritted his teeth and ordered his heartbeat back into submission. "Working on some bumps," he responded. "But yeah, ready to go."

"You need to be solid on that green light, Slash." It was Zeke's voice this time. "Because Sharif's exiting the jeep now and—"

"Shit!"

The expletive was repeated in its English and Indonesian forms at least a dozen more times over the radio. Kellan watched a viler version of it burst off Sharif's lips before the man disappeared from his scope, apparently rushing after something.

Not something. Someone.

The mystery woman had broken free from the clutches

of the driver and started running across the town's square. Since nearly every civilian in the area was not only aware of the covert ops mission but sympathetic to it, a crowd quickly formed, urging her toward them. But it was swiftly clear that Sharif had jacked up more than the woman's face. She couldn't move faster than a painful shuffle.

Sharif, as spry as he was ugly, grabbed her before the townspeople did. As he stopped and secured her in his hold, his crooked police force spilled out of the station house, armed with rifles to keep the crowd at bay.

"Slash and T," Franzen seethed. "We can give you another twenty seconds on this—*maybe*."

"Take the damn shot!" Zeke bellowed.

"Working on it," Kell bit back. "Talk to me, T-Bomb. *Now*. I'm dialing in on Sharif's new twenty. I'll do it without you, but I'd really like it if you're along."

All that answered him from five feet away were vicious huffs. Fuck. Hyde was back, and he wasn't pretty. "If you're dialed in wrong, you'll hit *her*!"

"So get me lined up right." He rechecked his coordinates. There were only a thousand and one things that could go wrong with the trajectory of this bullet in four hundred yards. *This* bullet. He was only going to get *one* shot. "I've got the wind and humidity figured in. And the MOA—"

"Is too low," Tait cut in. "Higher, Kell."

"What?" He rapidly did the math again. "No, T. It's right. Minute of angle goes one-point-oh-forty-seven for every hundred yards. So I've adjusted—"

"Incorrectly."

Tait's snarl was so full of conviction that Kell was induced to do something really stupid. He looked up. His partner's stare waited for him, not blinking and not backing down. The rest of his face was stamped with the same determination.

"The humidity's going to drag it." His tone walked on a solid slab of careful enunciation. "And twilight's coming, affecting that tiny little factor called gravity."

The clench under his jaw betrayed that he had more to say, but they didn't have time for the sharing-is-caring therapy hour. Fuck, there wasn't even time to clear up whether it was Jekyll or Hyde on tap now, and that scared the crap out of him. He had to simply trust that whoever was here had brought enough of his wingman and friend along—the guy in whom he was now sinking a terrifying chunk of trust.

Within three seconds, he was back at the riflescope, hitting the new coordinates, confirming Sharif hadn't moved.

He pulled a long breath in. Squeezed a little on the trigger. Breathed gently out.

"Taking the shot...now."

He didn't hit the woman.

He didn't hit Sharif, either.

"What the hell?" came Zeke's growl. "Slash, did you... Where'd it—"

"Oh, my God." The hoarse interjection was from one of the Indonesian squad leaders. Shouts from his squad were a chaotic din in the background. "Man down! One of ours. Sharif and his people have seen us too. They're onto us. They know we're covert and are taking measures!"

"Move in!" Franzen's shout was garbled by the force of his vehemence. "Altered alpha formation. I repeat, altered alpha formation flies now! We just treat Sharif as one of them now."

"Roger," came Zeke's boom. "Zsycho and team are good to go from the northwest."

"Do it," Franz ordered. "Try to capture, not kill. Repeat, do not kill Sharif unless absolutely necessary. Turning this freak into a martyr while his men watch will only win new zealots for their cause. We'll have to do this the messy way, but we're gonna get it done."

Kellan pushed to his feet and stumbled from his rifle on weak legs. He'd missed shots before; everyone did. But not like this. *Not like this.* As he blinked in slow horror, he prayed that every time he reopened his eyes, the world would be different. He wouldn't be standing here unable to control his breathing anymore—or the fury of glaring over to the man who'd once been his sharpest wingman. The guy he'd made the supreme mistake of trusting again.

Tait still sat on the ground, back propped against one of the tower's parapets. The guy was silent and had the gonads to look stunned, even a little contrite. *Very* good thing. If he said a word right now, Kell was pretty sure he'd ram the spotting scope up his goddamn ass.

He was certain there'd be time for conversation soon enough. As soon as Franzen finished with the "messy" shit in the square, he'd be calling for Kell's and Tait's asses, front and center. Kell wouldn't be surprised if the man met them holding a huge knife—and a bucket in which to toss their balls as soon as he sliced the fuckers off.

★ ★ ★ ★ ★

"I'm actually gonna give you guys ten seconds not to feel like the biggest bags of fuck-up fudge on the planet."

It wasn't the opener Kellan had expected from their CO, who'd kept his formidable features in an impassive mask since entering his temporary office at the training base. Franzen gave little else away with the neutral tone of his statement, but the fact that he made Tait and Kell maintain their at-attention stances sent up another warning flag. Yep. The man was just biding time before whipping out the blade and ordering them to drop trou for the big slice.

"So," Franz began, "our friend from the Indonesian force was only nicked. The kid's gonna have a nice gouge in his ear to show off for the ladies, but other than that, he's all right."

"Thank fuck." It rushed out before he could stop it. "Sorry, Captain," he followed up in a rush. "It was a weight."

"I know, Slash." The man's voice conveyed real empathy. "And your concern was relayed to him."

"What about the town?"

They were practically the first words out of Tait since shit had gone sideways. Though they were quiet, communicating the guy's respect about the situation, they still made Kell want to indent T's jaw with his fist. "What about the *town*?" He settled for a low snarl instead. "Don't you mean what about her? The stranger in the shroud for which you compromised the entire op? The squirrel that had you running so far off track, you nearly calculated a bullet to hit one of our friendlies?"

Franz shoved to his feet. "Sergeant Rush, that's enough."

"Squirrel." Tait's lips twisted. "That's your little nickname for a woman now, huh, Kell? Well, did you see what that cocksucker did to that *squirrel*? How she could barely take a step because of the damage he'd done to her?"

"To save them, you have to ignore them." He drilled his glare into his friend, noticing for the tenth time in the last twenty-four hours that Tait's eyes were really different now. Those dark-gold depths used to sprout lasers of focus on a mission like this. Now, they looked like glazed donuts. "Compartments, T-Bomb. Remember those? They're not just necessary for your sanity. They're necessary for your efficiency."

"And become a disconnected bastard like you?"

"You think every inch of my gut didn't feel like barbed wire when I saw her face too?" He pushed back his shoulders and squared his stance. "I thought you knew me, asshole. But I thought I knew you too. The Tait Bommer I used to serve with wouldn't have displaced his issues about one woman's death by compromising an entire team mission."

Tait narrowed his gaze. "You have no fucking clue about my issues—which I at least have the courage to look at. When was the last time you took *anything* inside you out of its *box*, Kell?"

"When you're out there"—he jabbed a finger toward the window—"the shit stays inside the goddamn box!"

"Sure," Tait scoffed, "if you want to be a robot."

"Better a robot than a donut, assface."

"What the fuck does that—?"

"Enough." Franzen's bellow rattled the shoddily-installed window. Their CO crossed the office in three pounding steps, arms spread and face thunderous. "Corners." He pointed to the opposing sides of his desk. "Now!" After they'd shuffled into place, he swung a glare between them. "What the hell happened to you two?" When he saw them both pulling in air for comebacks, he rammed out his arms again. "No. Forget it. I don't want your whiny-ass excuses. It's by the grace of the goddamn angels I'm not shipping both of you back to Lewis-McChord to pull a month's worth of cleaning latrines with toothbrushes. You have Hayes to thank for that. Zeke rallied

the Indonesian forces to a brilliant take-back on the police station, turning all those local boys into stud heroes who are probably all getting laid by willing partners as we speak."

Kellan was compelled to ask his next question. "What about Sharif?"

"Bugged out into the jungle with his crew of rats. They'll no doubt try to seize power again. They'll be on high alert after this."

Kellan nodded, processing the information. Even if he'd gotten Sharif, there was no guarantee the radicals wouldn't make like cockroaches and grow another head to take the bastard's place. But knowing the man still walked the earth, raping and extorting again, chafed at his spirit in the worst places.

Franzen didn't give him long to wallow in the rage. The man turned around and braced himself against the desk between them, arms folded, head shaking. "Now I'm left with a dilemma. I can't send your asses back to Tacoma, but I'm sure as hell not putting either of you back in action."

Kellan shot up a glower, making no effort to hide his outrage. "*Either* of us? Wait a second. I'm not the one doing the twelve-step program for grief here."

Tait chuckled. "Stages. They're called stages, man. The twelve-step crap is for addiction."

"My point exactly."

"All right," Franz snapped, "cut it out!" He huffed and leaned forward on the desk. "I've reffed spats more civilized than this between my *keiki hanaunas*."

Tait's scowl conveyed the perplexity for them both. "Your what?"

"It's Hawaiian for nephews, though I wish we also had

a word for *brats* because it often applies to those two. But their bickering is a goddamn kumbaya hug compared to you dickwads."

Kellan peered at him. "You're Hawaiian?"

"Half," Franz explained. "My dad was German-English, but my mom was a full-blooded islander." His eyes widened as if those words were actually news for him too. "And *that* gives me an idea. A fucking brilliant one, if I say so myself."

Kellan exchanged a glance with Tait that was oddly bonding due to its trepidation. Okay, many of Franzen's "ideas" were notorious for being on the "brilliant" side, but many of them were a straightjacket buckle short of crazy. Why did he sense, and could see Tait agreed, that this one was going to slide into the second column?

"After my mom passed, we inherited her land," Franz explained. "There's a house and several acres not far from the beach on Kauai. It's pretty. And secluded." The man nodded at them. "And the perfect place to focus and get your shit together."

Kellan's eyes widened as comprehension wound a sneaky path into him. "Whoa. Wait. Are you saying—?"

"That the two of you have just earned yourself two weeks of mandated leave and a retreat vacation on the lovely garden island of Kauai? Ding ding ding; yep, that's exactly what I'm saying." He swung an arm toward the door. "Now go see the girl in the evening gown for your prize. Nah, kidding. I'll give you all the details and directions."

"Captain." It was gratifying to see that Tait looked like he'd been sucker-punched too. "You can't be serious."

"As a fucking heart attack." The man straightened and braced his legs wider, adopting a battle-stance pose. "You two get your asses onto that beach and fix your heads, or I'll execute a mental-health leave for you both faster than you can say *Aloha, pupule 'uku.*"

Kellan sucked in a breath. This had to be some surreal illusion, though his rising fury was very real. And his fear. As a sniper, getting his ass pulled on a psych disability probably meant he wouldn't shoot at the elite military level again. Which meant he was hauling said ass onto a plane for Hawaii as soon as he could, with T-Bomb along whether he liked it or not.

Hell.

He wished Franzen had simply brought the knife and bucket.

★ ★ ★ ★ ★

Two nights later, paradise still felt like hell.

He wondered if Tait agreed. Actually, he wondered if Tait was capable of forming a coherent thought. The empty vodka, bourbon, and tequila bottles around the house gave him good reason to assume otherwise.

The guy's slide into oblivion had begun about two hours into their commercial flight to Honolulu, after a steady flow of Luna photos and an iPod full of music that had been special for the two of them. Luckily, neither of them were in uniform, because Kell was certain that by the time they boarded the puddle jumper to Lihue, Tait's blood alcohol level had revised the *T* in his call-sign to stand for *Toxic.*

On top of all that, hurray of all hurrays, they had to stop and pick up the keys to Franzen's place from his buddy Kaipo— who owned the local liquor store. Fifty bucks later, they walked out with at least a hundred G's worth of hootch, thanks to the man referring to Franz as his *hoaloha*, his brother in everything but blood. Really. Fucking. Awesome. Kell had rolled his eyes, climbed into their rental, and hoped that T endured such a brain-blaster of a hangover that he left the bottles in the bags for the rest of their stay.

So much for hoping.

After indulging in a late-afternoon nap, Kell awakened to notice a couple of the bags from Kaipo's place were only half-full now. After shrugging into a shirt but not buttoning it, he took several conscious breaths, concentrating on tamping his wrath enough to search for his friend. His partner? Battalion mate? What the hell *were* they to each other these days? And why should he care, when it was clear Tait didn't?

Might as well resign yourself to that psych card now, man.

"Olly olly oxen free," he grumbled into the thickening twilight. "Ready or not, asshole, here I come."

First things first. He made a mental note to call Franzen out as the biggest liar of the year when he'd told them his house was "not far" from the beach. Less than fifty paces down a flagstone path, Kell found himself ankle-deep on a stretch of pristine white sand that sloped down to gentle waves glowing deep purple beneath the clouds of a waning thunderstorm. Deciding he'd at least enjoy himself while following a self-imposed APB on his friend, he started down the beach.

Less than a quarter mile later, he spotted a figure sitting on the sand in a slump...tipping a bottle to his lips. As he drew near, Tait slanted a glance up at him. Kellan couldn't figure out whether the brief gleam in the guy's gaze was scrutiny or greeting, but he didn't care. A gleam meant there might still be something to work with, conversationally speaking. And if they could talk, maybe they could start working on things.

So what if T likely wouldn't remember it tomorrow morning? Maybe it would feel like progress. *Maybe.*

Kell dug his heels into the sand and rocked back on them. "So are we having fun yet?"

Tait looked down the neck of Mr. Grey Goose and then tipped up the bottle again. "Is that...a trick question?"

Kell was surprised the words weren't more slurred. On the other hand, maybe T was well practiced at the binge drinking game by now. "You look like a damn hobo."

"Uh-huh." Tait belched. "So do you. Only...I'm the cute hobo."

He'd probably said it to diffuse things with a laugh. Kell couldn't give him what he wanted. As he stared down at the shell of what used to be his best friend, he could barely manage any reaction outside a short grunt. He wanted to punch the bastard. He wanted to hug him. He wanted to fight for him. He wanted to fucking give up.

"What's going on, Tait?" he muttered. "What the *hell* are you doing?"

At first, all he received was one of those long, somber silences the guy had down to an art form. That was fucking terrific for the mood...not.

"Me?" T growled at last. "Just watching the sunset, dude." Surprisingly, he extended his free hand, his fingers weaving and grabbing at the air. "And...wanting to touch it."

Kellan studied his friend carefully. Christ. Was T concocting shit from thin air now? His eyes had surpassed donuts for the glaze factor, and Kell couldn't tell if it was delusion or tears. "Are you serious?"

Tait nodded slowly. "It looks like her hair...doesn't it? I—I miss her hair."

He looked out past T's hand with fresh consideration. Of course. The thunderheads from the storm, now streamlined by the wind into black ribbons, were interspersed with the lavender and purple glow from the fading sunset.

He did the conscious breathing thing again, but the technique was growing thin as his patience. "It's pretty. I'll give you that."

"It's beautiful. Just like she is."

"Just like she *was*." Screw the Zen shit. It was time for an old-fashioned dose of tough love, perhaps for both of them. He stepped forward, swiped the bottle out of Tait's hand, and gave it a hard Hail Mary into the palm trees. The waves etched on the bottle were caught by the light reflecting off the real swells behind him, deep purple and gold, before it flipped over and dropped into the foliage. "Just like she *was*, Tait," he repeated from bared teeth. "It's time to wake the fuck up and let her go."

Tait swayed to his feet and glowered into the trees. Back at him. Into the trees. He was wearing a snarl when he swung toward Kell again. "What the fuck did you do that for?" His voice dragged on the *f* in the profanity. It was the perfect fuel for Kell's indignation, at just the right time.

"Did you hear anything I just said?" he fired. "Do you remember anything of what Franzen told us before we got banished here?" He stomped over to Tait, sand flying in his wake. "If you don't get your shit together, you're taking me down with you. And goddamnit, Tait, that makes me seriously crave slamming my fist down your throat right now."

He grabbed the drunken bastard by the neckline of his T-shirt, forcing himself to ignore the agony in Tait's features. A year ago, this guy could've been the poster boy for golden surfing god. With his flirtatious smile and whip of a wit, Tait Bommer could walk into any bar and have half the women pickpocketing his phone in order to program in their digits. Now, he literally hung in Kellan's grip, lips twisting in heartbreak, tears brimming in his eyes.

"I loved her." He pulled in a jagged gasp. "I loved her, Kell."

"I know you did. And I don't care." Kell added his other hand to the hold. "I *can't* care. And damn it, I'm here to make you see that you can't anymore either."

He saw *that* hit a target in the guy. Tait's eyes screwed shut. He yanked at one of Kell's wrists. "Get away from me."

Kellan tightened his grip, digging his feet deeper into the sand to back it up. "No fucking way. I'm not going anywhere." As the words left his tight lips, new understanding blared into him. "It's why Franzen sent me here with you, asshole. He knew I'd be the only one who wouldn't. That I'd refuse to see you ruin yourself like this. And your career—"

"My career." Tait fired a bitter laugh. "Yeah. My goddamn career. Going back to that worked out real well, didn't it?" He flung his head from side to side. "My career is fucking poison. *I'm* fucking poison. My choices that day...led Luna to that soundstage...and put her in that coma..."

"No, T. *Her* choices. What Luna did was heroic—but it was her choice to run with that bomb. *Her* decision, made with full knowledge of what the consequences could be." He grabbed Tait's head and lined up their stares. "Listen to me. If it'd been the other way around, do you think you'd want her doing this? Pining for you like this?"

"It *should* have been the other way around." Tait jerked his head away and let out an open growl. "Don't you see? It should have been me. *I* should have died! They pay *me* to die, damn it!"

Each word bashed Kellan like a brick laced with lead. He released Tait and stumbled back from the impact. "Is that how you really feel?" he grated. "So...taking the fast track to pickling your liver is just your way of telling me to let you die? You're going to throw away all the good you've done for this world, and all the good you still have left to do, because of one fucking woman?"

Tait laughed again. The sound was softer this time, like he'd heard the punch line to a joke Kell couldn't possibly understand. "Therapy session's done for the night, Doctor Rush."

He turned and started for the water, but raw rage spurred Kell to chase him and seize him by the shoulder. "The fuck it is."

Tait stopped. Swiveled his face, carved in hard angles of rage and misery, back at Kell. "Get your hand off me. I said we're done."

Kellan took his turn to get in a smug laugh. Right before doubling the pressure of his grip.

Tait reacted how he'd hoped. As the guy's fist drove into his gut, Kell reminded himself that he'd asked for this. And aside from the pain, this was pretty damn good, at least for a start. Getting Tait to get mad at anything besides himself and God was a step in the right direction. Besides, the guy was shitfaced. That much was evident when Kell was able to knock T to his back with one well-placed head butt to the ribs. With one, maybe two more moves, he'd have the guy pinned, seething, and finally experiencing life outside his grief for the first time in six months.

Maybe they really were getting somewhere.

It was the last cohesive thought in his brain before the

damn thing was flipped along with the rest of him. The forced body roll had him catching air before landing flat on his back in the sand. Good Christ. How had Tait pulled *that* move out of his half-tanked ass?

Easy answer: he hadn't.

T's grunt came from the sand directly next to Kell's head, prompting him to glance at his friend. Tait was still in the prone position in which Kell had dumped him. But now, Tait's stare was riveted on something over both their heads. And shit was he transfixed. As in, not audibly breathing because of the damn trance.

Kellan followed the guy's line of sight—and said goodbye to the air in his own chest.

The moon had just peeked over the ocean, outlining the woman's curves in stunning silver clarity. *Holy fuck.* The last time God made figures like that, he gave them the names of goddesses like Brigitte, Marilyn, Raquel, and Sophia. The black bikini on this deity—because that was seriously what she must be—left little to doubt about her place right next to those icons of sensuality. Endless, strong legs. Soft, graceful shoulders. Full, amazing breasts. A waist with curves that all but demanded his mind to join them in fantasies of pulling her close, bending her back, sinking his lips to the beautiful column of her neck...

He wouldn't stop there, of course. Why would he, when her brilliant, nearly silver gaze ordered direct contact from his, commanding his respect like a mythical queen? She had the shimmering waterfall of hair to back that part up too. It was so black that as the moon climbed higher in the sky, it reflected the light as streaks of silver and lavender. *Hell*...just like the clouds at sunset that Tait had desperately wanted to touch. He couldn't believe he was admitting it, but shit did he understand the fantasy now. With painful intensity...

Her mouth, curved as a bow but set in lines of take-no-shit attitude, parted to reveal the tight lock of her perfect porcelain teeth. Whatever inch of his cock hadn't stood up and taken notice before was sure as hell at attention from her ballsy move now.

Ballsy. Yeah, he'd really just gone there. He'd stand solidly by the call too. How this flawless representation of her gender could also represent for solid steel *cojones,* Kell was mystified to explain—but he prayed to learn that secret. He longed to know *all* her secrets.

"Holy fuck," Tait murmured.

"Uh-huh," he muttered back.

It was only then that he noticed the goddess brandished an accessory besides that body, those eyes, those lips, and that hair. She handled the twelve-inch diving knife like an expert.

A pissed-off expert.

"Either of you move a muscle, your testicles are fish food."

He forced himself to heed the words instead of letting her silken alto wrap its magic around his dick. Too late. His crotch was the first stop on her voice's magical mystery tour through his body. His nerve endings begged his ears for more. His chest pounded, held mercy by the crazy cavalcade of his heartbeat.

Christ. He'd never experienced anything like this before. Had some alien taken over his body and hardwired it for servitude to every sound, stare, and move this woman made?

This woman. How the hell was *a woman* doing this to him?

"Hey," he shocked himself by locating his voice. "We don't want any trouble, okay?"

"Is that so?" She flipped her hair from one shoulder to the other, making the lavender lights dance all over her head again. "Maybe you should've thought of that when you trespassed on my property, threw a vodka bottle into my garden, and started fighting like drunk asses on my beach." She crimped that gorgeous bow mouth at him. "Oh, you've got trouble, buddy. It's me."

He and Tait went back to not breathing again. Finally, Tait broke their silence. "I—I think I'm hallucinating."

Kellan swallowed hard. "I think I'm in love."

Continue the Honor Bound Series with Book Five

Wet

Keep reading for an excerpt!

EXCERPT FROM *WET*

BOOK FIVE IN THE HONOR BOUND SERIES

CHAPTER ONE

"Perhaps I didn't make myself clear the first time, gentlemen. If either of you moves, I cut your balls off. Got it?"

The two men sprawled at Lani Kail's feet—and the end of her Bowie diving knife—gave instant silent nods. *Hell.* Why did she have to have trespassers stumble onto her West Kauaʻi beach tonight? And why did they have to be a pair of the most beautiful males she'd ever laid eyes on?

Trepidation gripped her again. Maybe they hadn't stumbled at all. They were breathtaking, the kind of hunks a resort developer bully like Gunter Benson liked on his support team. The first of them, though clearly between three and thirteen sheets to the wind, was a mesmerizing mix of rugged and beautiful. His blazing amber eyes were framed by a messy head of hair in a slightly darker shade. The other filled out the yin to that yang, his silky gray gaze and spiky dark hair no less arresting. They were both built like the walls of Waimea Canyon, huge and hard and covered in taut bronze skin. Their open shirts, thrown over wrinkled khaki shorts, made it sinfully easy to confirm the conclusion.

Throwing them into a comparison with her island's stunning tourist attraction brought a warning pulled straight from the canyon's hiking brochures. *Distracted by the scenery? Prepare to fall to your death.*

She gulped, tightened her grip on the knife, and re-firmed her face. No sense in letting the hulks think their presence here was a shock, despite the fact that it was. Since the main highway ended a mile away, the sunset-seeking tourists kept mostly to the beaches south of the Barking Sands base, and thrill-seekers on their way to Na Pali usually only made breakfast stops here. So where had these two come from, and why had she found them in the middle of a fight that looked like a failed audition for a UFC slot?

There was only one answer that made sense. They had to be part of Gunter's goon squad, sent out here in preparation for the "casual meeting" their boss had requested for tonight up at the ranch's main house. And this move just screamed *casual*, didn't it?

She glowered harder, though she thanked the gods she'd discovered the intruders now, thanks to being paranoid enough to conduct a preliminary property sweep. The only thing she regretted about the decision was not thinking out her wardrobe better. With her mind consumed by anxiety about the appointment, she'd walked out of the house without thinking, still dressed in nothing but her bikini and thigh sheath—a factor clearly noticed by her detainees.

Damn it.

The gray-eyed stranger tried playing chief negotiator. He raised a placating hand, as if her knife was nothing but a quill pen. "We got the message loud and clear, sweetheart. So why don't you just lower—"

"I'm not your sweetheart." She flicked the knife, making sure the blade reflected the light back into his face. But that meant she had to meet his gaze once more. *Why* did the man have to possess such mesmerizing eyes?

He lowered the hand. "Fair enough. Maybe you have a real name I can use?"

"Nice try." Like he didn't know her name already. The man's persistent sociability, even with her Bowie at his nose, answered that well enough. What the hell was Benson's game this time? Why had he sent in a pair of his "cabin boys" to act like drunk frat brothers on the beach like this? Did he think she wouldn't see through this game? That she wouldn't see him trying to "survey" the beach that wasn't even his yet?

She winced at her mental default.

His *yet*?

No. *No.* This battle was far from over, no matter what Benson believed or connived to make *her* believe. There was nothing on this ranch—*her* ranch—that belonged to Benstock Development, including this sand. And, she vowed with renewed determination, no grain of it would. She knew what the man and his company did to the lands they gobbled, to the people they took from their homes in the pretty and *not* so pretty ways.

Right now, Benson was making a run for the "pretty" angle. Shallow, devious coward.

"All right," she snapped. "Stand up. Both of you. Slowly. Hands visible. No funny shit. I can gut a bluefin in two minutes with this thing, and your testicles won't be half the challenge." She rolled her eyes as Golden Eyes mangled his obedience, staggering more than straightening. "Okay, the act's going to get old real fast, pretty boy."

"Huh?" It was the first thing she'd heard out of the guy since she'd found the pair wrestling out here, pretending they were out for each other's blood, even hurling booze bottles into her garden during the performance. But she knew better.

"The *soused and stupid* act?" she countered. "It's all right to cut it now. I know what's really going on here, okay?"

"Oh?" He managed a sarcastic grin that looked lopsided due to a slightly crooked canine tooth. "Hmmm. Maybe you can fill me in, dreamgirl, 'cause I'm a little lost."

He leaned over, forcing her to deny better sense and steady his gait with a hand to his waist. He really was as solid as a granite cliff. Thanks to the wind, she confirmed he really had hundred-proof vodka breath too. *Aue*. She didn't know whether to slap him or laugh at him. Normally, guys who did "drunk with a twist of cute" were more tempting to her than chocolate, but right now, she was much more ready for a Godiva than *any* of Benson's brutes. Still, a new resolve took root. She'd have to keep her guard up with *both* these bozos.

"A 'little lost,' huh?" She shoved him away and pulled up on her stance again. "And I'm the goddess Hina, newly awakened for my nighttime adventures."

"That explains a few things." Mr. Intense Eyes and Dark Hair—and, she observed now, Endless Legs—surrendered that in a tone of a thousand nuances. She dared a glance at his face, to find his stare still fixed on her, looking like he deliberated the pieces of an intricate jigsaw puzzle.

She looked away before the man evoked the pull of a god in his own right. Just as fast, she added an angry huff. *God?* He barely should've gotten the courtesy of "man." Both of these hulks were on Benstock's payroll, which placed them somewhere between banana slugs and heroin dealers in the evolution chain.

"I'm taking you both back to the house," she declared. "Sorry to cut your romp out here a little short, but since our friend arrives in less than fifteen minutes, you've given me no choice."

"We're goin' to your place?" Golden Eyes cracked a woozy grin. "Suh-weet."

To her surprise, McDark-And-Dreamy was just as ready with his hospitality. "Like *I* said before, we're not here to cause trouble. And I'm sure any friend of yours will be a friend of—"

"Save it." She hardened her posture, still baffled by the angle these guys were playing. Usually Benson selected his groupies for the clean-and-cute image so he could be the alpha dog with his fitted suits and expensive charm. These two apes didn't fit an inch of that MO. But Gunter had never sent any of his men to play real-estate recon on her beach before, either. The bastard was busting out an arsenal of new tactics, which only made her queasier about his agenda for the upcoming meeting itself. "Let's go." She pulled Gray Eyes forward by fitting the knife's tip into one of his shirt's button holes. "You're taking lead, Yin-man."

Confused crinkles appeared at the corners of his eyes. "Huh?"

"Yin and yang. It fits you two, in a demented way."

He smiled. The look wasn't a copy of his cheeky smirks so far. It grew from the middle of his mouth and then moved outward in an ocean-like undulation...wreaking strange havoc on her stomach in the process. "Yeah. It probably does."

His voice was different now too. A little more serious. A

lot more velvety.

Guard up, Hokulani!

"The path to the house starts there," she ordered, "between the two papaya trees. Look for the bamboo planks. Got it?"

"Had it scoped about five minutes back, sweetheart." He turned and trudged toward the trees, flexing calves the size of hams. For once, Lani was thankful for his strange cockiness. It made her consider the logistics of her order. *Damn.* The path was only wide enough for single-file travel, meaning there was no way to police both the men at once.

Or was there?

"Stop." Her slam on the syllable was sufficient to freeze them both.

Yang swiveled his amber gaze back at her. "Dear Christ, I like the way she says that."

"Down, T-Bomb," cautioned Yin.

"Well, don't *you*?"

Gray Eyes didn't say anything—until he looked again to Lani. Though his lips remained motionless, his answer slammed through every inch of her body like a tidal wave of fire. *Gods.* The man wanted her. To be honest, that part would be easy to handle, if this was just a case of a jerk letting his dick control the guidebook. But the way he took her in, as if he'd never seen a woman before and marveled over everything about her, was something she'd never experienced from a man before. From another *person* before.

What the *hell* was he doing this for? He didn't relent, freezing her in place, binding her—terrifying her.

And elevating her next command to the stratosphere of crazy.

"Give me your pants."

Golden Eyes slid out another smirk. "I like the way you say *that* even better."

Gray Eyes glowered. "What the fuck?"

"You heard me." Lani jerked her chin, making sure to keep the Bowie directly in his view. "Benson sent you down here ahead of the meeting for a reason. I don't know what that is yet, and I'm not going to risk finding out when one of you runs ahead to warn the man. Your shorts are my insurance against that. Hand them over."

Golden Eyes, having already shucked his khakis, finished tearing off his shirt, as well. His new outfit, nothing but his black briefs, left no doubt in her mind that every part of him was as mighty as a boulder. He extended both with another crooked grin. "Do I qualify for extra credit?"

Hell. How the man could make her want to scowl and smile in the same reaction was a mystery she didn't have time to untangle. She diverted her attention by turning to his friend, who still shifted uneasily on the sand.

"You sure about this?" Gray Eyes finally charged. "You already have his. Do you really need both—"

"Take them off or I'll cut them off. Your choice."

The tension continued in his face for another two seconds. When it suddenly disappeared, she wondered why a thread of uneasiness dragged through *her* nerves now—thickening to straight-up alarm as he drawled, "Your mandate, sweetheart."

Hell. He justified her anxiety the next moment—in hard, huge, and damn near erect detail. And the man, with that sensual smirk again sliding across his lips, just let her stare as he dropped the shorts, blatantly revealing he was a commando kind of guy.

This story continues in Wet: *Honor Bound Book Five!*

ALSO BY ANGEL PAYNE

The Misadventures Series:
Misadventures with a Super Hero

Honor Bound:
Saved
Cuffed
Seduced
Wild
Wet (February 2018)
Hot (February 2018)
Masked (February 2018)
Mastered (Coming Soon)
Conquered (Coming Soon)
Ruled (Coming Soon)

Secrets of Stone Series:
No Prince Charming
No More Masquerade
No Perfect Princess
No Magic Moment
No Lucky Number
No Simple Sacrifice
No Broken Bond
No White Knight

**For a full list of Angel's other titles,
visit her at www.angelpayne.com**

ABOUT ANGEL PAYNE

USA Today bestselling romance author Angel Payne loves to focus on high-heat romance starring memorable alpha men and the women who love them. She has numerous book series to her credit, including the Suited for Sin series, the Cimarron Saga, the Temptation Court series, the Secrets of Stone series, the Lords of Sin historicals, and the popular Honor Bound series, as well as several standalone titles.

Angel is a native Southern Californian, leading to her love of being in the outdoors, where she often reads and writes. She still lives in Southern California with her soul-mate husband and beautiful daughter, to whom she is a proud cosplay/culture con mom. Her passions also include whisky tasting, shoe shopping, and travel.

Visit her here:
www.angelpayne.com